## "Why do I feel like we're leaving for a date?"

Caleb laughed. "And your friends are the parents telling you to get home by ten?"

"Something like that. But I doubt they'll ground me if I stay out after curfew."

"That's good to know." His deep voice rippled over her skin, leaving warmth behind.

When they reached the makeshift dance floor and he pulled her in to move to the slow song the band was playing, Maya really did feel like it was a first date—butterflies, goose bumps and all.

For a moment Maya closed her eyes, breathing in Caleb's salty, soapy scent, the heat that seemed to roll off him in waves. The way that heat seemed to permeate her and make her want him close like this, every day of her life.

His arms were so thick and strong around her back. What would it be like to finally give in?

Dear Reader,

Welcome to Shelter Creek!

Nestled in the rolling hills of Northern California, just inland from the Pacific Ocean, Shelter Creek is a quaint ranching town where locals care deeply about each other, their traditions and the land around them.

But sometimes even the most beautiful place doesn't feel like home anymore. That's how Caleb Dunne feels. He's spent over a decade serving in the Marine Corps, and now he's desperately trying to save his family ranch from debt and ruin.

Shelter Creek isn't home for Maya Burton anymore, either. She left town right after high school, when a terrible tragedy destroyed the love she and Caleb shared. Now she's a wildlife biologist, back in Shelter Creek to spend time with her grandmother and help ranchers like Caleb protect their livestock from predators. Only, sometimes the ranchers don't really want her help!

I loved writing this emotional, complicated story. Maya and Caleb are strong and tough and used to taking care of themselves. Yet with the help of Maya's grandmother, her Book Biddies book club, and a few other human and animal friends, Maya and Caleb learn to lean on others just a little more. In the process, they finally face their past and heal the hurt between them.

I hope you enjoy *Reunited with the Cowboy*. It's the first book in my new series, Heroes of Shelter Creek. If you'd like to keep up with what I'm writing next, or just say hello, please look for me on the web at clairemcewen.com. I always love hearing from readers!

*Claire McEwen*

# HEARTWARMING

## *Reunited with the Cowboy*

——

*Claire McEwen*

**HARLEQUIN® HEARTWARMING™**

Recycling programs
for this product may
not exist in your area.

ISBN-13: 978-1-335-51073-0

Reunited with the Cowboy

Copyright © 2019 by Claire Haiken

Printed in U.S.A.

**Claire McEwen** writes stories about strong heroes and heroines who take big emotional journeys to find their happily-ever-afters. She lives by the ocean in Northern California with her family and a scruffy, mischievous terrier. When she's not writing, Claire enjoys gardening, reading and discovering flea-market treasures. She loves to hear from readers! You can find her on most social media and at clairemcewen.com.

### Books by Claire McEwen

### Harlequin Superromance

*A Ranch to Keep*
*More Than a Rancher*
*Convincing the Rancher*
*Wild Horses*
*Return to Marker Ranch*
*Home Free*
*His Last Rodeo*

Visit the Author Profile page
at Harlequin.com for more titles.

This book is dedicated to my father.
He wouldn't have enjoyed the romance much,
but I think he would have liked the cowboys.

# CHAPTER ONE

MAYA BURTON HAD always loved being alone in the wilderness. But after three hours of climbing through steep, dense, shadowy forest, it occurred to her that this nighttime hike through mountain lion territory might dim that love, just a bit.

It had felt like a good idea, back in Shelter Creek. The odds of meeting a mountain lion on the trail were low, and facing a lion seemed a lot less scary than facing the memories waiting in her hometown.

But Maya had forgotten that forests in this part of California were full of oak and bay trees that sent their branches arching right over the trail. And mountain lions loved to hang out on branches. Shining her flashlight to make sure she was safe still didn't ease the prickly feeling on the back of her neck as she passed underneath.

When she finally reached the edge of

the forest, stepping out onto the wide-open ridgetop was sheer relief. She loved studying mountain lions, but she was glad to be in a place where they couldn't drop on her from above. Maya took in the full moon beaming in the sky, tinting the grassy meadows and scrubby slopes with silver. So much moonlight, she could put her flashlight away.

They were out here too though. Mountain lions, pumas, cougars, catamounts, ghost cats, panthers…maybe the big cats had so many names because they were so mysterious. Able to exist alongside people without anyone realizing they were even there.

Except lately the mountain lions in this area had been attacking livestock on local ranches. And people definitely noticed that.

That was why Maya was here, in the coastal hills surrounding her hometown of Shelter Creek, on a two-month assignment for the Department of Wildlife. She was going to try to find pumas. Photograph them. Count and classify them. Assess the population's overall health and figure out why they were eating so many sheep.

But she'd rather not meet any big cats out here in the dark. "Okay, pumas," she said to the shadowed spaces just past the moonlight. "If you're out there, beat it. I'm coming into your territory and you are not allowed to bother me."

She was being silly. Most big predators would prefer not to run into any humans. Usually people were a meal they didn't have much appetite for, though once in a while…

Ugh. Don't think about *that*.

What was wrong with her tonight? Maya spent weeks at a time living in remote wilderness, studying predators. She rarely worried about being attacked. But tonight she was nervous. Maybe because she was used to the Rocky Mountains, and the way mountain lions behaved when they lived in truly wild places.

Here in Northern California, the mountain lions' habitat was broken up by ranches, towns, cities, roads, wineries and farms. Pumas with limited territory were less predictable and less afraid of people, and this knowledge made every rustle of grass blown by the breeze off the Pacific travel straight up Maya's spine.

Or maybe she was jittery because this afternoon she'd come home for the first time in thirteen years. And promptly had a huge panic attack. That was enough to make a gal nervous. To make her decide that it would be better to jump straight into work than to sit in her grandmother's house, bombarded by memories of the accident that had changed her life forever.

The night she'd lost control of her car and her boyfriend's sister had been killed.

It had all come flooding back today, as Maya drove past the vintage clapboard buildings and flower-filled yards of Shelter Creek's Main Street. Each memory was etched with vivid clarity, a high-definition slide in a tragic slideshow. The click of Julie's seat belt as she freed herself in the back seat. Her drunken refusal when Maya told her to put it back on. Her final words, "No one wants to hear Nirvana," as she flopped into the front seat to change the music. Her shriek of startled laughter as she lost her balance and fell onto Maya. Her weight, her flailing limbs knocking Maya's hands off the steering wheel, blocking her view of the road ahead.

Memories of panic. Of slamming on the brakes, hitting them too hard, sending them into a skid. And one final image, the single strobe-like flash of trees looming in the headlights.

Pulled over by the side of the road today, bracing her weight on the old sign that read Welcome to Shelter Creek, Maya had gasped for breath and tried to remember what a long-ago therapist had taught her about panic attacks.

*Notice what's real. Notice what's around you.*

Maya had tried to focus on the bumpy gravel beneath her sneakers. The warm, dry air of the summer afternoon. The oily, metallic smell of her truck engine, hot after three days of driving west from her home in Boulder, Colorado. The scolding shriek of a Steller's jay in a nearby tree.

She'd calmed herself down, but she was desperate to be alone. To have quiet. She was falling apart, and wilderness, solitude and work were the glue that could put her back together.

Luckily Grandma understood. When she'd opened her front door and found her grand-daughter sitting on her front porch, stuffing scientific equipment into her backpack, she'd just given Maya a giant hug and gone to pack her some food. Grandma had accepted Maya's quirks a long time ago.

Maya scanned the moonlit landscape one more time. No critters that she could see, though surely there were all kinds of nocturnal animals roaming these fields. "Ready or not, here I come!" she called, just to make some more noise, and started out across the ridgetop, trying to relax and finally enjoy the night.

At least being home gave her a chance to walk this trail again. She'd hiked these hills every chance she'd had when she was young. Peaceful, wild places had always called to her. Maybe because her early childhood had been filled with so much chaos before she'd come to live with Grandma in Shelter Creek. Maybe because, in wild places, things were simple. One foot in front of the other. Look, listen, think. Alone in the wilderness, other peoples' decisions, their random acts of craziness, couldn't affect you. Couldn't turn your entire life upside down in an instant.

Maya shook her head, trying to shake off the memories, the feelings. *Think about science, think about pumas, think about this trail and what you remember about it.* At the other end of this meadow, there was a steep hill, thick with shrubs. It was the perfect place for pumas to hide while they waited for their favorite food, mule deer, to leave the safety of their thickets and venture out to graze.

That interface between shrubby hill and open grassland was where she'd set up the first motion-sensitive camera.

Hopefully she'd get a few cameras up and running tonight. They'd feed into her computer and give her a sense of the wildlife in the area. No one had surveyed these rugged hills for mountain lions in years. This would be one step toward figuring out how many of the big cats were living around here.

A swishing sound sent Maya's pulse racing. She glanced over her shoulder. Not a lion. Just the shadowy shape of an owl, launching from the trees behind her. It soared out over the ridge and circled, eerily silent. Maya pulled in a deep breath, filling her lungs with the soothing scents of coyote brush and sage. The smell was pure memory, each inhalation bittersweet.

For so long she assumed she'd never breathe this air again. When she'd bought a one-way bus ticket to college, and what she'd prayed would be a fresh start, Maya swore she'd never look back.

But last month, when her boss at the Department of Wildlife in Boulder had mentioned this job, a short-term attempt to reduce mountain lion attacks on livestock in the area, it had felt almost serendipitous.

Maya was in a lull between research projects, and she'd been worried about her grandmother, who still lived in Shelter Creek. This past year Grandma Lillian had stopped coming out to Colorado to visit Maya, saying she was tired of traveling. She'd even stayed home for Christmas and skipped their annual spring break adventure.

Clearly Grandma was slowing down. This job could be Maya's chance to check on her, to make sure she was still able to live on her own and care for herself.

And maybe it was time to do what her grandmother had been telling her she needed to do for years. To finally face the memories that waited for her in Shelter Creek.

That part hadn't gone so well, so far. Maya would have to be stronger, or she'd never survive the next two months.

The terrain around the trail was changing. The brush was thicker here, providing good cover for various animals. She'd catch coyotes on her cameras for sure. She'd heard a few of them yipping and yowling in the woods about a mile back. She'd probably see plenty of skunks, raccoons and foxes on the feed too. And with good camera placement and a lot of luck, she might get footage of mountain lions.

A sharp sound cut through her thoughts. Maya froze, heart hammering, listening so hard that the silence felt loud. The sound was gone now. But there had been something. The crack of a stick underfoot. *Something.*

Another noise—closer this time. A rustling in the bushes. Whatever it was, it was big. Normally a mountain lion wouldn't be this noisy, but what else could it be? Stray cattle, maybe?

The crisp snap of a branch shattered her fragile composure. Maya whirled to face the threat. A shadow loomed up from the brush. With a shriek, Maya leaped back and stumbled on the raised grass that edged the trail. Arms flailing, feet staggering, she fought for balance as her backpack pulled her down.

*Oomph.* Air shot from her lungs as she hit the dirt hard. She lay on her back like a stranded turtle, arms and legs useless as her pack held her down.

Clawing her way out of the confining straps, Maya jumped to her feet, groped for her safety whistle and blew hard. The shrill sound sliced open the night.

*Pepper spray.* It was in her belt. Wrenching it from the holster, Maya held out the can and slowly backed away from the dark shadow emerging from the bushes.

"Hang on! It's okay!"

The unexpected voice stopped her in an instant. It wasn't a mountain lion. It was a man.

"Who are you?" Her voice quavered, weak and thin. But she couldn't be weak here, alone on a trail. She drew herself up to her full five-foot-one frame and gripped her pepper spray a little tighter, her pulse pounding in her ears.

The man stepped slowly onto the trail from some low bushes, where he must have been hiding. In the dim moonlight he was a dark shadow. Maya could see the outline of his cowboy hat, but not much else about him. Except in one hand, he held…a rifle.

Maya froze—the gun changing everything.

"It's okay." The man's voice was low and steady, like he was trying to be reassuring. "I'm sorry if I scared you."

Maya's heart wouldn't slow. Her breath

wouldn't fill her lungs. She needed to calm down, to get back in control.

But it was a strange man. With a *gun*. On a hiking trail. At night.

This wasn't good. Worse than a lion. Her thoughts sped, frantic. This trail wasn't that far from the highway. Was he some kind of homeless wanderer? A serial killer?

She had to get a grip. She'd spent her entire adult life in the wilderness. Had never met a problem she couldn't handle. But that wilderness had been remote and isolated. Not like this area, so close to cities and towns. And people.

She tried to put authority in her shaking tone. "I'm with the Department of Wildlife. Lower your weapon."

He lowered it to his side and pointed it toward the ground.

"Is it loaded?"

"Yes."

Maya's blood chilled when she heard the safety click. He'd been ready to shoot. Could so easily have ended her life with just a twitch of a finger. The knowledge rippled down her spine, and one of her knees started shaking like it had a mind of its own.

The man spoke quietly. "Did you get hurt when you fell? Do you want some light?"

Her flashlight. She should have reached for it right away. Maya grabbed it now and directed its beam straight at his face.

"Hey!" He tilted his head down and brought a forearm across his eyes. "Can you shine that somewhere else?"

"Not until you put the gun on the ground." She shoved every ounce of confidence she'd ever felt into her voice.

"Not easy to do when you're blinding me."

"Just put it down." Her heart was going to pound right through her ribs if he didn't get rid of that gun.

"Okay! Hang on." He walked a few steps backward and slowly bent to set the gun on the ground. As he straightened, he tilted his hat back and looked right at her, squinting to protect his eyes. "Can you move the light now?"

She couldn't move the light. Didn't know if she'd ever move anything again, because now she could see his face, and it was Caleb. Caleb Dunne.

A metallic taste coated her tongue, and she swallowed hard. Both of her knees were shaking now, and the flashlight beam quivered with her trembling hand as if her entire body was rebelling at the sight of him. Rebelling against this homecoming, which was already turning into the disaster she'd always assumed it would be.

She had to lower the light. It was wrong to keep blinding him. But if she lowered it, he'd realize who she was. And Maya already knew what his reaction would be. Rage. Disgust. Horror. Because she was the last person Caleb would want to meet on this trail, or anywhere else.

Still, they couldn't stay like this forever. Maya forced her hand down, every millimeter of motion triggering an exponential increase in dread. She had no hat brim to hide under, and the moon was rising higher, the pearly light bathing them. As the beam reached the ground, she heard Caleb's sharp gasp of recognition. He took a stiff step forward. Then another.

"Maya?" His voice was hollow, as if just the sight of her gutted him.

There was nothing she could do but stand there while he stared, his dark eyes burning into her, branding her a murderer. The name

he'd called her the last time she'd seen him,
so many years ago.

There was nowhere to run this time, no
bus to catch, no remote Colorado wilderness
to hide in, as she'd done for almost a decade
now. A strange, slow feeling seeped through
her, resignation so strong, it was almost relief,
easing the turmoil in her mind, allowing her
to move a step or two toward him. This meeting she'd feared and dreaded for so long was
right here upon her, and there was nothing
she could do but accept whatever came next.

"Yes," she said softly. "It's me. Maya. I'm
home."

FOR A SPLIT SECOND Caleb wondered if Maya
was actually real. Still as prey, with moonlight painting shadows around her eyes, she
was almost ghostlike. Fitting, since she'd
haunted him for all these years.

His hands had become fists, and he carefully unclenched them, trying to fathom her
presence on this trail. "Why are you here?"
It came out in a hoarse whisper.

"Work." She twisted the light nervously
in her hands, casting wild shapes across the

ground between them. "And to see my grandmother. Why are *you* here?"

He heard the question, knew he should answer, but it was *Maya*, standing right here in
front of him, and his words were boulders
lodged in his throat. Caleb swallowed hard
and tried to take her in. He'd never thought
he'd see her again.

A thought skittered around his mind like
a panicked rabbit. He'd almost shot her. If it
had been a darker night, if she hadn't fallen
and let out that yelp, if he'd been a different
rancher, less patient and more trigger-happy…
There were so many scenarios in which he
could have shot her. If he had, he'd be standing over her bleeding, broken body right now.

The image sent the night reeling, the moon
spinning, his heart pounding through his
veins. He'd wanted that mountain lion, had
been looking so hard for it that a part of his
brain had assumed that was exactly what she
was. Fear blazed into anger. "You're crazy,
walking out here on your own."

Her shrug dismissed his worry like it meant
nothing. "I've spent most of my adult life outside, on my own."

She reminded him of how little he knew her now. And how well he once had.

"I could have shot you," he blurted out, not in control, not able to decide which of the words, dislodged now and tumbling through his head in a landslide, he should actually say out loud.

He could hear the shaky breath she drew. "Do you wish you had?"

"What?" Aghast, he took a step closer. "No. Never. I'm not a murderer."

As soon as he'd spoken the word, he froze. *Murderer.* He'd called Maya that the last time he'd seen her. He'd been called that himself, a few times since. And the irony wasn't lost on him. She hadn't been a murderer, hadn't even been guilty. But he probably was.

Of course the military shrink had told him different. But Caleb had made mistakes in Afghanistan that he couldn't forgive. He'd hoped to leave them behind now that he was home for good, but he hadn't known then that regret had no borders. How things you put aside in the daytime ran rampant in your mind at night. Another reason he was out on the trail tonight. It was easier out here, hunting, protecting his livestock, than tossing and turning, desperate for sleep, even while dreading the dreams that sleep might bring.

"I don't wish you harm, Maya."

She huffed out a shaky laugh. "Well, seeing as we're alone out here, and you have a gun, I'm glad to hear it."

"I'm after a mountain lion. It's been killing my sheep."

She stilled then—nothing he could see, but something he could sense.

"Really?" She gave a strange little hollow laugh. "Well, isn't that just perfect?"

Her sarcasm baffled him. Then he remembered what she'd said moments before. That she was with the Department of Wildlife.

"I have a permit. A depredation permit. To kill the lion."

"I'll need to see it."

It was like looking into a twisted carnival mirror, where nothing was as it seemed. Maya, on a trail near his ranch, in the middle of the night. Maya, suddenly sounding official and asking for his paperwork. Which, of course, he didn't have with him.

Not for the first time, Caleb wished he'd reenlisted. Just stayed in the Marine Corps forever and never come back to Shelter Creek.

Home, ranching…it was supposed to be simple. But every day brought a new complication. "I left the permit back at the ranch."

She sighed as if she couldn't believe his incompetence. "Okay. Well, please don't shoot anything until I've seen that permit."

It was sinking in now, this bizarre situation they were in. "Let me get this straight. *You're* in charge of permits? I have to answer to *you* if I need to shoot a mountain lion?"

"I'm the temporary field biologist for this area, in charge of wildlife management, among other things. So, yes, you'll need to clear the use of that permit with me."

Her words filtered through his denial. "You can't be serious."

She sounded resigned. "I'm afraid I am."

"I never thought I'd see you again." The words tumbled out, rough and raw. He'd loved her. So damn much.

A pained smile twisted the corner of her mouth. "Don't worry. Once I know for sure that my grandmother is doing well, I'll leave. This job is just a temporary position for the summer."

It was probably rude to feel so much relief. She had every right to be here, and if her grandmother needed her, then she *should* be here. But it didn't mean he wanted Maya anywhere near him. All they could do for each other was bring up old hurt and brutal memories. And feelings. So many damn feelings that his throat burned with them, like they *wanted* to be shared, *needed* to be shared. But how could he? It was all so long ago. The damage he'd done had solidified into concrete. Had become the foundation on which they'd both built new lives.

He wanted to go, to retreat, to put at least a few miles between them. He took the first steps away. "Well, good luck with your grandmother. And the job."

"I'll need it." Her mouth hinted at a wry smile. "Especially because Grandma is as stubborn as ever. And because I have to try to help ranchers like you with predator management."

He couldn't work with her. "I don't need any help. A mountain lion killed my sheep. I have the right to shoot it. End of story."

Maya made no sign that his tone bothered her; instead her voice remained steady and calm, like nothing about this meeting or this conflict shook her. "There are new regulations in place. You have to try to manage predators without harming them. Shooting is a last resort now."

Worry settled cold in Caleb's stomach. He couldn't afford to lose one more animal. "What do I have to do?"

"Well, it depends on what you're already doing. We can talk more about it when I visit your ranch."

"Visit my ranch?" Caleb ran a hand over the film of sweat that was coating the back of his neck despite the chill night. Maya on his ranch. Maya seeing how run-down and ruined it was, how low he'd ended up. "Why do you need to visit my ranch?"

"To see where attacks have occurred. And to figure out how we can prevent any more of them."

*We?* There could be no *we* here. "What do you know about ranching?" He was being rude, but he didn't care. He didn't want a visit. Didn't want help. Didn't want anything to do with her. Already he felt the pull, like she emitted some kind of memory-inducing pheromone that allowed him to see their past so clearly. Maya laughing by the swimming hole, water droplets clinging to her tanned skin. Maya riding these hills, next to him, reaching her hand out for his. Each image crystal clear, each memory so good.

Until it had all gone so bad.

She was silent for a moment, as if gathering up her next arguments. She'd always been stubborn, and it seemed like that hadn't changed.

"Look, Caleb. We both know I'm not a rancher. But I know a lot about wildlife management and predator-prey relationships. So I'll probably have some useful advice."

He caught the edge of frustration in her voice. He was being a jerk, but maybe that was okay if it would help keep her from coming out to his property. He didn't want time with her. Didn't want to face everything he'd lost when he'd told her to leave. "We shouldn't even be around each other."

"Trust me—I was hoping to avoid you. But here we are." She gestured around them, at the trail, at the night, in a sort of helpless way. Like their meeting was a fate she didn't want but had already accepted.

Caleb didn't want to accept it. Because he was already torn, wanting her to stay away and wanting to see her again. Because she was Maya and no one had ever made him feel the way she had. Even now, here, arguing, he felt some part of himself wake up, like it had been sleeping all these years, dormant. Waiting.

Maya reached for her pack and swung it up onto her back in an effortless motion. Though how someone so tiny could carry that much gear was beyond him.

"I'm going to be hiking out here for the next couple of days. I'll stop by your ranch later in the week to talk about your options. How about Thursday?"

"Thursday," he repeated stupidly. Because the whole idea that he and Maya were standing on this trail, in the middle of the night, making plans, was surreal. He didn't want plans, didn't want her help, and he opened his mouth to tell her, but she was already talking.

"Until then try not to shoot any lions. If you need to scare them off, blow a whistle. Bang a few pots and pans. Spray water. Get creative."

Before he could answer, she gave a little wave, like they'd just run into each other on the street or something. Then she walked off into the darkness as if it was perfectly normal for her to head out into wild places, by herself, at night.

Maybe it was. He didn't know her anymore. Not at all.

Caleb listened to her footsteps until they faded to nothing and she became just another part of the ghostly moonlight. Like she hadn't been real. Like she'd never been here at all.

Except she was real. And when she showed up at his ranch, there'd be no hiding the mess there. She'd see it all. The leaning fences, the overgrown fields, the ruined barns, the neglected house. The visible evidence that his family had shattered beyond repair, on the night Maya drove into a tree and killed his sister.

# CHAPTER TWO

CALEB THREW A dollar tip on the bar and took a gulp of his second beer. Dex's Alehouse was busy for a Tuesday night. The usual customers crowded around the beat-up dartboards and pool tables. Ranch hands, workers from the vineyards, mechanics and store clerks—the regular folks of Shelter Creek—all showed up here.

Most of the town's wealthier residents would be over at the new craft brewpub, or one of the wine bars that had opened up in Shelter Creek over the last few years. Change was coming, courtesy of better roads and direct flights from Los Angeles to the nearby city of Santa Rosa. Ranch land was being plowed under for vineyards. Big tasting rooms and cute inns were drawing weekend tourist crowds.

If he could, Caleb would pick up the whole town and move it a few hundred miles north, away from all the tourists. He'd keep it small and simple, just the way it had always been. Dex always said that Caleb lived in the past, and maybe that was true. So far the present hadn't shown him much to get excited about.

Except now Maya was back. Though that wasn't exciting. It was so many feelings, he didn't even have words for them all. The combination was irritating, like a horsefly that kept buzzing around his head no matter how many times he slapped it away.

Why the hell did she have to be so…so Maya? Even on a dark trail, with a huge backpack on her back, she'd been achingly familiar. The flashlight had caught her long brown hair, woven into braids, the way she used to wear it when they went riding or did stuff around the ranch. He'd seen the shadows below her cheekbones and the light in her eyes.

He'd thought he'd never have to see any of that again. Figured it was for the best. Whatever had been between them was in the past. Separated from the present by the massive chasm of his sister's death in Maya's car.

He'd raged at Maya after the accident.

Raged and blamed and thrown his grief like grenades, destroying everything they'd had.

Still, somehow, last night on the trail, there'd been this thread, this connection. A tenuous glimmer of remembered love and shared pain that had linked them together.

He hadn't felt linked to anyone since he'd said goodbye to the guys in his platoon and left for home. And even those connections had been different. Camaraderie. Teamwork. Friendship.

What he'd felt last night was far more confusing. A vague sense that, on some deep level, she knew him and he knew her. And even if what they knew about each other contained so much that was bad, it still made him feel less adrift.

He practically lifted his hand to swat that last thought away. Darn horsefly.

Where was Jace? He'd talked his buddy into meeting him here, hoping his old friend would lighten his dark mood. He needed the distraction. He couldn't stand here thinking about Maya for another second.

Caleb pushed his way through the crowd and wrote his name on the chalkboard near the pool tables. Then he leaned on the wall to watch the play. A guy he didn't recognize lined up his cue to take a shot. He was going for the eight ball, and no way was he going to make it. Caleb bit back the urge to help him out and watched him miss instead. Watched his friend clap him on the back in triumph and go on to win the game.

Winners and losers. Life had clearly defined boundaries about that. And Caleb knew which category he fit into. He'd tried to come to terms with losing everything. Tried to be okay with wanting nothing more than a clear deed for the ranch and a few beers at the end of the day.

Ever since he'd come home from Afghanistan, he'd tried to believe it was enough.

Glancing toward the door, Caleb spotted Jace heading for the bar, well-dressed as always, in dark jeans, polished boots and a plaid Western shirt. The former bull rider had been a total ladies' man on the circuit, and he still dressed the part.

Glancing down at his own worn black T-shirt with the feed company logo chipped and faded across the chest, Caleb figured he had a ways to go in that department. Which was okay by him. Women wanted things he couldn't give. Money. Stability. Fun.

There were a few empty tables, and maybe he should grab one, but Caleb was too wired to sit. He'd been fired up ever since he'd run into Maya last night.

She was coming by his ranch to give him advice on Thursday. That was rich. His townie ex-girlfriend had gone off to college to become an expert on ranching? *She* had the authority to tell him not to shoot the mountain lion that threatened his sheep?

He drained his beer. When he'd finished, Jace was just a few steps away. "You look like hell."

Caleb set his empty down. "Glad to see you too. I wasn't sure you'd get away from the rug rats tonight." Jace was the brand-new foster parent for his nieces and nephew, and he had shadows under his eyes to prove it.

Jace smiled wearily. "I just hope they're not tearing up the place. Carly said she'd get them to bed on time, but I have my doubts."

"Well, from what you've told me, Carly is used to being responsible for the other kids."

"Yeah, but that doesn't mean she likes it." Jace took a gulp from his beer, like he had to fortify himself just to think about his fifteen-year-old niece. "Teenage girls are scary."

"Well, scary or not, I'm glad she took over tonight. It's good to have you back in town."

"I won't have a lot of time for bars, but you're always welcome to stop by. Come for dinner. Though I can't promise much. My cooking skills are still pretty hit-or-miss." Jace grinned. "Mostly miss."

Caleb tried to meet his friend's smile. He should be going by, should be helping Jace out. But the whole family thing made him uncomfortable. What would he say to a kid? What would he talk about at a family meal? His own family had fallen apart after Julie died—his parents had split up and first Mom, then Dad, had left town. It had been over a decade since Caleb had sat down to a family dinner.

"Have you heard anything about your sister's trial? Is she really in jail for the long haul?" Caleb still couldn't believe it. Jace's older sister, Brenda, had always seemed so sophisticated and smart. Then she'd gotten hooked on drugs and started a relationship with her dealer.

Jace leaned on the wall beside him. "Twenty

years for drug manufacturing, distribution, weapons, all kinds of stuff. On top of neglect of her kids."

"That's rough. How are the kids doing?"

"Let's just say it's an adjustment period for all of us." Jace took a long pull of his beer, then swiped a sleeve across his mouth in a careless gesture that spoke reams about his state of mind. "I just wish I'd paid more attention. Figured out what was really going on. Those kids have seen way too much. It messes with them."

Caleb cast around for some words of reassurance. He was rusty at any kind of real conversation. The weather, livestock, the cost of feed… He could talk about all that. But he'd learned a long time ago that his own inner world contained troubles too big to share. They stopped conversations. Made everyone look miserable. So he avoided talking about anything heavy. Better to stay on the surface than drown in the depths.

He surveyed the bar, looking for a new topic. They could always talk cattle. Jace had recently purchased an old ranch, and he could go on for hours about the bucking bulls he planned to raise once he got the place fixed up.

A woman sitting at the bar looked familiar. She turned to say something to her companion, and her name hit Caleb like a blow to the gut. *Trisha Gilbert.* Julie's best friend growing up, who'd been with her the night of the accident. Who'd survived.

He hadn't run into Trisha since he'd been home. What was going on? First Maya, and now this? Was there some cruel alignment of the planets that was bringing these women back into his life? He didn't need reminders of the accident. He had plenty, every day that he lived and his little sister didn't.

As Caleb watched, Trisha slid off a stool and walked toward the restroom. She moved with a slight limp and Caleb wondered if that was her souvenir from that horrible night. Trisha's leg had been broken in a couple of places.

The guy she was with—kind of a skinny, ratty-looking dude—glanced furtively around the bar, reached into his pocket, took something out and dropped it in Trisha's drink.

"Holy hell," Caleb murmured, taking a few steps forward. He set his beer down on the nearest table, ignoring the protests of its occupants.

"What's going on?" Jace moved to stand beside him.

Caleb pointed to the bar. "That guy right there? He drugged Trisha's drink."

Cold fury flooded Caleb's system, pressing out from inside his chest, and he was moving, shoving aside chairs and people until he was in front of the ratty man. He grabbed the guy's collar. "What did you put in it?"

"Get off me," the guy spluttered. "I don't know what you're talking about."

"I saw you," Caleb ground out, gripping him even harder. "I saw you put something in that drink."

"Is there a problem?" The bartender, Royce, was Dex's nephew. Small, young, not much help in a fight.

"This guy spiked his date's drink." Jace handed Royce the glass. "Save that. Call the cops."

Royce eyed the man in disgust and put the drink out of sight, behind the bar. "I'm calling." He pulled a cell phone out of his pocket.

"I didn't do anything." The man's whine scraped away the last shreds of Caleb's civility. Men like this hurt women and there were too many of them out there, wreaking havoc. Older guys had gotten Trisha and Julie drunk, the night Julie died. And now this jerk was hoping to do God-knows-what to Trisha.

The idea of some guy targeting Julie, in some future that could never happen, curled Caleb's fingers tighter around the man's coat. "Don't ever come back here." Caleb pulled him off the stool, shoved him toward the door, once, twice, herding the stumbling, stammering scum.

"Back off," the man squeaked as he crashed into a table.

Caleb grabbed the weasel one more time and hauled him out into the night.

In the parking lot, the man tried to break free, but Caleb held tight and raised his fist. Trisha could have been his sister. She could have been Julie.

Someone grabbed his hand and forced it down. "Get a hold of yourself," Jace commanded, low and stern, wrenching Caleb's arm behind his back. "You've done enough."

The weasel saw his chance and ran for his vehicle.

Headlights lit up the night as a sheriff's car turned into the parking lot and pulled alongside them. The window lowered to reveal the scowling face of Adam Sears, now Deputy Sears, a friend from high school. "I heard there's a problem. And look who it is. I should have known I'd find you out here, Caleb."

It was hard to look dignified when your buddy had you in an arm lock, but Caleb tried. "It's that guy over there, getting into the silver pickup."

"Caleb, were you beating on the guy? I warned you last time. No more fights."

"I just chucked him out of the bar." The irritation was back, several horseflies now, buzzing wildly in Caleb's mind. Adam was wasting time while the jerk got away.

Adam shook his head like a disappointed dad. "This wasn't your problem to solve."

"I don't see *you* solving it." Caleb tried to break free, but Jace wouldn't budge. "Why don't you do your job and stop him before he drives off?"

Adam pointed toward another car pulling into the lot, lights flashing. "He won't get far. And my job is to keep the peace. Right now that means stopping you from doing anything stupid. I don't want you back in my jail. I don't want to charge you with assault. So calm down. Okay?"

Breath coming in ragged gulps, Caleb jerked his head toward the silver truck. "Shouldn't you be talking to him?"

"I will be. But I also want to talk to you. Tomorrow morning. Meet me at the diner at nine."

"I've got a ranch to run." No way did he want a heart-to-heart about his wrongdoings with Adam, who made straight and narrow look so easy.

"Just meet him," Jace said in a low voice. "You're lucky he's not arresting you." He loosened his grip, and Caleb's arm flopped back down to his side, the blood flooding in with pins and needles.

"Fine." Caleb's vision was clearing, the laser focus on his quarry easing. He suddenly noticed all the people who'd followed them out of the bar. They were standing around, gaping at him. Once again, he'd provided the entertainment at Dex's. He should start charging admission. He glared at Adam. "But you're buying."

"Just be there." Adam finally turned to look at the man who'd tried to drug Trisha. The coward had his hands on the truck while the newly arrived deputy frisked him. Adam took his microphone off the dashboard and his voice blared through the loudspeaker, silencing everyone in the lot. "Okay folks, that's a wrap. Time to go inside."

"Show off," Caleb muttered as Adam drove off across the lot to help arrest the guy. "Come on. I could use another drink. And we should check on Trisha."

"Hang on." Jace put a hand on his arm to stop him, jerking it back when Caleb whirled to face him.

"What? Are you gonna give me a lecture too? I'm pretty sure Adam will take care of that tomorrow."

"C'mon. I've known you forever. What is wrong with you?" Jace looked tired all of a sudden, and Caleb remembered everything his friend was dealing with at home. He'd lost his rodeo career, his entire life, when he'd taken on his sister's kids.

"Nothing's wrong." Just saying the words felt like effort. The rage that had powered him into overdrive was fading. Now even the air felt heavy, weighing down muscle and bone.

"*Nothing's wrong,*" Jace mimicked. "You sound like a teenager. And I've already got one of those in my life. Seriously, what happened? Why are you so angry all the time?"

Where the hell to start? All the problems on the ranch that he couldn't find the money to repair? The nightmares that stole his sleep? Or he could always blame Afghanistan, and everything that went down in that dusty hell-hole.

Talking about that kind of stuff was impossible. So he'd blame the most immediate issue. "A mountain lion has been killing off my sheep. I got a permit, and last night I went out to shoot it. I ran into Maya instead."

"Maya Burton?" Jace stared. "What was Maya doing near your ranch?"

Haunting him. A beautiful, brainy, scientist-ghost. "She's some kind of expert on mountain lions. She said she was tracking them."

"Sounds like she can't be as smart as we all thought if her job involves chasing lions."

"Maybe." Caleb glowered, too much feeling coursing through him to appreciate the lame joke. He'd almost killed her. Almost shot her out there, on that trail. "She wants to come by my ranch and tell me how to keep them away."

Jace blew out a breath. "That doesn't seem

like a great idea. You could tell her you'd rather not."

"Trust me, I tried. But there are new laws, and apparently listening to her is one of them." But there was more. Maya wasn't the only reason to lose it. "Then Trisha tonight… well, it felt almost like someone was trying to hurt Julie." Caleb ran a hand through his hair, trying to bring his thoughts into some kind of order. "Coming home, being on the ranch, seeing Maya and now Trisha, it just brings it all back."

"I get it," Jace said quietly. "I really do. But you've got to find a way to keep the past from messing up the present."

Caleb eyed this new, mature version of his friend. "Not too long ago you would have landed a punch or two yourself."

"Not too long ago I didn't have three kids to think about," Jace countered. "I've had to change. Maybe it's time you grew up too."

The old sorrow knotted in Caleb's stomach. "I kind of feel like I grew up a long time ago. But I skipped the fun part and went straight to being the bitter old guy hunched at the end of the bar."

"You've got to get over the things that are

eating at you. Adam isn't going to let you off with a chat over breakfast if this kind of thing happens again. You're not a Marine anymore. You can't deal with your problems via combat."

Jace was right. But sometimes it was hard to stop fighting, after he'd spent so many years doing just that.

Caleb looked over at Adam, still across the parking lot, talking to the other deputy. His old friend had locked him up once already, a few months ago, the day Caleb realized that his dad had stopped paying taxes and the state was about to take possession of the ranch. Caleb had gotten drunk and disorderly at Dex's as he tried to absorb the news—that his beloved Bar D Ranch, which he'd held in his mind like a precious prize to claim once he'd finished his final tour, was about to slip out of his hands.

He'd never told Adam or Jace the reason for his binge that night. He was too ashamed of the poverty, the way that his family, once respected and influential in Shelter Creek, was about to lose the very ground beneath their feet. Instead he'd sobered up in the drunk tank and gone home to figure out how to save the ranch.

And he had. Sort of. He'd worked out a payment plan with the state that could save the Bar D, eventually. But making those payments was a challenge, especially when the ranch also needed so many repairs. So when a mountain lion had taken a couple of sheep last week, it had felt even more personal than it might have otherwise. Those sheep were Caleb's only hope of income, his chance to get himself out of this financial mess.

Jace cleared his throat. "Want to see if we're up at the pool table yet?"

Good old Jace. Knowing when to stop lecturing and have some fun. "Okay." Caleb clapped his friend on the shoulder. "Thank you."

"Don't mention it." Jace pulled his phone out of his pocket and glanced at it. "I've got to be home in an hour. And you should go home then too."

"Yes, Dad." Caleb winced as Jace landed a punch to his shoulder. "Ouch. I thought you were a pacifist now."

"Mostly. But as your friend, it's still my duty to hit you when you're being an idiot."

"Then I guess you've got yourself a new punching bag."

"You've got to grow up. I'm serious."

"I'm grown. I promise." Caleb followed Jace back into the bar, knowing his friend was right. Adam was right. He had to stop fighting. He had to stop drinking so much. But if he did, what would he have left?

Nothing but troubles he didn't know how to solve and memories he didn't want to face.

## CHAPTER THREE

MAYA HEAVED HER backpack through Grandma's front door, inhaling the scent of the lavender sachets Grandma put in every drawer. It was the same smell Maya had noticed when she'd first come to live here as a scared, sad five-year-old. Peace. Comfort. Safety.

Funny how Maya hadn't noticed the lavender when she'd stopped by briefly on Monday. She'd been too busy trying to figure out how to get away from town again, as fast as possible.

She unlaced her dusty hiking boots and set them back outside on the porch before stepping inside and closing the front door behind her. "Grandma, are you here? I'm home!"

"In the living room!" Grandma Lillian's voice was light with laughter, and suddenly the meaning of all the cars parked in front of the house sank in. It was Wednesday evening. Grandma's book club was here. "Come on in and say hello to The Book Biddies," Grandma called.

Glancing down at her dusty clothes and scraped-up legs, Maya winced. She needed a shower desperately after spending two nights and days on the trail. "I'm really dirty!" she called back.

"Ooh most people don't admit that outright," came a sardonic voice Maya didn't recognize.

A roomful of giggles followed the quip. They must have busted out the drinks already. So many of Grandma's stories about The Book Biddies involved alcohol, Maya teased her that they should change their name to The Booze Biddies.

"I'm going to shower first!" She made it to the first landing on the stairs before Grandma appeared at the bottom, hands fisted on her hips.

"Maya Burton, are you hiding from a bunch of old ladies?"

"No." Her face heated. "But I've been camping for two nights. I need to get cleaned up."

"Come say a quick hello. Everyone is so excited to see you. It's been thirteen years."

"Exactly. So can't we wait twenty minutes more? I look terrible."

"No one cares how you look. And we're going to get into our book talk soon. Just come?"

Maya's feet were reluctant weights as she stomped back down the stairs. "I'm probably covered in poison oak and ticks."

"Then a few of my friends shouldn't scare you." Grandma folded her arms across her pink-flowered bosom and set her lips in the stubborn line Maya recognized as the ancestor to hers. "I know you're anxious about being home again. But my book club is the perfect place to dip your toes in the water."

"I'm not ready to dip my toes anywhere but the shower."

"Don't be silly," Grandma said and turned around with the confidence that Maya would follow.

Which she did. This was Grandma asking, so she'd do what would make her happy. As she followed her grandmother down the hall, Maya noticed how light on her feet the older woman was. Grandma wore hip fake-leather leggings today, a top covered in pink flowers and sparkly flat shoes. She moved like a much younger woman. Why had she stopped traveling? Why hadn't she wanted to come see Maya anymore?

Maya had assumed it was because her grandmother was slowing down physically. But she sure didn't seem slow. She was practically skipping. And judging from the laughter in the next room, Grandma wasn't lacking in friends. She didn't seem lonely or depressed.

Just before they reached the living room, Maya paused, heart thumping against her ribs, the air suddenly thin. It was one thing accidentally running into Caleb; it was another to deliberately meet a bunch of people who all knew her past. Maya had never had to do it before. Leaving town so soon after the accident had given her a fresh start where no one knew her story. No one knew that her bad driving had killed her boyfriend's sister, the town's sweetheart, Julie Dunne.

Of course Maya knew. Shame and regret ate at the edges of even her best days, and devoured her entirely on others. But she'd never had to be around anyone, except Grandma Lillian, who *also knew*.

Her heart kicked up another notch, and Maya inhaled a shaky breath, trying to calm down.

Grandma must have heard, because she paused, her face set and stern. "Chin up," she said softly. "You can do this. It's time to stop hiding."

Maya wasn't sure about that last sentence. Hiding had served her pretty well for over a decade.

But her grandmother had been so devoted over the years, traveling to see Maya wherever she was. The very least Maya could do was meet her book club friends.

Grandma took Maya by the hand. Wrapped in her soft grip, Maya trailed into the living room behind her, feeling like the lost kid she'd been when Grandma had taken her out of foster care and given her a home.

Once inside the doorway, Grandma released her hand and Maya stepped forward on her own power. She was instantly met with a chorus of "There she is!" and one "Oh my goodness, what happened to you?"

Maybe she should have showered first.

Heart thrumming an uncomfortable bass in her chest, Maya broke through the wall of exclamations. "I've been out hiking the past couple of days." She looked around the room, recognizing most of the women sitting on Lillian's comfortable sofas but feeling suddenly shy about greeting them. "Hello."

Grandma gave Maya's shoulder a quick, bracing squeeze. "Maya was out tracking mountain lions."

"Why in the world would you want to do that?" A woman in a red sweaterdress, her platinum hair coiled in a perfectly styled chignon, raised her penciled eyebrows.

Grandma gestured in the elegant woman's direction. "This is Monique Lawrence. She owns Monique's Miracles. It's a wonderful salon."

Not that Maya spent any time at salons. But Grandma was forever hopeful.

"Nice to meet you, Monique," Maya said.

Monique gave her a beautifully manicured wave. "So nice to finally meet you."

"Maya!" Mrs. Axel, Maya's former teacher, heaved herself out of Grandma's coziest armchair. "How wonderful to see you!"

Maya went to Mrs. Axel and hugged her gingerly, trying to keep her dusty clothes away from the other woman's flowered cardigan sweater. Mrs. Axel had always been small, but she felt frail now, and that one change drove home all the other changes Maya must have missed while avoiding Shelter Creek. Changes that Grandma had experienced, without her, because Maya had been too scared to face her past. She cleared the lump of guilt in her throat. "It's great to see you too."

Mrs. Axel held her at arm's length, her pale blue eyes swimming with tears. "Look at you, all grown-up."

"Grown-up and absolutely beautiful!" The exclamation came from Kathy Wallace, Grandma's next-door neighbor, who'd babysat Maya and been on hand for every one of life's occasions, from dance recitals to holiday meals. "It's amazing to see you again," Kathy said, reaching out her arms. "The photos your grandmother shares with me just haven't done you justice."

Maya hugged her, blinking back the sting of her own tears. Ever since she'd left, all of her thoughts of Shelter Creek were about what she'd been trying to avoid. Not about people like Kathy, who'd invested so much in her as a child. Who'd believed in her as she was growing up.

"I'm sorry that I haven't been in touch," she managed to say. "It's so good to see you, Kathy."

When they pulled apart, Kathy's cheeks

were pink and she dabbed at her eyes. "Now, let's not get all weepy. I wasn't trying to make you feel guilty. It's just wonderful to see you again. It's been so many years, I thought… Well, never mind what I thought. It's just so good to have you home."

Maya tried to tamp down the emotion threatening to overwhelm her. "I know it's been a long time. But Grandma was always so great about coming to see me, I guess I never needed to come home." It was a weak lie and as soon as it was out, Maya felt like an idiot. "But I should have," she corrected.

"Well, you've always given me a reason to have an adventure somewhere new," Grandma chimed in, kind as ever. "There are benefits to having a granddaughter who won't settle down." Grandma gave Maya a glass of white wine and a quick kiss on the cheek. "Still, it's very nice to have you home."

"It sure is." Annie Brooks rose from where she'd been sitting in the far corner, by Grandma's piano. Annie had been a close friend of Grandma's since the two of them were rivals for Miss Shelter Creek Rodeo, back when they were in high school. Now she came forward and clasped both of Maya's hands in her own. "Welcome home, Maya."

"Thank you." Annie's face was the same, with just a bit more weathering from all the time she'd spent out on her ranch. Her hair had more salt than pepper, but her warm smile hadn't changed. "It's so nice to see you again."

Annie just nodded, gave Maya's hands one more gentle squeeze and then retreated to her seat. She never was a person to express her emotions in words, but Maya had always loved her. Annie had taught her to ride horses, had encouraged her passion for the outdoors and had shown her an example of what a strong woman in a nontraditional job was like.

Maya took a sip of wine to soothe the roughness in her throat and perched carefully on the arm of the sofa next to where Grandma sat down. Hopefully her dusty clothes wouldn't do too much damage.

"How was your hike, dear?" Kathy asked. "Did you see any lions?"

"I saw one in a tree, early yesterday morning. I got a few photos, actually. And I set up several motion-sensitive cameras in the area. Hopefully I'll catch some more photos with that."

"Did you hear that?" Mrs. Axel waved her wineglass at the group. "I was her teacher, you know. And third grade was a big year for studying animal habitats."

Maya laughed. Mrs. Axel had been a great teacher, taking the kids on nature walks and getting them excited about the local flora and fauna. "It's true. Grandma, next time you get mad at me for chasing lions, you can blame Mrs. Axel."

"You should call me Priscilla." Mrs. Axel poured herself a generous refill of wine. "And I'm proud to play a part in your pursuit of lions."

"Well, then when she gets bit by one, I'll know who's responsible." Grandma sighed. "Maya, when you became a biology major, I assumed you'd end up teaching at a university or working in a laboratory. Not crashing through the woods, searching for predators."

"I like the woods," Maya said. "And predators."

"You always loved animals," Kathy added. "Remember, Lillian, when she found those abandoned baby raccoons? And tried to raise them herself?"

"Oh my goodness, I'd forgotten." Grandma giggled. "And remember when she tried to pet an otter in the Russian River?"

"Oh no." Maya put her free hand up in protest. "Do we have to talk about that?"

"Oh yes, we do," Kathy said with a chortle. "That thing chased you all the way up onto the beach."

"I never knew otters had fangs like that," Grandma added. "I thought it was going to bite you for sure."

"So did I." Maya was laughing too. She'd been so silly, thinking somehow that just because she loved animals, they'd all want to be her friends. Grandma had probably let her watch *Snow White* too many times.

"You know, a lot of locals aren't happy to have so many mountain lions around here these days." The speaker was a severe-looking woman with dark hair pulled back in a tight bun and purple reading glasses perched on her nose. "I'm Eva Rosen, by the way. We haven't met. I'm pretty new to Shelter Creek. I own an art gallery in town."

Maya smiled at her, grateful for the change

of subject, even if it wasn't a happy topic. "Good to meet you." It was so strange to think of art galleries in Shelter Creek. But she'd noticed several as she drove through town.

"Eva is right, you know," Grandma cautioned. "You may run into some unhappy folks while you're doing this study."

Ha. She'd already met the unhappiest of them all. And he'd made it clear he didn't want to work with her. Didn't want her around here at all. "Well, it's not like people in this town are going to welcome me back with some kind of celebration anyway." Maya flushed at the hint of bitterness that had seeped into her tone and the silence that instantly coated the room in awkward truth.

"Now, Maya." Mrs. Axel broke the silence to offer comfort. "The accident was a long time ago. Most people probably don't even remember it. They definitely don't blame you for it."

"They did though," Kathy said sharply. "All that nasty stuff about apples not falling far from trees. I gave a few people a piece of my mind about that."

"I've heard about the accident," Eva said.

"But I'm sorry—I don't understand about apples. Unless I'm prying…"

Grandma sighed. "It's okay, Eva. It's not a secret. Everyone knew that my daughter and her husband, Maya's parents, were drug addicts. That's why Maya came to live with me in the first place. After the accident, a rumor got started that Maya had been drinking when her car hit that tree."

"Oh no." Eva looked at Maya, her dark eyes bright with compassion. "I'm so sorry to hear that."

"Tests were done that night," Grandma went on. "We proved there was no alcohol in Maya's blood. The coroner ruled the death accidental."

"But rumors have a way of sticking to things," Annie said. "While boring old facts just blow on by."

"Plus Trisha and Julie, the two girls riding in Maya's car, *had* been drinking that night," Kathy added. "So maybe that's how the rumor got going."

"I didn't live in town back then," Monique said. "But once in a while, gossip resurfaces in the salon. I don't think most people believe that old rumor now, Maya."

"Good to know," Maya mumbled into her wine. Talking about all this was knocking her off-balance. They were all so casual, just chatting mildly about the thing that had shattered her heart and her world.

"Most?" Grandma looked at Monique sharply.

"Well, I've heard a few things I don't like," Monique admitted. "And I've always addressed it when I hear it. Unfortunately there are people out there who prefer their own version of things to the actual truth."

Her words settled like mud in the bottom of Maya's stomach. She'd known, of course, that there were people who'd happily resurrect old gossip. It was a small town and they needed something to talk about. But somehow the fact that Monique had witnessed it made it a lot more real.

"We need to help you face those people, Maya," Annie said briskly. "We need to support you. I wish I'd supported you better back then."

Eva lifted her glass toward Maya. "I'm happy to do whatever I can."

"Me too," Monique added.

"I'm okay," Maya assured them, her skin

going prickly with discomfort. "I'm used to handling things on my own. I'll be fine."

"But you don't have to handle this on your own." Kathy rummaged through her purse and pulled out a packet of tissues. She used one to dab her eyes. "I'm sorry. It just gets me very emotional."

Her tissues had ducks on them. It was an unimportant detail, but Maya focused on it because seeing Kathy cry made her want to cry too.

"I feel the same as Annie." Mrs. Axel's voice was husky all of a sudden. "Maybe if more of us had gathered around you and spoken up for you, you would have felt like you could have stayed. Or at least come back to visit once in a while."

Grandma wiped her eyes on her sleeve. Oh no, if she started crying, then Maya would lose it. And she *didn't* lose it. Well, except for her meltdown by the side of the road the other day. She'd learned a long time ago that crying didn't help. Mourning was a void she could get stuck in forever, because there was no closure when you'd been responsible for a death. Every day you lived was a day the other person didn't. If you allowed yourself to cry, you might just never stop.

It was better to keep busy, stay focused, work hard and avoid other people and their emotions as much as possible. Because emotions were unpredictable. Look at her and Caleb. One day they'd been madly in love. Then the accident happened, and he'd instantly despised her.

That was why Maya had chosen a career that let her work alone, in the wilderness. In a solitary life, she couldn't be hurt that way. And, most importantly, she couldn't hurt anyone else.

The room had gone quiet, and the silence finally permeated Maya's thoughts. She glanced around and saw that The Biddies were watching her expectantly, like she was supposed to say something.

"It's okay," Maya tried to reassure them. "I'm okay." Really, she wanted to sink into the floor, down to the nice, cool, dark dirt of Grandma's crawl space. Anywhere but here, with everyone's pity and regret. "I'm sure it will all be fine. And I'm only going to be in town for a couple of months anyway."

She wished suddenly, fervently, that she

was still on the trail, setting up cameras, looking for scat and tracks. Those were things she could see and record and make sense of. That was peace. This was like standing in a hot spotlight, itchy and alone, picking at scars that never healed.

Kathy cleared her throat. "Just know that we are here for you. That if there is any gossip, we'll try to stop it."

"Anything you need—support for your work, someone to talk to, company if you are planning to go out—you just call one of us," Mrs. Axel said.

Annie chimed in. "If you have trouble with any of the local ranchers, I'm your gal. None of them will give you a hard time if I'm around."

Their kindness loosened the tears Maya had been holding back ever since seeing Caleb out on the trail. The salt stung her eyelids, and she reached for one of Kathy's duck tissues.

"We may just be a bunch of Book Biddies," Eva said, "but I think everyone in this room would like to help you feel at home here, in Shelter Creek."

Grandma patted Maya's knee. "You see? You're not alone. You've got all of us."

They were all being so wonderful, but they were seeing her as the sad, pathetic girl she'd been when she'd left this town. She'd changed since then, she was strong and independent. Why couldn't they see that?

That was the danger of coming home. All that you'd become, all that you'd worked so hard for, wasn't anything anyone could see. All they could see was a familiar face, and then they made familiar assumptions.

Still, all this was kindly meant. "Thank you," Maya managed to say. "I appreciate it."

Grandma's soft hand reached for hers. "I'm sorry if we are too much. I guess we are all too old to ignore the elephant in the room."

Maya scrubbed her palms over her eyes, wishing she could rub all this pity off her skin. "It feels a little like an intervention. Are you sending me to rehab?"

"Guilt rehab," Kathy said. "You deserve to be comfortable in your own town. You may not choose to stay in Shelter Creek, but we don't want you to live in exile."

If only it was so simple. Was there really any rehab for the guilt and regret? Those things were just givens in Maya's world. They wore away at her the way the Pacific's waves eroded the cliffs by the coast. Little by little. Every day. All the time.

"This town needs to do better by you," Annie said. "You're brave to come home. Let us help while you're here."

Maya looked at The Biddies sitting there, with wine and books, and love in their eyes. She couldn't tell them no, despite every instinct insisting she was better off alone. "I don't think I could ask for a better set of bodyguards than you all."

Monique let out a guffaw of laughter. "This town won't know what hit them. Maya Burton's home, and The Book Biddies have her back."

It was what they all needed to lighten the mood.

It was also a good moment to escape. "I think the town, and all of us, would be better off if I had a shower now."

"Just remember that we're here for you," Eva said. "And stop by my gallery sometime. Your grandmother told me that you take really beautiful photos. I'd love to see them."

Maya's cheeks flamed. "Grandma!"

Her grandmother's smile was totally un-apologetic. "You're my granddaughter. I'm entitled to brag sometimes."

"They're not art," Maya tried to explain to Eva, in case Grandma had built up her expectations. "They're just something I do when I'm in the backcountry. To pass the time."

"Well, whatever you call them, I'd love to see them," Eva reassured her. "Come on by. We'll have tea."

"Okay, thank you." Maya raised her wine-glass to the rest of the room. "Enjoy your booze… I mean, your book club. And thank you for making me feel welcome."

"Feel free to join us when you get cleaned up," Grandma told her with a mischievous twinkle in her eye. "We haven't even talked about the book yet."

Curiosity caught at Maya's bookworm heart. "What did you read?"

"That romance book they made into a movie," Kathy said. "You know, the one with the naughty businessman and the college student?"

Horror heated Maya's cheeks. "Not… *Fifty Shades*?"

"That's the one!" Grandma fanned her hand in front of her face. "Oh my, it was spicy!"

"Absolutely." Monique put her palms to her cheeks. "That Christian Grey fellow—I wouldn't mind an older version of him showing up in my shop."

"Okay." Maya was pretty sure her face was beet red. Thankfully she was almost out the living room door. "I'm going to leave you ladies to it. I've got some field notes to catch up on after my shower."

Maya went to her grandmother and kissed her on the cheek. She waved at the rest of The Biddies. "Have a good time," she told them and made her way upstairs. She could hear them talking and laughing, even from her room. And for the first time since she'd come home, she felt a little stronger. A little more like the person she normally was.

*Maya Burton is home, and The Biddies have her back.* She smiled, imagining pulling up to Caleb's ranch tomorrow with a car full of Book Biddies. He'd at least have to be polite.

Somehow she had to find a way to work with him. But how could she work with him when he had such a good reason to hate her? He'd made it so clear, years ago, that he wanted nothing to do with her. He'd made that clear again when she saw him on the trail the other night.

She wasn't great at working with people in the best of circumstances, which was why she spent most of her time doing research alone, in the wilderness. How was she supposed to work with Caleb?

Maya turned the shower on and peeled off her filthy clothes. The steaming water felt delicious as it washed away the layers of dust. If only it could wash away the worry too.

# CHAPTER FOUR

"CALEB? CALEB, ARE you okay?"

The words seemed to come from a distance, as if the owner of the voice was on the other side of a wall. Caleb tried to move toward the sound. The voice was sweet, compelling, but his mind was thick with fading dreams, caught in a dark and unfamiliar place.

"Caleb, wake up!" A hand gently shook his shoulder, jolting him the rest of the way out of sleep. Caleb opened sandpaper eyelids, saw Maya's concerned face peering down at him, and quickly shut them again.

"What are you doing here?" he tried to ask, but it came out more like "Whar—oo-rooing-ere?" and he plastered his hands over his eyes, over his face, trying to bring life back to skin that felt numb. In fact his entire body felt cold and stiff.

"Caleb, are you sick?" Maya shook his shoulder again.

What was she talking about? Why was she here? He felt like he should know, but his head was pounding too hard to think. He opened his eyes again and noticed she was pale, her eyes dark, wide and very worried.

"Wha's up?" he managed to say and glanced around at his sagging porch, surrounded by thick fog that must have blown in from the ocean last night. Understanding trickled slowly through his murky mind and Caleb shoved himself upright in the old wicker chair he'd flopped down in last night, somewhere past midnight, when he'd given up on ever falling asleep.

He'd stumbled out here after one of his nightmares, grabbed a bottle of rye and tried not to think. Just sat here, drinking and listening to the crickets and petting Hobo, an orange cat with a tattered ear, who'd been Dad's companion the last couple of years he'd lived out here on the ranch. Hobo had adopted Caleb now that Dad had moved away.

He'd meant to just drink enough to help him settle, help him drift off. But there were so many ghosts around. Julie playing on the tire swing that used to hang from the old fir tree. His mom riding up on her favorite horse, a paint named Rocky Road. His dad coming in every evening, swooping his mom up in a hug and kissing her cheek. Memories of when this ranch had been full of life and laughter.

And the memories he didn't want. Of Mom crying for days in the kitchen after Julie died. Of Dad walking through his ranch chores like a zombie. Memories of Afghanistan and of the moment he'd seen the shadow running toward him, bulky around the middle, and he'd thought *suicide bomber* and fired until the shadow was still.

Memories that had Caleb finishing off the bottle in hopes he could erase them, even for just a little while. He glared at Maya. "Why are you here?" His words came out a little more coherent this time.

"We had a plan to meet this morning, remember? I figured I'd catch you during morning chores. You weren't at the barn, so I came up here." She stood, glaring at him. "I thought you were dead for a second there. What happened to you?"

"Nothing." He shifted in his seat and his foot made contact with something hard that slid across the porch with a hollow sound, hit the railing and bounced back.

He and Maya both stared at the empty bottle of rye as it revolved slowly, then stopped.

"You drank all that?" she asked quietly.

Caleb searched his ego for a little bluster, some way to pass this off as no big deal. "Looks like." He leaned forward, elbows to knees, head in hands. "Might not have been one of my better ideas."

"No." She knelt before him, so he was forced to look up and meet her eyes, so wide and dark, so full of sadness that they condemned more than her words. "Caleb, this isn't like you. This isn't who you are."

His skull might crack open, the pounding was so bad. Her reminder of better times, when he was a better man, didn't help. "You don't know who I am now."

She flinched, then rose to her feet. "Let me get you some water."

Caleb held up a hand to stop her. "No. I'm fine. I'll be fine. I've felt worse." He didn't want her to see the state of his house. A broken, run-down mess. Just like him.

"I'm not sure that's anything to brag about. Why did you drink so much?"

He stared up at her, wondering how to answer that. *Because I wanted oblivion* seemed the most accurate response, but probably wouldn't go over so well. "I don't know," he finally said. "Couldn't sleep. It was a bad decision."

That's what Adam called it, Caleb remembered, at their come-to-Jesus breakfast yesterday. "It's horrible that your sister passed," Adam had said, leaning into the table, all earnest like the Boy Scout he'd been. "And I'm sure you've got scars from your service to our country. But you've got to face up to those memories, deal with them and stop making these bad decisions. You're way too old for all the drinking and fighting."

Caleb hadn't appreciated the lecture. He faced the memories every day. Here on the ranch, and now with Maya. She made him think of what they'd had, of what they'd lost and how they'd lost it.

Anyway, it was easy for Adam to say. He'd married a girl he met at community college, had two kids with her, and was raising them surrounded by his parents and more brothers and sisters than Caleb could keep track of.

But there it was again. His self-pity. The fact that Jace and Adam could both see it was embarrassing. But Maya bearing witness to his weakness? Humiliation had him burying his face in his hands again.

He had to salvage this situation and muster some kind of dignity. Pulling in a deep breath, Caleb put his hands to the arms of the chair and shoved himself up to a standing position. The world spun and he braced a hand against the wall of the house to steady himself.

"Caleb, sit down." Maya's voice was sharp. "You're ill."

He glared at her. "I'm fine. I just need a minute to get cleaned up and I'll meet you at the barn."

"If you're sure you're—"

"I'm fine." He practically growled the words at her. "I just need a few minutes."

"Okay." She backed away, palms up. "I can come back another day if you'd rather."

He'd rather she never come back at all but that wasn't going to happen, so he might as well get this over with. Then he'd do the chores and sleep the rest of the day. "Ten minutes. By the barn."

She turned and jogged down the porch steps. He heard a car door slam, the engine start and the crunch of tires. He was relieved she was gone and that he had a few minutes to himself.

How unbelievable that she'd shown up here. That she'd seen him like this. Though maybe it was good. Maybe she'd write him off as a lost cause and go focus on other ranchers. Maybe she'd leave him in peace to deal with his ranch and any predators who threatened it, as he saw fit.

Caleb staggered inside, drank water and poured some over his head. Downed a couple of aspirin and some antacids. He should probably eat, but when he opened the refrigerator, the sight of food made him gag. Hoping his head and stomach would settle down, he changed into clean clothes and started for the barn, amazed that he was up, walking in sort of a straight line down the lane.

He was late feeding, but the animals would just have to hang on a few minutes longer. He'd talk with Maya first. His head pounded in time with his footsteps. Maybe he should have taken her up on her offer to come another day.

A green pickup was parked alongside the barn, and Caleb tried to steady his thoughts. He had to keep his cool with her. He'd show her the permit he'd shoved in his jacket pocket before he left the house just now. She'd lecture. He'd pretend to listen. Then she'd be gone, out of his life again. It was all pretty simple, as long as he kept his mouth shut and nodded a bunch.

A small squeak behind him had him turning to see Hobo trotting up, his green eyes meeting Caleb's in cat-concern. The cat trailed after Caleb most of the time. He'd even taken to riding on Caleb's shoulder while Caleb worked around the barn. Which was kind of cute, though it had Caleb worrying that he was turning into the male equivalent of a lonely cat lady. But mostly he was just glad to have the company.

Not too many people visited their ranch these days. The little guy probably thought he needed to protect Caleb from this intruder.

And maybe the darn cat was right. Though, for his dignity's sake, Caleb wasn't sure he wanted his little buddy along with him right now. "Shoo," he told the cat, flicking his hand back toward the house.

Hobo stopped, one paw in the air, uncertain. Caleb kept walking, feeling oddly guilty. Hobo had sat with him and his bottle last night. He always stayed by Caleb when night-mares hit, when things got bad. But, sheesh, he was a cat. He should be able to handle a little time on his own.

The driver's side door of the truck opened and Maya hopped lightly down. Caleb was glad to have a moment to take her in from a distance, now that his head was clearing a little. Her fitted jeans ended in hiking boots. She wore a dark green jacket, and when she spotted him and waved, he could see the lines of her waist, the curve of her hip. Not something he should notice or care about. He'd lost that right when he drove her out of his life. Still, he was surprised he could notice any-thing through his hangover haze. Maybe the aspirin was helping a little.

Maya stopped a few paces from him and waited, the keys she twisted in her fingers be-traying her emotion. "You're looking a little better," she said.

"Thanks. Feeling a little better too."

She nodded. "Look, it's not my business, but are you okay? You were pretty out of it."

"I'm fine. Just spent a little too much time with a bottle of rye, that's all." No way was he going to have some heavy discussion with her just because she happened to find him passed out on his porch. Getting drunk was his prerogative. He'd fought for his country—had the nightmares to prove it—and if a little alcohol helped keep them at bay, she didn't have the right to judge. Plus he didn't need her judgment. He was pretty sure he had enough self-loathing for both of them.

"Where are your parents?"

"Divorced. Gone. My mom lives in New York City. Dad left a few weeks after I got home to live with one of his sisters in San Diego." He didn't want to talk about that. How Mom and Dad had put Shelter Creek, this ranch and him behind them.

He pulled the permit out of his pocket. "Here. You wanted to see this, right?"

Nodding, she unfolded the paper and studied it. Then pulled out her phone. "Mind if I grab a photo of it?"

He shrugged. "Suit yourself."

She snapped the photo and handed him back the paper. "All right. This permit looks good."

The sun was pushing tentative rays through the fog, casting her skin in gold, illuminating the freckles it had scattered across her cheeks.

It caught the interest of his tired mind, lured it away from the topic at hand.

How could the years have changed her so little? Time had left only light tracks. A few lines around her eyes, a lean, strong look to her, and a way of moving that made him think she could easily out-hike, outrun and maybe even out-lift most people. He'd been a Marine, and he still kept in shape, but she had a feral strength that spoke of a life spent in constant motion.

But despite these subtle changes, she was still Maya. Long brown straight hair pulled into a ponytail beneath her baseball cap. Brown eyes that had always reminded him of the color of the bark on the redwood trees that covered the hills just a little inland from Shelter Creek.

He shouldn't pay such close attention. Shouldn't look at her at all. Because memories were rushing in so rapidly, so vividly, he was surprised she couldn't see them too, crashing against him in waves of color and feeling.

There was the first time he'd realized that they were more than just childhood friends. She'd hurt her hand while they were trying to finish a science project in seventh grade, and he'd grabbed it to stop the bleeding. And realized he never wanted to let go.

They had their first date at the school Christmas dance. He'd bought her a gardenia corsage and she'd giggled at his awkward moves on the dance floor.

His throat felt thick and he cleared it, hating the magnetic pull of the past that had him gripping a bottle of whiskey most nights, in a desperate attempt to stay anchored in the present.

"So, you've seen the permit. Can I hunt my lion now?" His tone was curt, rude, but he wanted her gone—her and the memories she brought. Memories that made him want that innocent time more than he wanted a drink even. More than he'd wanted anything in a long time.

A shadow of something flickered across her eyes and was gone. If he'd struck a blow, she wasn't going to let it slow her down. Instead she turned smooth and professional. "You don't even know what lion you're hunting, I suspect. I saw a few different sets of prints out on the trail the other day. There are at least three mountain lions living around here. We have no way of knowing if any of them killed your sheep."

That stopped him. He'd assumed that whatever mountain lion had gone after his sheep would be the one he met up with when he went hunting. Though, now that he thought about it, that was a pretty lame assumption. "You're saying that if I'd found a lion that night, I might have shot the wrong one?"

"It's very possible. Your lion could be long gone by now, especially if it was young and in the territory of another male."

It was sobering. Caleb wasn't a sport hunter. He didn't enjoy killing wildlife just for the sake of it. "So, what do I do now?"

"You work with me. Let me help you make some changes that will deter lions in the future."

"Why don't you just tell me what to do? Don't you have some literature or something you can give me?" He didn't want to spend more time with her. Didn't want to see the way the growing sunlight lit up strands of gold in her hair. Didn't want to think about how no other woman had caught his attention for long, since her.

Except part of him, that boy he'd been

when he'd loved her, *did* want her here. It was ridiculous. Some ancient fantasy of happily-ever-after that his brain was revisiting.

"I have literature, yes. And I'll leave you with some. But the best way I can help you is if we walk around your ranch together and talk about what you can do to prevent any further attacks."

As if on cue, Hobo leaped onto Caleb's shoulder, startling him so badly that he jumped a couple of feet to the right. "Jeez, Hobo!"

Maya burst out laughing, the sound ringing like a pretty bell in the quiet. "Wow! That is one agile cat!"

This was great. More indignity to add to the morning. Caleb's face warmed and he resisted the urge to bat the cat off. But it wasn't Hobo's fault that Caleb was an idiot who'd passed out on his porch last night. Or that Maya had found him there.

Plus Hobo was stubborn. He'd probably just jump right back on anyway. Best to play it cool. "Yeah. This is Hobo. He likes to hang out with me when I'm working."

"I see." Maya's lips quivered as if she

wanted to laugh again, and Caleb got it. He must look quite the fool. The big, hungover, grumpy dude with a small orange cat along for the ride.

Hobo stuck his head under the brim of Caleb's hat and shoved, knocking it askew.

"Hey!" Caleb set his hat to rights and moved Hobo off his shoulder, tucking him under his arm instead. Darn cat. Except he was pretty cute, the way he was snuggling up into Caleb's chest. It was hard to stay mad. Which was strange because Caleb was pretty sure that mad was the main emotion he'd felt ever since he'd come back to Shelter Creek.

"So, why don't we take a look around the property?" Maya glanced around. "Do you still have cattle too?"

"Just a starter herd of Angus." *Starter herd.* He almost laughed at the ridiculous term he'd pulled out of the blue, in some stupid attempt to impress her, or at least make his situation a little less pathetic.

When he'd left the Marines, he'd had big plans for running cattle, until he'd gotten home and seen the state of the ranch and found out about the unpaid taxes. Because of that, all he'd been able to afford were a half dozen Angus. It was kind of silly to buy any at all, but he wanted them here to remind himself of what he was working toward. To help him feel like he was on his way to the ranch of his dreams. Even if it was just a few cattle, it was something.

"How many sheep? Any other livestock?"

And so it began. The revelation of just how far down in the world the Bar D Ranch had fallen. Caleb tried to deliver the news as if he didn't care. "About thirty sheep. Two horses."

Her eyes went wide. He didn't blame her. It was so far from what his family used to own.

"Okay... Well, with such small numbers, it should be pretty easy to protect them. It could actually be a good thing because you can test out some different methods before you increase your herd size." She glanced at him, a wealth of questions in her eyes. "Assuming you are going to increase your herd size?"

"Eventually. Yeah." Caleb led the way down the rutted dirt lane, trying to ignore the way the old barn seemed to lean a little harder toward the left now that Maya was looking at it.

Maya fell into step beside him. Gosh, she was tiny, just coming up to his bicep. He'd forgotten how small she was.

He couldn't miss her stricken gaze as she took in the ruin of his ranch. Back in high school, the Bar D had been the biggest operation around, with a few hundred sheep and almost as many cattle. Shame flared itchy beneath his skin. But it shouldn't. He hadn't run this place down. That was Dad's fault. Or Dad's depression's fault. His old man had never been able to recover from losing Julie.

Maya started talking, oblivious to his dark thoughts. "With your permission, I'd like to set up some motion-sensitive cameras around the property so we can see what kind of critters you're getting around here at night. Coyotes are a big issue around here, as well as mountain lions."

"Cameras." He liked the idea of knowing what kinds of predators were showing up. But cameras would cost money he didn't have. And even if she paid for them, that meant she'd be here, checking on them. And he'd have to see her. He didn't want to see her. Not when she brought so much emotion along with her. "We'll see," he grunted.

"It's up to you." She gave him a neutral, professional smile.

She was a good actress. Better than him.

For so many years, she'd haunted him. Her voice. Her laugh. Her touch. And all the horror and loss of the accident that had broken them apart. And now she was here and he was supposed to act like it was no big deal. Apparently she could do it. Him, not so much. He'd keep this tour short.

Caleb turned onto a narrow trail that took them away from the barn. He didn't want her seeing it up close, with its broken boards, missing doors, the rotting roof and the corral fences he'd patched together with whatever he could find lying around.

Hobo wriggled out of his arms to sit on his shoulder again and Caleb sighed. He'd just have to resign himself to looking like a fool in front of Maya long-term.

They reached a field of long golden grass and tangled weeds that had once been neatly sheared pasture. Caleb pointed to the far side. "I see coyotes over there a fair amount, in the early mornings."

"If you're not grazing this, mow it," Maya said.

"I know. It's a fire hazard." Caleb wasn't going to mention that his tractor had been broken for weeks. Or that he was too broke to get it fixed.

"Well, yes, though fire isn't really my area of expertise." She pointed to the field. "But all of this—the long grass, the bushes—has become wildlife habitat. Just walking over here, I spotted three different areas where you've got mule deer bedding down."

He glanced around, wondering if she was making it up. He hadn't noticed anything. "You sure about that?"

"One is just before that scrub oak back there."

Caleb looked at the stubby little oak he saw every day. Though clearly he hadn't looked closely enough.

Maya went on. "The problem is mule deer are mountain lions' favorite food."

Caleb looked out over the golden grass, flowing gently in the rising breeze. "I didn't realize."

Maya raised her hand to encompass the field. "This is a twenty-four-hour buffet. And not just for mountain lions. I'll bet you this field is packed with rabbits and ground squirrels. Those coyotes you've been seeing love to eat them. Which isn't a problem right now, but with all this great food available, your resident pack will grow and pretty soon they'll be helping themselves to lamb for dessert."

He didn't want to admit it, but she had a point. "So, you're saying I need to mow."

"As soon as possible."

Now that Maya pointed it out, he could see that this abandoned pasture was alive. There were squeaks in the grass to his left. A family of quail was crossing the trail a few yards in front of them, the male leading the way with his fancy feather bobbing on top of his head. Lizards sunned themselves on the fence posts.

He'd been so busy trying to keep this ranch, and himself, above water the past couple of months, he hadn't seen the obvious problem right in front of him.

Of course seeing the problem didn't mean solving it. He was down to just a few bucks in his bank account. Maybe he could hit the junkyards in Santa Rosa tomorrow to try to find a tractor like his. Then he could pull the water pump. He hated to lose the day it would take to make the trip, but better to lose a day than any more livestock.

Maya put a hand to his arm. Just a brief

brush to his forearm but it was warm and unexpected. Like a quick visit from a bird.

"Look, I know you don't want to take my advice. But this is what I do. I have my PhD in wildlife biology. You don't have to like me, but I wish you'd let me help you out."

"You have a PhD?" It was one small detail of what she'd said, but it stood out. Another symbol of how little he knew her.

"Yeah." Her chin jutted out defiantly. "I'm actually considered an expert on predator behavior. And here I am, offering my services for free, so you should take advantage of them."

"It's not often a woman invites me to take advantage of them." It was a stupid thing to say and he regretted it the instant it was out. An insecure fool's effort to bring her down a peg, now that he knew just how smart and accomplished she really was.

"If you're going to act like an idiot, you won't have my help."

"I never asked for your help," he reminded her.

"You clearly need it," she shot back. Then she paused, like she was counting to ten before she said anything more. When she spoke, her voice was quiet and calm again. "Look, I know you hate me, Caleb. You made that very clear years ago. But that doesn't mean you can't listen to my advice. I do have expertise that could help you."

He stared, letting her words filter in. "I don't hate you."

"Well, you told me you did, after the accident. And you certainly act like you do now." He could see tears building in her eyes, the way she blinked them back, to stop them from falling.

"It's complicated." He tried to find the words in his whiskey-blurred brain. But his lack of sleep, his hangover and all the memories she stirred up just by standing here in front of him knotted in his mind and left him with nothing.

"We have a complicated past. But this is about helping your ranch and protecting your livestock. And preserving the local mountain lion population too. So why can't we just keep those things separate from what happened between us?"

He stared at her, fighting the urge to yell at her, chase her off his property and out of his life. Because she was flinging open doors he'd tried to keep shut for so long.

"I don't know." It was one of the few honest things he could say. "I don't know if I can work with you."

Her face paled and her small fists clenched. "You're not the only one having a hard time with this situation. When I came to see you after I got out of the hospital, you said horrible things. You broke my heart. But I'm still trying to work with you."

Caleb recognized the sick feeling in his gut. He'd felt it that night she'd come to see him, after Julie died. He felt it now. Emotions, so many, so mixed up, it was impossible to untangle any of them into coherent thoughts or words.

"I'm sorry. I never meant to hurt you."

Her short, harsh laugh startled him. One cynical beat of sound. "We both know that's a lie. You blamed me. And I took it. I took all the blame, because how could I not? I was behind the wheel that night. I lost control of the car. And your sister died.

"But I've had a lot of time to think about it, Caleb. And there are a couple of things about that night that you and your parents and half this town conveniently forgot when they all pointed their fingers at me."

He gaped. She'd dropped the professional demeanor and was pure emotion. Pure anger, pure sorrow and regret so profound he felt it in the air between them. "Maya, I—"

"No. If you want to let our past get in the way, fine. That's your choice. But I won't let you label me a murderer again. I went to pick up Julie from that concert that night as a favor to you. Remember? Your sister called *you* for a ride, and you asked me to go instead because you wanted to hang out with Jace. And Julie was drunk and she would not listen to me. Do you even know that?"

"Of course I know." But he tried not to think about the horrific details of that night— only looked back in brief glances. Now here she was, the scientist with her microscope. Magnifying guilt.

"You don't know my view of what happened though. Because you wouldn't listen. You just told me we were over. As if all of our years together meant nothing. As if I'd crashed that car on purpose. You acted like you believed those rumors around town. That I was drunk. And since you seemed to hate me, a lot of people assumed those rumors were true."

Tears were pouring down her face now and Caleb blinked back his own. "I was overwhelmed by it all." He was overwhelmed now, by what he'd done wrong back then, and all that he should have done right.

"What feels so unfair sometimes, is that Julie would have listened to you, if you'd gone to pick her up. She would have kept her seat belt on and she would never have tried to climb into the front seat. Has that *ever* occurred to you?"

She backed a few steps away from him and swiped at her wet cheeks with her sleeve. "I'm not shying away from the blame. Believe me, I carry more guilt and regret than you can ever imagine, every single day of my life. But maybe it's time you were honest about your part in it. And about Julie's part. Her actions helped cause that car accident."

"Go." It came out like a growl from somewhere deep and raw in Caleb's chest. She was hacking at bone with her words, excavating pain he'd buried deep for a reason. "This isn't going to work, you and me. It could never work. You want to leave me something to read about managing wildlife? Fine. But don't come back here, trying to tell me how to run my ranch. Or how to remember my sister."

She stared at him, stunned and stricken, and he remembered that look. Because he'd put it there once before, on the night he'd accused her of killing Julie. The night he'd destroyed what was between them. And now, just as they'd been maybe making a few tentative repairs, he'd put it there again.

But last time, she'd turned and run out of the room. This time she held her ground. "There you go again. Laying all the blame on me. Well, you know what? Blame me for the weather, for the mountain lions, for whatever you want, because there is one thing different from the last time you treated me this way. This time, I don't care."

She turned so quickly, dust rose from the path beneath her feet.

Caleb watched her walk away, across the field, past the barn, until she was just a speck getting into her truck and driving away. Good. They were fools to think that they could be around each other at all. She'd shown up here, unwelcome. She'd brought up the accident and so much he didn't want to think about.

As he started up the path, he saw Hobo sitting just a couple of yards away, staring at him reproachfully. "What?" He faced off with the animal as if it could speak.

But Hobo didn't need words. He just turned and stalked away, paws lifting high, as if the very ground that Caleb owned disgusted him.

Shamed by a cat. Shamed because he'd had a chance to do the right thing. To give Maya the apology he'd owed her for years now. But instead he'd made it all much, much worse.

Ever since Afghanistan, ever since his own terrible mistake there, he'd had a self-destructive streak in his soul a mile wide and just as deep. When there was something that mattered, he broke it.

Maybe he felt like he didn't deserve anything good. Maybe he felt like he'd ruin it anyway, so he might as well get it over with.

Today, for a few minutes anyway, talking about predators and deer and Hobo the cat, it had felt like maybe he and Maya had built something. A small bit of trust, or at least an ability to be around each other and maybe solve the problems on his ranch.

For a few minutes there, he'd envisioned what it would be like to have her help, to learn from her, to get to be around her again, after missing her so much, for so many years.

For those few minutes, he'd felt hope. So unfamiliar, it startled him. So inspiring, it scared him.

So he'd brought his angry words crashing down like fists, to shatter it into pieces. Because without hope, he had nothing to lose. And he'd lost enough to know that life was a whole lot safer that way.

# CHAPTER FIVE

THE RATTLE OF Maya's truck down Caleb's rutted driveway was almost soothing. It jostled Maya's bones, bounced her in her seat, forced her to hold tightly to the wheel and concentrate while she navigated the more cavernous potholes. She welcomed the effort. It forced her to stay alert, to push back the tears that kept sliding down her face, no matter how many times she wiped them away.

She'd promised herself she'd stay professional. To ignore their past and focus on her work.

It wasn't just his anger and his obvious dislike that broke her resolve, though that had slowly and surely gotten under her skin the more time she'd spent at his ranch.

It was the way he'd lain broken on that beat-up porch chair, his spirit shuttered by the whiskey. The shame on his face when he'd woken to find her there, and the desperate attempt to cover up, to pretend like that kind of drinking was no big deal. Her parents were addicts who'd lost everything, including her, to get their next fix. So she knew firsthand that being that drunk was a really big deal.

He'd brought her back there. To those times as a tiny little kid, when she'd try to wake her parents up. They'd be passed out just like Caleb, and wake up angry and swearing. It was all too familiar, and the fact that he'd forced her back to that place and those memories had upped her anger to the boiling point.

But it wasn't just worry and anger that had her losing control. It was the way his ranch, so beautiful when they were young, had fallen to pieces. It felt like her fault. She might be angry, she might stand up to his blame, but she knew—of course she knew—that she'd been the only one behind the wheel the night Julie had died. And the demise of the Bar D, his parents' divorce, his drinking—it could all be traced back to that accident eventually.

Maybe that was why she'd lashed out. Tried to shove the blame for the accident on to him just as he'd done to her so many years ago.

But it had been wrong to do, especially when she was supposed to be working. She

was supposed to be helping him; she was supposed to be a professional.

Maya slowed partway down the drive to
calm herself before she hit the main road.
Fields of dry grass ranged out on either side of
her—all that open space giving her comfort.
The Bar D had been one of the most beautiful ranches Maya had ever seen. Hundreds of
acres of rolling hills, green and lush in winter and spring, bleached to gold in summer
and fall. The property extended west toward
the Pacific and the eastern edge connected
to the open-space preserve, where Maya had
run into Caleb the other night.

But it was so different now. The Bar D
that Maya remembered was neat as a pin,
the house painted a cheery yellow, the barn
a classic red. The fences, the outbuildings
and the roads were constantly maintained by
Caleb's father and the many ranch hands he'd
employed.

Today Maya had barely recognized the
place, with its leaning fences, rotting posts
covered in lichen and barbed wire lying hap-
hazardly and hazardously on the ground.

The lambing shed, where she used to love
to go with Caleb and greet the new arrivals,

was propped up on one side by huge beams, and the roof was entirely gone. The main barn, though still standing, was patched and faded, the red paint almost gone, the doors barely hanging on to their hinges and the entire structure leaning inland, as if giving in to the winds that blew from the coast.

It was as if the ranch had lost hope and was collapsing into the earth. Just like its owner.

Maya scrubbed the last tears off her face with her sleeves. Enough. She'd learned to be strong in the years since Caleb had turned his back on her, and she'd rely on that strength to get her through these months in Shelter Creek. She'd focus on her work, just like she always had. She'd advocate for the predators who were so often blamed for what was not their fault.

Killing a sheep wasn't a decision for a puma; it was instinct. Hunger had to be satisfied, and a mountain lion made no distinction between a deer on one side of a fence and a sheep on the other. Surely there were other ranchers in Shelter Creek who would understand that. If Caleb wasn't able to, well, there was still a lot she could do here.

After a long, shaky breath, the tears seemed

to be truly gone, so Maya turned onto the road toward town, the truck suddenly, oddly quiet on the smooth pavement. Caleb's face rose in her mind, unwelcome and unbidden. That moment when his cat had jumped onto his shoulder, and his expression had gone from surprised to sheepish… It was as close to a smile as she might ever see on his face.

She wished she could unsee it. Because Caleb was still so beautiful, with his startling dark brown eyes, his black hair, his tall, bulky frame carved with visible muscle. He'd always been handsome, but now he'd been honed into something raw and rugged, with a barely contained bitter energy that couldn't be all about her and the ranch. What else had happened to him in the years between then and now? She'd heard from Grandma, at some point, that he'd joined the Marines. Maybe war had changed him. He certainly wouldn't be the first to come home different.

His seemed a hard life, a scarred life. She'd caught a glimpse of it on the porch when he'd shoved out of the chair only to reach for the wall. His story was imprinted on his forearms with black tattoos, the patterns mostly abstract, probably meaning something only to him. Only one patch of ink was starkly clear. Julie's name, scripted on his wrist.

Her cell phone rang, jolting her out of her thoughts. The call was probably about work, or from Grandma Lillian. Maya slowed, put on her signal, waited for a turnout to pull off the narrow winding road. She hit the hazard lights so anyone coming up behind her would know she'd slowed down. She'd always been a pretty cautious driver. Since the accident, she made the slowest granny look like a daredevil.

A wide gravel verge came into view, and Maya pulled her truck over and stopped under the arching branches of a bay tree. Craving fresh air, she stepped out of the cab, and answered.

It was her boss here in California, Cooper Peyton, calling from the Sacramento office. When he asked her how she was, Maya had to cross her fingers before she answered. "Fine. Everything's good."

Cooper didn't waste time on small talk. "Listen, Maya, on a short assignment like this, it's important to reach out to as many people as possible, as quickly as possible. We need to educate the community about living with predators and preventing predation."

"Okay," Maya answered. "What do you suggest?"

"I encourage you to take advantage of some of the summer events around the area. I know the local rodeo must be coming up soon. Can you get a table there? And see if you can attend a town meeting, the local rancher's association, anything you can think of where you can make contact with a lot of community members at once."

Maya's stomach did a few flips and flops at his words. Of course she'd known she'd be reaching out to ranchers in this position, but she'd assumed it would be one-on-one. She was an introvert, someone who'd spent most of the last decade on her own, in the wilderness, not talking at all. "Um…of course," she answered, swallowing panic. "It makes sense."

"Great. Listen, email Barb, she's our administrative assistant here in Sacramento. She'll mail you a few boxes of information to distribute. We've got pamphlets, posters, all kinds of stuff you can use to connect with people."

"Okay, sure." She could do this. Her worst fears, of being judged or rejected or reminded of her past, were just that. Fears. She'd faced down Caleb. Yelled at him, even. If she could do that, she could do anything.

"There's also a slideshow about preventing predation. I'll email that."

"Right. A slideshow." Her words came out stilted as she tried to picture herself presenting at a town council meeting. Would people listen? Would they whisper gossip about the accident?

Cooper reminded her of a few other administrative details, like turning in her time sheet. While she listened, Maya noticed a sound coming from some low blackberry bushes on the other side of her truck. She walked around to look, but didn't see anything but dusty brambles.

When the conversation was over, Maya put her phone in her pocket and went to kneel by the bushes, trying to see underneath the tangled canes. They were swaying now, like whatever was in there was moving around, maybe stuck in the thorns. She heard a low whining noise. "Who's there?" she called.

Another whine and the brambles shook

wildly, then parted, and a black nose poked out. It was attached to a light brown muzzle, framed by a big square head. Dark eyes peered at Maya hopefully, and fuzzy ears perked up and then forward.

"Hey, it's okay. You can come out of there." The dog crawled out into the open. It was all angles and bones and scruffy brown fur, covered in foxtails and burrs. With a jolt, Maya realized that it was missing its rear left leg. An old injury, thank goodness, but still...the poor dog. It crouched before her, cowering a little. One big ear flopped forward like a folded napkin.

"Holy smokes, look at you." She held out her hand, knuckles down, and kept as still as she could, crouched there in the gravel, eye to eye with the dog, who, now that it had her attention, was watching her warily.

"It's okay. I won't hurt you," Maya promised. Gray hair flecked its muzzle and etched the brows above its eyes. Eyes that held a world of hurt. The poor creature had probably been abandoned somewhere on this road.

"You're safe," she promised. "Come with me. I'll take care of you." This guy needed a rescue. Good thing Cooper had called when he did, and that she'd pulled over here.

The fuzzy, lopsided ears came up, and the dog rose and took a few tentative steps forward, until its nose, cold and damp, snuffed at Maya's knuckles with a few loud breaths. It retreated, growled low and regarded her with a suspicious glare.

"You're confused. Wondering if I might hurt you," Maya said. "I won't." She turned sideways, put her hand out again and waited. This situation felt familiar, and then it hit her. Caleb was like this dog. Wounded. Trying to reach forward for connection. Retreating back into his fear. Growling to cover it up.

Though somehow it was a lot easier to be compassionate with a dog than with an angry man who'd broken your heart.

She could rescue this dog, but who could rescue Caleb? He'd made it clear he didn't want *her* help, but maybe she could speak with someone else who could try. Was he still friends with Jace? Grandma had mentioned that he was back in town. Or maybe Caleb would listen to Grandma? They'd always really liked each other, before the accident.

And then she knew the right person. Annie,

from The Book Biddies. Annie was one of the most respected ranchers in the area. Caleb would listen to her, if he was going to listen to anyone. He needed help with his ranch *and* with his life. If anyone could set him on the right path with both, it was no-nonsense Annie Brooks.

Relief that she had a plan, a way to possibly still help him, took away some of the tension Maya had felt ever since she'd left the Bar D. She'd phone Annie, just as soon as she got this dog figured out, and ask her to go see Caleb.

And indirectly, by sending Annie to help, maybe Maya would be able to make some amends for her role in Julie's death, and all the ruin that had come after it.

Hope rose and lifted some of the strain off Maya's shoulders. What did Grandma always say growing up? Grandma had a saying for every occasion. Oh yes. *Where there's possibility, there's hope.*

The big dog, as if sensing that, crept closer again, its broad pink tongue swooping over the back of her hand. Like he'd finally decided he could trust her.

"Hey." Maya smiled at the rough tongue

and the bushy tail that had perked up and was wagging over the dog's back like a flag. "Are you going to let me take you home?"

She stood slowly, ran a hand gently over the dog's head and down its back, wincing at the knobby backbone and the sharp ribs. The dog was thin, but as far as she could tell, he— she peeked underneath to confirm—yes, *he,* wasn't injured. A bath, a vet trip and a few good meals, and he might be just about fine.

Maya wasn't sure what her grandmother would think about a three-legged canine visitor, but there was no way Maya could leave the poor animal here. Maybe if Grandma didn't like him, one of The Book Biddies would have an idea of where he could go. Maybe Annie would fall for the old dog and want him to keep her company out on her ranch.

Because how could she not fall in love with those floppy, fluffy ears and the dark yearning eyes?

"I'm calling you Einstein," she told the dog. "You look wise and those gray eyebrows… well, they're very distinguished."

Maya went around to the passenger side of the truck and pulled an old towel out from behind the seat. She laid it down before looking back at the dog. "Want to get in?"

The dog shambled over, moving pretty smoothly on three legs. At the truck, it eyed the height into the passenger seat with a dubious expression and turned to look up at Maya, the question clear in his big brown eyes.

"Really? You want a lift?" Maya sighed. "Well, I suppose a missing leg gets you certain accommodations in life."

She ran her hands over the dog's body, trying to see if he flinched at all. He seemed like a big teddy bear, but she didn't want to assume that and then have him turn around and bite her.

He didn't seem to mind her touch. In fact he leaned into her, as if, now that he'd decided to trust her, he was relieved to have her take some of his weight. Or maybe he was just relieved to not be alone anymore. Maya knelt and wrapped an arm around his big chest and another around his backside. He was a big dog—he had to be part German shepherd—and she wasn't actually sure she could lift him.

"Small but mighty," she muttered, her motto when she was on the trail with her

backpack full of gear. Pushing off with her
legs, she stood, staggered, but managed to get
the dog level with the passenger seat and ma-
neuver him close enough that his front paws
were on the towel.

With a wiggle and an awkward kick with
his one back leg, he was on the seat. He sat
down like he belonged there and looked over
at Maya with a concerned expression wrin-
kling the fur between his eyes. As if he was
asking, *Well, what are you waiting for?*

"I'm coming." Maya wiped her hands on
her jeans and shut the truck door, walking
around to the driver's side again. She fastened
her seat belt and glanced at her new companion. "Ready?"

She could swear that her new friend nodded, his eyes so full of soul and so oddly
human that it was easy to imagine he knew
exactly what she was saying.

"Okay. We're going to stop by the vet and
see if they can check you over. Then we'll go
home and meet my grandmother."

The filthy brown fur ball blinked once.
And then calmly watched the road ahead as
Maya drove them into town.

Strange how one morning could have so

much to it. The horror of finding Caleb on the porch. A little hope when it seemed like they might work together. And then despair when their past came crashing down between them. A work mandate from her boss that she wasn't actually sure she was capable of. And then this dog here, who needed her immediate help and reminded her that Caleb did too, even if he didn't want to admit it yet.

She looked over at Einstein. "Things have been a little rough for both of us. But we're going to be just fine. Don't you fret."

The big dog flopped down on the seat and put his head in her lap. Either he trusted her promise or he was just too tired to stay awake any longer. Or maybe he felt like she did. That he belonged here, with her.

# CHAPTER SIX

CALEB HAULED HARD on the wire, bracing himself against the fence post, driving the staple into the splintery wood. It would be a whole lot easier if he had someone to help him with this task, but that required a budget he didn't have.

And maybe this was better—therapeutic—his body braced, pulling wire, leveraging the post, muscles straining until his triceps, biceps, lats and pecs were all on fire. Pain was good; it grounded you, distracted you and reminded you that you were still here. Not dead and buried out on this empty ranch.

He hadn't minded the quiet out here so much at first. After years of shared barracks, shared tents and shared dirt under a desert sky, he'd been ready for solitude. For a night unblemished by other men's snores and grunts and all that breathing.

The ranch had been blissfully quiet. Soothingly peaceful. There was all that space and it was all his.

But after Maya had left here two days ago—so furious, so upset—the solitude had felt a little less comfortable. Too much quiet let your thoughts get loud. And his weren't just loud; they were as tangled and twisted as this wire. Weighed down with the terrible things he'd said. And she'd said.

And all the things he didn't say. The things he'd wanted to.

He got tongue-tied around emotion. Like he wasn't fluent in the language. His had never been an effusive family. Mom and Dad were both quiet, hardworking, practical people. Caleb had been expected to grow up and man up and deal with whatever came his way.

Which was good in some ways. It helped him through years at war. But in the moments that mattered, when there was something big that needed saying, he got stuck. Like he didn't have the vocabulary for what was going on inside him.

And because of that, he'd ruined something with Maya on her visit. Some chance at contact, some chance at a change in the old hurt between them.

He drove the heavy staple into the post with one blow of his hammer. It wasn't just the emotions that ruined him. He'd lashed out—at her success and his failure, at the way she'd found him, passed out like some derelict on his porch. The image of that empty bottle had been slowly spinning in his head ever since. And the horror on her face when she'd realized what it meant.

Caleb reached down for more wire, carefully avoiding the sharp points. A metaphor for his life, because avoiding pain was pretty much what he did now. By drinking. By fighting. By pushing anyone who might cause him any hurt right out of his life.

Just like he'd done with Maya.

Adam was right. He had to grow up, he had to face what was going on with him. He'd been a Marine, a soldier, and that was still the kind of man he should be. Not a coward who hid in a bottle because he was afraid of his memories. Not a loser who refused to shoulder blame that was his.

Ever since Maya had come and gone, Caleb had been trying to do things differently. Instead of the bottle before bed, he'd gone for a run, done pushups and worked on fixing up his house, until he was so tired, his mind had no choice but to let him sleep. And when the nightmares came, he refused to medicate. He'd drunk water, read a book or cuddled Hobo, and somehow he'd eventually dozed off.

Of course he'd woken from a dream, twisting and sweating, at 4:00 a.m. today, knowing there was no way he was getting back to sleep. So he'd come out here to work, to watch the foggy sky go from dark to gray, to feel the thick marine layer—a dense, wet summer fog—coat everything in refreshing dampness.

The sky, the horizon and the newly mowed field beyond—it was all waking under the mist. It might have been a rough night, but this was a good way to start the day.

The sound of a truck in the driveway had him straining to see who might be coming out here before seven o'clock on a Saturday morning. It was a pickup he didn't recognize at first, a deep gray color that instantly classified it as not-Maya's, which should have been a relief but somehow tasted more like disappointment.

The truck pulled up by the barn, and a lone figure jumped out of the driver's seat and started toward him. A tall, thin woman, holding something in each hand and a bag on her arm.

Caleb blinked through the blowing mist and started toward her, wiping his filthy hands on his jeans.

"Good morning," she called cheerfully. "I thought you might want some coffee."

It took him a moment to recognize her. Annie Brooks. Head of the local ranchers' association and breeder of some of the finest wool sheep on the West Coast. They'd met often when Caleb was young, when Annie and his dad would stop by each other's ranches for a chat and a little friendly competition. But he hadn't seen her since he'd been home. What was she doing here now?

Then she handed him a cup from the Creek Café, and he inhaled the strong coffee scent, and he didn't care why she was here. "Thanks." He raised his cup in a salute to hers. "What brings you to the Bar D?"

"I wanted to see how you're doing." She walked toward the fence he'd been working on. "It's not easy, bringing a place like this back to life."

He followed, trying not to notice the bag

tucked under her arm, because maybe she'd picked up a few pastries from the café as well, and suddenly the breakfast he'd never had didn't seem like enough.

She must have read his mind, because she handed him the bag. "Danish. Wasn't sure what you'd like, so I got a few types."

His stomach rumbled loud enough for her to hear. He hadn't eaten since the can of chili he'd heated up last night.

Annie grinned. "Guess I got here just in time."

Caleb tried to remember what he knew about Annie. A fixture in the ranching community around here since well before he was born, a fierce advocate for sustainable ranching practices. He knew that because she wrote a column in the *Shelter Creek Sentinel* once a month. She'd been on the town council, never had kids that he knew of, was a widow and was good friends with… Maya's grandmother. Caleb remembered seeing her at Maya's grandma's annual backyard barbecues.

"Did Maya send you?"

Annie shot him an amused glance. "She mentioned your meeting didn't go so well.

But I wouldn't be here if I didn't want to speak with you myself." A thin spark of a smile added dimples to her weatherworn cheeks. "Is that okay with you?"

Caleb felt his face get warm under its coating of mist. "Of course." He set his coffee on the fence post and reached in the bag for a Danish. He took an enormous bite of the sweet bread, and what seemed like apricot and blackberries, and just about passed out from the perfection. "And if you bring these, you can come anytime," he mumbled through the crumbs.

Annie laughed. "I'll keep that in mind." Then her tone dipped into serious. "I'm here because, frankly, I'm a little worried about you. This ranch needs a lot of work, and if the rumors are true, your dad didn't leave you with a lot to work with."

Shame washed most of the taste out of the pastry and Caleb swallowed it in a lump. Chased it with a gulp of coffee before he let himself answer. "I don't know who's been spreading those rumors, but I'm fine."

Annie nodded thoughtfully, but didn't answer. Instead she surveyed the field on the other side of the fence. "Looks like you mowed this pretty recently."

"Yup." After a few hours in the junkyard, searching for the right water pump, and a few hours more putting it in, he'd gotten the old tractor running again. He'd mowed yesterday afternoon, trying not to feel guilty about the various critters who'd taken off running when they'd heard him coming. Maya had been right: that field had been a small animal buffet, an open invitation to predators to take up residence on his ranch.

She'd been right, and he'd been a jerk.

"So, look," Annie said briskly. "I'm here because I want to see you succeed. I want the Bar D to make a comeback. I can offer you advice, I can lend you a ram or two if you need them at breeding time and the Ranchers Guild has money available. It's set aside for hardships, and son, you've got a fair number of them here. If you need some money, you just say the word."

Caleb's whole head was on fire—he was so damn embarrassed. "I know you mean it kindly, Annie, but I don't want to be the local charity case."

She puffed right up like an indignant hen.

"You are not that, Caleb Dunne. You spent over a decade serving our country. Risking your life and dealing with God-knows-what. Now you've come home to a property that's been long neglected and the community would like to help you fix it up a little. That's all. It's not charity—it's common decency. So please don't let your pride stand in the way."

He felt about ten years old, with her scolding him like that. And part of him—the soldier, the warrior—wanted to tell her to get off his land. Because accepting her help felt like accepting defeat.

She must have read his mind because she said quietly, "When you were out there fighting, were you expected to do it alone?"

"Of course not." He picked up his shovel, leaned on it, wanting something to do—anything—because this was so uncomfortable. What was it with the Shelter Creek women anyway? So much meddling and prying. And the worst thing was he probably really did need their help, and the fact that they could see it made him all the more pathetic.

"So, why do you need to do *this* alone?" She gestured to the barn behind them, the downed fence at their feet. "People would love to help you. We'd love to have a chance to thank you for your service and get you back on your feet. You're born and raised in Shelter Creek. You're one of us."

Caleb cleared the ache out of his throat. "I don't know, Annie. I appreciate the offer. I really do. But I have to think on it."

She nodded. "Okay. I get it. But don't think too long. Summer's rolling on, and before you know it, we might actually get some rain. And I'm not sure your barns will last through more than a storm or two without some reinforcement." She glanced at the lambing shed in the distance. "Or a roof."

She was teasing him just a little and Caleb couldn't help but smile back. It was so derelict, it was almost funny.

"And before I go, there's one more thing." Annie eyed him sharply. "And it's about Maya, who I love very much, so think before you speak."

She was refreshingly straightforward. She reminded him of one of his drill instructors. "Okay. Shoot."

Annie let out a long breath. "I know that what's between you is impossibly hard. I can't begin to imagine what it's like. But I know that Maya wants to help. She didn't mean harm by coming out here the other day."

He nodded. "I know."

"And she *is* knowledgeable. She came out to my ranch yesterday and taught me a thing or two. She's going to be at Juan Alvaro's ranch later this week and Brian Silva's the next. Us ranchers tend to get set in our ways, but times are changing. We have to change too. And if it means we lose less livestock in the process, so much the better."

Caleb nodded, not trusting himself to speak. He was young compared to most of the other ranchers around Shelter Creek. He shouldn't be this resistant to new ideas. Shouldn't be so stuck.

Caleb looked out over the field with its broken fence. His pride hurt like hell when he thought about how people saw him. Poor. In need of rescue. But he also knew how pride could get in the way. Had seen it firsthand in guys who'd failed out of boot camp because they just couldn't let go of their own egos.

He didn't want to fail, yet failure was right around the corner. His bank account was empty, and he and Hobo had been living on canned food all week. Well, he had. Hobo was probably supplementing his diet with mice in the barn. Caleb wasn't ready to go that far, but he'd been considering venison. After all, Maya had mentioned he had a whole lot of deer on his property.

Annie was waiting, sipping on her coffee, looking around, with curiosity and concern writing equal stories on her features. He had to say something. To at least be polite and acknowledge all she had offered. "I'll think about it, Annie. I will. And I would like your advice down the road, if you have time to give it. I want to breed for wool, and you're the best around for that."

"I'd be happy to give any assistance I can. Why don't you swing by my ranch sometime soon and we'll chat."

"I'd appreciate that."

"And just remember, you're not the only person who has ever needed a little extra help. You're not that special, Caleb Dunne."

He hadn't laughed in so long, it sounded rusty. "Good to know," he told Annie, who was smiling at his reaction. "Very good to know."

"I'll see you soon." Annie turned to go and almost tripped over Hobo, who'd emerged from a clump of brush with the stealth of the mouse-hunter he was. "Oh! Look at you!" She reached down to pet him, but the orange beast made a beeline for Caleb and jumped up to his shoulder.

"Well," Annie said, watching them with a surprised smile. "Would you look at that? Good to see you're not totally alone out here, Caleb." She waved and strode back up the lane toward the barn, hopped into her truck and was off, leaving Caleb with his pride at his feet, but his heart warmed by a glimmer of something he'd forgotten. Kinship.

He had one relative left in town, his mom's sister, Aunt Loreen. He was scheduled to take her to dinner next week, but it felt more like a duty, not like a real connection.

But Annie just now… Well, maybe he was nuts, but her driving out to check on him today, bringing him a treat and an offer of help—it felt a lot like what family would do. And he hadn't felt anything like that in a long, long time.

## CHAPTER SEVEN

"WELL, I THOUGHT that went very well. I'm so proud of you." Grandma Lillian led the way out of the town council meeting, where Maya had just given a short presentation about what her job was and how her work could help the people of Shelter Creek.

Maya stopped outside the town hall to zip up her fleece jacket. The fog had rolled in while they were in the meeting, and it wrapped the cute Victorian buildings on Main Street in mist, giving the town a mysterious aura, like Brigadoon in that old movie Grandma loved. A couple walked out of Shelter Creek Coffee Roasters, to-go cups in hand, but other than that, the street was quiet. Maya had forgotten how picturesque the town was. When she'd first moved here as a child, she was sure she'd landed in the middle of a storybook, everything was painted and landscaped so nicely.

"I think the meeting went okay," she told

Grandma. "They seemed to like the idea of doing a town-wide educational campaign about mountain lions and coyotes. But I don't know if I'm up for doing an assembly at the schools. I'm not a teacher. I'm barely a people person at all."

"Priscilla could help you," Grandma said. "In fact, if you told her what to say, she'd probably do the whole thing for you. I think she misses teaching."

Maya glanced at her grandmother in admiration. "That's brilliant, Grandma. I wouldn't have thought of asking Mrs. Axel."

"Well, don't forget, I managed a busy office for many years. So I learned how to delegate."

Before she retired, Grandma managed the town credit union because, as she used to like to joke to Maya, bossy came naturally to her. Once, just once, Grandma had confided in Maya that she worried that her strong personality might have been the cause of her own daughter's addiction. Mostly, though, they avoided speaking of Maya's parents. That subject, as Grandma liked to say, was all questions and no answers.

They had made efforts to find them over the years. When Maya was in high school,

Grandma got word that they were out of jail and living in a homeless shelter in San Francisco. Maya, with dreams of helping them out, talked Grandma into visiting the city to try to track them down. After days of leaving word at shelters and on street corners, they'd realized that Maya's parents just didn't want to be found.

A couple of months later, Grandma got a postcard from them, saying they were living in a camper van and driving it to Florida to have good weather year-round. Neither Maya nor Grandma had heard from them since.

Maya reached out and squeezed her grandmother's hand, so grateful that this wonderful, bossy woman had kept her out of the foster care system and raised her as another daughter. "I appreciate your advice, Grandma. I am definitely going to ask Mrs. Axel if she'll help me with the school presentations."

"Look at you," Grandma teased. "Asking for help twice in a week. First getting Annie to help with Caleb and now this. It's a miracle."

"Desperation makes people do crazy things," Maya muttered. Remembering her nerves before she spoke at the meeting tonight, she added, "Maybe I'll get really wild and ask Mrs. Axel to give *all* of my presentations for me."

"You did just great," Grandma assured her. "You may get nervous but you're a natural at explaining these animals so that people can understand them better."

"I guess." She'd have to take Grandma's word for it because she'd been so terrified, the audience had been a fuzzy blur. She'd managed to build her professional reputation mostly by writing articles about her research. Back in Boulder, it was easy to find graduate students or interns who were eager for experience. They were happy to take care of any requests for presentations.

"I was surprised to see Caleb in the audience," Grandma said.

"Me too. He certainly wasn't interested in learning about predators when I visited his ranch." Maya had noticed him the moment she stood up to speak and had almost lost the last shreds of her courage. He'd been sitting in the back, but his big frame and brooding expression were impossible to miss.

"Are you okay?"

"I'm fine," Maya fibbed. She would probably never be okay when it came to Caleb. Yes, she could be strong. She could get her work done, spend time with Grandma and The Biddies, and play with Einstein. But coming home had taught her something. She could never think of Caleb without something aching in her heart. There was a part of it that had never healed, and maybe never would. "I can't imagine why he was there tonight. I was afraid he was going to stand up and start yelling at me in the middle of my talk."

Grandma smiled. "He may have been difficult that day on his ranch, but I don't think he'd do that. Annie says she went out there last Saturday, and had a very nice chat with him. Maybe he's coming to his senses. Maybe he showed up tonight because he's finally ready to learn something about wildlife management."

"I suppose it's possible." Maya had no way of knowing what was going on in Caleb's head, and maybe it was better that way. Better not to guess or wonder or worry about him and just focus on the work she was meant to do. Now, if she could just convince her mind of that...

"I thought that was you."

Maya and her grandmother both turned to face the voice behind them. It was high summer, so there was still enough light left in the evening to see that it was Loreen Brockman. She was Caleb's aunt, his mother's sister, and she'd doted on Julie. She had loved taking her niece on shopping trips to San Francisco, and at least once a month had insisted that they get their nails done together.

Maya remembered Julie saying that, while she loved her aunt and appreciated the attention and care, she wished they could just go riding together. Julie had lived for horses and would have appreciated a pair of new riding boots far more than perfect nails or the fashionable clothes her aunt bought her in the city.

"Hi, Loreen. How are you?" Maya tried to keep her voice steady and pleasant.

"I'm doing okay." Loreen sighed loudly. "You know, one day at a time."

Maya didn't actually know, but figured it was safer not to ask. The last time she'd seen Loreen, it had been right after the accident. Loreen had come to Maya's hospital room and demanded to see her. Grandma had told her a firm no, and hospital staff had escorted the distraught woman off the premises.

Maya had caught a glimpse of Loreen's furious, grief-twisted expression as she scowled at her through the doorway of her room.

"Were you at the council meeting tonight?" Grandma Lillian asked.

"I was. I saw Maya's name on the agenda and wanted to hear what she had to say. I wanted to see what she'd been doing with her life since she left Shelter Creek. I hope you've made every single day count—" her voice dripped sweetness that felt anything but sweet "—since my precious niece didn't get to have any of those days."

"I'm very aware of that," Maya assured her, the granola bar she'd nibbled on before the presentation rebelling in her stomach.

"I miss her every day. I hope you realize what you took, not just from Julie, but from so many people, when you got behind the wheel of the car that night."

"Loreen." Grandma's voice was sharp. "Watch what you're saying. Everyone knows that accident wasn't Maya's fault."

"She drove my niece into a tree."

"Perhaps—" Grandma's voice was icy "—you aren't familiar with the actual circumstances of the accident?"

"I know that my niece died because your granddaughter lost control of the car. And I know her mother had problems too."

"That's enough." Maya realized it was true as she said it. *Enough.* For so long she'd been afraid to come home, to hear people like Loreen make these kinds of accusations. Now that she was here, it wasn't as frightening or as hurtful as she'd imagined. It mostly made her mad.

But she wouldn't yell, no matter how much she wanted to. That was what people like Loreen expected her to do. So Maya brought her voice lower and forced herself to speak politely. "Loreen, when you say things like 'got behind the wheel' and 'lost control,' I assume that you're implying that I was drinking. I was not. It's all in the sheriff's report, if you'd like to read it."

"How can you be so cool and calm about it?" Loreen's voice shook. "A beautiful young girl died because of you."

Maya could see tears in Loreen's eyes. All the woman's anger and accusations came from pain and loss, and that knowledge had Maya's temper cooling to a low simmer. She understood pain and loss, had felt plenty of it herself.

"Aunt Lor, *stop*."

Maya started at the deep voice. Her attention had been so riveted on Loreen that she hadn't heard Caleb approach. She turned and there he was, taking up space with his height and breadth and that tough, dark magnetic field that he seemed to have acquired in the years since she'd left. It messed with her breathing and made it hard to look away.

"Hello, Caleb," Grandma said, and Maya was sure she spotted a twinkle in Lillian's eye. She'd always had a soft spot for him and had treated him like family all the years he and Maya had dated.

"Hello, Mrs. Burton."

"You always called me Lillian, so please don't get all formal on me now."

One side of Caleb's mouth curled in a half smile that took Maya by surprise. She'd only seen him looking stern, hungover and miserable. That piece of a smile was a shimmering reminder of all the times he'd smiled at her. Except he'd been smiling at Grandma, and it was gone now, as he turned to his aunt. "You told me you wanted to meet for dinner. Then you talked me into this meeting instead. How about you and I go get that food now?"

So much for Grandma's theory—that Caleb wanted to learn about predator management.

"Of course." Loreen softened when she looked up at her nephew. "I was just sharing that it's been hard, living without Julie. And that seeing Maya here, such a successful scientist, giving a presentation to the town, well, it just made me think about all of the things that Julie never got to do." Loreen glanced at Maya. "If things were different, she would have accomplished so much."

"Of course she would have," Grandma said kindly. "She was an incredibly talented young woman and her death is a terrible loss. But it's not fair to take it all out on Maya."

"Agreed." Caleb's eyes narrowed as he studied his aunt, who pressed her lips together and suddenly started rummaging in her purse for something.

Caleb's gaze drifted to Maya. "I enjoyed your presentation."

Maya stared at him, wondering what had happened between last week and now. Had Annie worked some mysterious rancher-to-rancher magic?

"Um…thanks?" Maybe it came out as a question because there were so many questions in her mind. Last time she'd seen him, he'd pretty much thrown her off his property. But it wasn't just that. Caleb looked different. He wasn't wearing a hat, so she could see his dark hair cropped close. He'd shaved off the thick scruff she'd seen out at his ranch, his eyes were clear and his skin was brighter. He seemed sober and alert and maybe even a tiny bit friendly.

And he was…Caleb. Not the shadowy figure on the trail or the ill stranger she'd tried to work with last week on his ranch. His face was sculpted with new lines and shadows, but he looked more familiar now. She could remember, as she studied him, how his expressions used to be. How his face looked when it lit up with humor and curiosity and love.

She would give a lot to see that Caleb again.

"Aunt Lor, let's go get that dinner you wanted." Caleb took his aunt gently by the arm, so careful with her, while still making it clear that they were leaving. Maya wondered how much he'd heard.

"Okay, yes." Loreen just looked lost now,

and Maya felt that too-familiar ache in her chest, the constant longing for things to be different. For that night, that accident, to never have happened.

Caleb nodded to Grandma Lillian. "Nice to see you again." He was politeness personified. He turned to Maya and gave another nod, only this time his eyes seemed to linger on hers for a moment. As if there was something he wanted to say to her. But all he said was "Good night."

Loreen leaned on him, just a little, as they walked away.

Maya watched them go, the sad, bitter older woman leaning on her tough rock of a nephew.

"Don't let Loreen get to you. Try to remember how kind everyone else was at the meeting tonight." Grandma put an arm around Maya's shoulders and pulled her close for a brief instant of comfort. "Most people are excited to have you here. They're excited to learn from you."

*But not the people who mattered.* The thought was so unexpected, it startled her. But years ago, Caleb's family had felt like hers. He'd given her a promise ring at junior prom and she'd been absolutely certain that promise would lead to a college engagement, which would lead to a postcollege happily-ever-after.

She'd felt so certain that his family would also be hers.

"I'll try to remember, Grandma." Maya took her grandmother's hand as they walked to her truck. "You're right. There are so many kind people. It's just that the angry ones stand out more, you know?"

"Well, as Monique always says, trouble likes to show up with big hair and a flashy outfit."

Maya giggled. "Like her?"

Grandma smiled. "Exactly. Now let's go home for some supper and then we'll take that sorry mutt of yours for a walk."

"You love my mutt. I know about all those biscuits you've been slipping him." Maya opened the passenger door and tried to help her grandmother inside.

"Well, he's skin and bones. Now, shoo!" Grandma flapped her hand at Maya. "I'm not too old to get myself into a vehicle."

Maya saw her opening and took it. "So, if you're still such a good traveler, why did you stop traveling to see me?"

Lillian settled herself in the seat and reached for her seat belt. "I guess I was tired of watching you hide from what happened." She reached out and patted Maya's hand. "You're certainly not hiding anymore. And you know what? Courage looks good on you. Now come on, let's get going."

Maya went around to the driver's side, not sure if she should laugh or cry. She'd been so worried about Grandma. So ready to come home and try to rescue her. When really it was Grandma who'd been on a rescue mission.

Maybe she should resent the deception, but she also understood why Lillian had finally put her foot down and forced her to come home. Because Grandma was right. It was past time that Maya faced all this. And even though facing it wasn't exactly fun, it was helping her feel a little stronger each day.

Still, when she plunked herself down in the seat next to Grandma Lillian and started the engine, she couldn't resist teasing her a little. "Big hair and a flashy outfit, huh? You're trouble, but that doesn't really describe you very well."

Grandma gave her a wink. "Maybe causing trouble to help someone you love calls for a more understated look."

"Ah, that explains it." Maya leaned over, gave her grandmother a kiss on the cheek and started them on the road home.

## CHAPTER EIGHT

CALEB FOUND JACE already by the chutes at the Shelter Creek Rodeo. "Sorry I'm late," he told his buddy. "Parking was insane."

"What's insane is that I let you talk me into this." Jace glared as he pinned his number to his shirt. "Me riding in a rinky-dink rodeo like this, well, it's kind of like setting up the tombstone to make sure everyone knows my career is dead and buried."

"Or maybe that's just your pride talking," Caleb shot back, craning his neck to try to get the pin through his shirt without stabbing himself. He'd had to park so far away, he'd barely had time to get his number.

He glanced around the arena. Not much had changed. The old weathered announcers stand was looking more rickety than ever, but the same golden hills rose beyond the ring, the same smell of dust, barbecue and excitement filled the air.

He'd been apprehensive about coming here today, afraid he'd miss his parents, Julie and Maya cheering him on from the stands. And he did miss that, right down to his bones. But it was still good to be back.

Maybe that's what healing was. Your losses still hurt, but you learned to live with them. You let the ache of them exist right alongside the good.

"Explain to me why you're so keen on us riding bulls today?" Jace tightened the buckle on his tooled chaps, looking every bit the professional rider.

Caleb went for the easiest answer. "Well, your nieces and nephew should see you do your thing. Then maybe they'll think you're cool and they'll listen to you more often."

"Well, if you're right, that might just make this whole fiasco worth it." Jace clapped him on the shoulder. "If it works, I will owe you, big-time."

"And folks will be pretty excited to see their local rodeo hero in action, right here in Shelter Creek," Caleb continued.

"Now you're trying to salvage a few shreds of my dignity. But that's not why you asked me to do this."

Caleb sighed. "Okay, the truth is, I thought if I did it on my own, I might just chicken out. It's been over a decade since I've been on a bull."

Jace gaped at him. "Then why the hell are you getting on one now? You know these aren't little kitty cats like that crazy scrap of orange that rides around on your shoulder. These guys are a ton of pissed-off muscle and they'd be happy to throw you into a fence or trample you to death."

Caleb glared at him. "I've ridden bulls before. Does high school rodeo champion three years running ring any bells? I kicked your butt each one of those years."

"It's been a long time since high school."

"Well, maybe I'm ready to revisit my glory days."

"Why?" Jace planted his feet and glowered at him. "Who are you trying to impress? So I know what cause to put on your death certificate."

Caleb wasn't sure how to answer that. Truthfully, he wasn't trying to impress anyone. He just needed to show himself that he could hang in there when things got rough. That he didn't have to numb himself with booze every time a difficult memory or complicated emotion wandered across his psyche.

Riding a bull was the opposite of numb. It was risking everything for nothing but an eight-second ride and a two-bit trophy. It was jumping right up on the tightrope between life and death and forcing himself to balance. It wasn't just facing fear down, it was spitting right in its eye.

"I've got no one to impress. I guess I just feel like beating you again, for old times' sake."

"Well, I hope you don't get yourself killed out there," Jace muttered. "I hope I don't get myself killed either. The purse just isn't worth it."

Caleb elbowed his friend in the ribs. "Yeah, but the glory is. Come on, you're the local hero. Show all of us amateurs how it's done."

"Fine." Jace elbowed him back. "But you owe me a beer or three after this."

Just the words were tempting. But Caleb had made a decision, haunted by that empty bottle on the porch. He hadn't had a drink in the two weeks since then. "How about a coffee instead?"

At Jace's questioning look, he tried to explain, without sounding too dramatic. "I figured I've had a few too many beers lately. I've been giving my liver a little vacation."

"Adam is gonna be so excited he got through to you." Jace grinned. "Watch it. He'll be so full of himself when he hears about this. Who knows what he'll start preaching about next?"

Caleb winced at the thought. "Maybe we can just agree not to tell him."

Jace nodded. "Though at some point, when he hasn't arrested you in a while, he's going to figure it out for himself."

Caleb's ability to laugh still surprised him. It did seem like, without the booze, the world got a half shade lighter every day. "Come on, they're starting to bring the bulls in. We'd better get over there."

They walked to the arena side by side. As they approached the chutes, Jace glanced his way. "You're sure you're ready for this?"

Caleb shoved down the unease that was starting to creep in and mess with his head. This was why he needed Jace here. Just like he'd needed his platoon in combat. Fear held less power when it had company. "Ready as I can be," Caleb told him. "Let's do this. Let's go ride some bulls."

IT WAS HARD to look away from the clowns running around the rodeo arena, one of them pushing the other in a wheelbarrow, blue-jeaned limbs flailing, but Maya pressed on through the crowd. The bull riding was going to start in a few minutes and she didn't want to see it, didn't want to be here, didn't want to be reminded of all the years she'd watched Caleb ride at this rodeo, and how much she'd loved it.

At least the crowds made it a little easier by blocking her view of the chutes, where bulls were being loaded and cowboys were getting ready to try their skill and luck. Maya hefted her folded table a little higher, trying to ignore the ache in her shoulder. She'd had to park almost a half mile away, and she'd been hauling the table and a couple of tote bags of information about preventing predation ever since.

Hopefully her arm wouldn't fall off before she got around the arena to the area where vendors were allowed to set up. She'd promised her boss that she'd host an information table here at the rodeo today. It was a great opportunity to educate ranchers about keeping their livestock safe from predators.

Because if there was one event guaranteed to get every rancher in the area into one place, it was the Shelter Creek Rodeo.

Though it might be hard to find the actual ranchers in this crowd. The rodeo was never this busy when she was young. Back then it had been a small, local event. Now it seemed to be full of tourists—parents with kids, and hordes of urban cowgirls in their lacy dresses and boots that were far too nice-looking to have ever walked on a ranch.

An itchy sort of crankiness seemed to be crawling under Maya's skin. Who wore white lace to a rodeo? And who were all these people?

Though of course, it wasn't the people that bothered her. It was the memories. Memories of being here with Caleb and their friends, every single summer since junior high. Memories of watching Caleb compete, of her pride in him, of the wonder that somehow this tough, fearless high school rodeo star had chosen *her*. Memories that had been hijacking her thoughts ever since she'd climbed out of her truck and started her long walk to the rodeo grounds.

She didn't want those memories. Didn't

want to remember what it felt like to be so in love, to be so sure of him. Not now. Not when he'd become a stranger.

Maya rounded the back of the metal bleachers to avoid the mass of people taking their seats for the bull riding. Back here the stubbled grass was uneven and the going slow. But at least she'd avoid seeing Caleb, if he was competing.

It was hard to imagine he wouldn't. If anything, he seemed tougher than ever, harder than ever, like all he'd have to do is stare down whatever bull he drew. The poor creature would probably just walk meekly around the ring, with that stern, angry man on his back.

The thought brought a smile that felt a little broken. Like her body didn't quite know how to associate Caleb with humor. Which made sense. There certainly wasn't anything funny about them, really. Except maybe that she was sneaking around the back of the bleachers to avoid the sight of him.

The announcer's voice boomed. "Ladies and gentlemen, please take your seats for the bull riding. These tough cowboys are going to put on quite a show for you folks. And to kick off the competition today, we have two riders who haven't set foot in this arena in many years. We sure are glad to have them home. Folks, let's give a warm welcome to our own PBR Event Winner, Jace Hendricks!"

The crowd erupted into chaos. People were standing on the metal bleachers, screaming and stomping their feet in an irregular rhythm that matched Maya's traitor heart. Because where Jace was, Caleb was. Which meant he was probably the second competitor.

Maya smacked her ankle against the folding table and gasped. The pain shot straight up her leg and seemed to seep right out of her eyes as tears.

No. Not going to happen. No crying over a stubbed ankle or an ex-boyfriend at the Shelter Creek Rodeo. In fact this was ridiculous. Skulking behind the bleachers like some heartsick adolescent. She was a grown woman, here to do a job.

And why would she get heartsick over Caleb? The first time she'd seen him since coming home, he'd almost shot her. The second time he'd been so hungover, he could barely see straight. A hand on the trigger and too much time with a bottle? That sounded an awful lot like her own parents, who'd chosen

their relationship with alcohol over a relationship with her every single time.

Another thing to mourn. Caleb hadn't been
much of a drinker when she'd known him.
Had Julie's death brought that out in him?
Was his drinking one more piece of the tragedy scattered across their lives like the glass
on the road?

Though he'd looked a little better when he
intervened with his aunt after the town hall
meeting last week. Healthier. Maybe even
happier.

The buzzer sounded, signaling the end of
Jace's ride and jolting Maya back to reality.
*Enough.* She and Caleb were an old story with
an unhappy ending. She had plenty to do in
Shelter Creek besides think of him. It had
been ten days since that town hall meeting,
and she'd been busy preparing school presentations with Mrs. Axel and working with a
few different ranchers around the area. It was
exciting; most people seemed relieved that
she was here, that she could give them ideas
on how to coexist more peacefully with the
wildlife that thrived in these remote coastal
hills.

But even though she was busy and had a

lot to think about, too often her mind went to Caleb. It was a bad habit, and the only way to break a habit was to persevere. Maya shook out her ankle, hefted the table and marched forward, emerging from the shadow of the bleachers to a perfect view of the action in the arena.

Jace was perched on the fence, waving to the cheering crowd as the announcer congratulated him on a fabulous ride. And then Jace hopped over the fence, disappearing from view, and Maya's legs suddenly refused to move. She set the table down, set her tote bags down, her eyes glued to the chutes, unable to make out the features of the big cowboy lowering himself over the bull, but sure that it was Caleb.

The announcer confirmed it. "Next up, that other local boy I mentioned, Jace's best buddy, former bull-riding champion of the Shelter Creek High School Rodeo Team, this man spent over a decade serving our great nation in the Marine Corps, and now he's home. Let's welcome Caleb Dunne!"

The cheers erupted all around her but Maya's ears were ringing as if she'd stepped into her own bubble of deafening silence. The chute opened, and there in her mind was the same prayer she'd said every time she'd watched him ride when they were young. *Please, protect him.*

It was a visceral prayer. It didn't matter that she had no right to it, no connection to Caleb anymore; it was just there on her lips as his arm went up and the chute opened and the big brown bull came hopping out like some kind of crazy crow on steroids, jumping and kicking. Somehow Caleb stayed with him, strong enough that he looked graceful where others would look like a ragdoll, riding *with* the bull until it did a strange sideways leap that left Caleb suddenly suspended in the air.

Maya gasped, the fear for him instinctive. But Caleb did what he'd always done when they were young. He got his legs under him and stuck the landing like an oversize gymnast.

No need to fear for him. He landed on his feet. Always.

Her odd, silent bubble burst as the crowd cheered and the clowns distracted the still-hopping bull. Caleb gave the bleachers a casual wave as the announcer said, "Seven-and-a-half seconds for Caleb Dunne. Not quite a winning ride but a stylish one. Let's give him another round of applause, people, both for his great ride today and for his service to our country."

Maya listened to the bittersweet enthusiasm around her. Yes, they'd both landed on their feet, at least somewhat, after Julie's death. But Caleb came home to cheering crowds, while she came home to anger and blame from him and his aunt. And she might have to face more of it today, at her wildlife-management table.

Though, as Grandma kept reminding her, most people had been kind. And it was easy to overlook kindness when meanness made such an impact.

Maya shook her head, trying to shake the gloom. She was here today to do a job. Not to wallow in the past or worry about what people thought. Not to stare at Caleb with a thick ache in her chest as he climbed the fence across the arena from her, accepting high fives and shoulder slaps from fellow cowboys along the way.

Hefting her table and bags one more time, Maya wended her way through the still-cheering crowd. She might not have Caleb's glory, but she had mountain lions and coyotes to protect. Thank goodness for work that mattered. It had eased her heartache many times before, and hopefully it would help again today.

# CHAPTER NINE

MAYA WAS SUPPOSED to set up next to the Wild Western Women hat booth, and sure enough there was an orange spray-painted $X$ on the ground, just as the rodeo organizers had promised. She unfolded her table and positioned it on the uneven ground so it didn't wobble too much. She was kneeling next to it, reaching for her bag full of literature, when a soft voice broke her concentration. "Maya?"

She looked up too quickly and smacked the back of her head on the table. "Ouch!"

"Oh no! Are you all right?"

Maya clutched her head and squinted at the speaker, her mind still reeling from the blow. It was a woman about her age, with long, thick honey-blond hair curled nicely around her shoulders and a pink blouse tucked into perfectly fitting jeans. Her pink sneakers matched her shirt.

"I'm okay." But that wasn't exactly true because Maya had just realized who this woman was. "Trisha." It came out a little more horrified than was probably polite. Trisha Gilbert. Julie's best friend, who'd been in the accident with them. Maya's mouth felt dry and she tried to swallow.

"Long time no see." Trisha twisted her fingers uneasily. "I was wondering if you'd like any help setting up your table. I'm just a couple of booths over, collecting for the scholarship fund."

Maya glanced where Trisha was pointing, and the throbbing in her head kicked up a beat. The sign above the booth read Please Donate to the Julie Dunne Rodeo Scholarship Fund.

No. Her biggest fear coming here today was that someone would get upset about the accident, the way that Caleb's aunt had. That someone would have heard and believed the old rumor that Maya had been driving drunk that night.

And here she was, with her assigned booth just two doors down from the Julie Dunne memorial.

Trisha was smiling, seemingly oblivious to Maya's rising panic. "Remember how much

Julie loved the rodeo? She was one of the top competitors on the high school girls' team."

Maya remembered. Julie was a gorgeous rider—so skilled, she was like an extension of any horse she rode. One entire wall of her bedroom had been decorated with ribbons. Maya had loved watching her ride, and was always a little intimidated when Julie joined her and Caleb for a trail ride on the ranch.

Maya dated Caleb for so long, Julie had felt like her younger sister too. When Caleb had asked her to pick up Julie and Trisha at the concert that night, Maya had felt a little proud, like she was family—like she was the responsible big sister, stepping in to help.

But after the accident, while Caleb and his family and Trisha and the town mourned Julie together, Maya had mourned alone.

"Anyway," Trisha went on, "the scholarship fund is to help girls who might not have the money to be a part of the rodeo team. It pays for their uniforms and transportation—things like that. Julie's mom started it a couple of years after Julie died. When Mrs. Dunne moved away from Shelter Creek, I took over fundraising for it." Trisha paused, a flush creeping across her pale cheeks. She looked so young, but she must be in her late twenties. "I'm sorry, Maya." Her bright demeanor faded out. "Is this really weird that I'm talking to you?"

Maya rubbed her hand against the ache in her skull. These were the kinds of social situations she dreaded. She was so rusty at platitudes. To be polite, she should probably pretend everything was fine. But that was also kind of a lie. "It's a little weird," she admitted. The last time they'd seen each other, Maya had stood in the doorway of Trisha's hospital room, flowers in one hand, the other in a sling to immobilize her broken shoulder.

"Maybe I was wrong to come over here," Trisha said. "But then I thought it would be odd to spend the day so close to each other without talking. Plus I've owed you an apology for thirteen years."

Maya's heart dipped like a barn swallow in her chest. "I'm pretty sure it's me who should apologize to you."

"You tried to, that day you came to see me in the hospital. I wouldn't listen."

The memory replayed, as it had so many times, like a clip from a surreal movie. Two days after the accident, Maya, released from her own hospital room, had gone to see Trisha, hoping to offer an apology, to commiserate in their grief for Julie, to say something— anything—to try to ease the agony twisting in her heart.

Instead she'd been met with accusations, pointed fingers and screaming fury from Trisha's parents. "Just tell the truth." Trisha's father had loomed over Maya, hands on his hips. "You were drinking that night, weren't you?" And when Maya had just stared, stunned and scared, he threw up his hands. "Of course you were. And we'll make sure the police know it."

Maya's blood had been tested at the hospital right after the accident. The results were proof that she'd been completely sober, and Trisha's father knew it. But those two words, *of course,* knocked the wind out of Maya's response. They both knew what he meant. *Of course you were drinking, because your parents are addicts and criminals. It runs in your family. Bad blood.*

But Maya hadn't had much time to process the insult.

"Don't you realize?" Trisha's mom had screamed, jabbing a finger toward Maya's chest. "She may lose her leg, Maya! And that's on you. That's on *your* shoulders."

Maya understood their grief; she'd been drowning in her own. But she hadn't been prepared for their fury, or the stony silence from Trisha. But when Maya sent her a pleading glance, wanting her to speak up, Trisha had turned her face to the wall.

Maya had dropped the flowers and fled.

Trisha took a step closer, her green eyes welling up. "I'm so sorry, Maya. For that day in the hospital. For the way my parents behaved. And the way I lay there like a coward and said nothing."

Maya nodded, not trusting herself to speak. She'd spent so many years trying to lock her emotions away so they wouldn't overwhelm her. Trisha's apology was a crowbar cracking the seal on the door. "It's okay," Maya managed. "We were so young."

"I was terrified of getting into more trouble. All they knew was that I was drinking that night. I didn't want to tell them anything else. So I stayed silent and let you take the blame."

Maya stared. "Trisha, what would *you* be

blamed for? You were just a kid catching a ride home from a concert."

Trisha crossed her arms over her chest as if she were suddenly cold on this hot afternoon. "Don't you see? The entire thing was my fault. There was this guy, an older college boy, who I had a crush on. When he asked me to the concert, I lied about my age. Then I talked Julie into going with me."

Trisha's voice was shaky, and she swiped at her eyes, but she kept talking. "If I hadn't been stupid over that boy, if I hadn't talked Julie into drinking—she'd never even had a drink before. Did you know that? Julie was such a goody-goody. I think maybe that's why the alcohol hit her so hard."

Words formed and disappeared in Maya's mind. Finally a few surfaced and stayed. "You think *you* were responsible? For the accident?"

Trisha buried her face in her hands. Her "yes" came out teary and muffled.

"No!" Trisha's distress pulled Maya out of her own. "No. Maybe you made a mistake in meeting those boys, but you called for help, which was exactly what you should have done under the circumstances. I was the driver. It was my job to get you home in one piece."

"But when Julie climbed into the front seat, when she fell...there was no way you could keep us safe. Julie was tall. Strong. You're..." Trisha looked up, and paused, as if worried about being rude. "You're petite. I tried to help. I tried to pull her away from you, but I couldn't. I wasn't strong enough, and she was so floppy and out of control."

It was just a tiny piece of information, but Maya felt it hit, land and then slowly sink into her mind. A cool, still piece of reprieve. "You...you couldn't move her?"

"No." Trisha's voice calmed a little. "I couldn't. And that's what makes what I did to you in the hospital even more wrong. I should have told anyone who would listen exactly what had happened. What Julie did and how it wasn't your fault. You couldn't have pushed her off, couldn't have kept control of the car..."

"I was still the driver. It is still my fault."

"It *shouldn't* be," Trisha said. "And that is what I should have said to my parents that day."

At a loss, Maya repeated something a therapist had told her once. "You did the best you could at the time."

Trisha let out a shaky breath. "I guess so. But my best wasn't very impressive."

It was hard to think straight. For so many years Maya had wondered if she'd just been stronger, more aggressive, maybe she could have shoved Julie away. But Trisha, even then, had been taller than Maya, *and she hadn't been able to get Julie to move either.*

"It helps, Trisha, to know what happened. Thank you for telling me."

"I wanted to tell you the other day, when you were at the vet with your dog. But I lost my nerve."

"You work at the vet? I didn't see you there."

"I'm an assistant, so I work in the back, mainly. But I heard that you were the one who'd found that sweet three-legged dog. How is Einstein doing?"

Maya smiled her gratitude that they were moving on to happier topics. "He's great. He has my grandmother wrapped around his paw. I swear she brings him a new toy almost every day."

Trisha laughed, and that too felt like a relief. "He deserves it, poor guy. He seems like he's had a tough life." She glanced at Maya's unpacked bags. "Can I help you get ready?"

Maya shook her head, her response automatic. "That's okay. I'm fine on my own."

"Oh okay." Trisha flushed, shy again. "Thank you for listening to my apology."

"Of course."

This was awkward. Emotion about the accident never came in small amounts. Talking about it was like trying to maintain some kind of normalcy while holding back a tsunami.

And when the talking was done, people expected closure. They wanted a "have a nice day," or an easy transition back to small talk. Which was just about impossible when your heart was brimming with endless longing for a different path through life. A path where Julie was still alive, Trisha was unharmed, and she and Caleb had stayed together.

Without that path, closure wasn't really possible. Living with a death on your hands was living with an open wound. And no one wanted to look at that.

"There she is!"

They both turned toward the voice and Maya was grateful for the interruption.

Grandma Lillian was bustling toward them,

with a big grocery bag from Shelter Creek Market in her arms. "And Trisha, you're here too! What a lovely surprise." She glanced from one to the other and Maya could see the concern behind her cheerful demeanor. "Are you two doing okay?"

"We are," Maya reassured her.

"Well, good. Now, Maya, I've brought some snacks in case we get hungry." Grandma plunked the bag down in the grass.

"We?"

Grandma didn't answer; instead she waved vigorously to someone she'd spotted across the field. That someone waved back. Whoever she was, she wore the biggest straw hat Maya had ever seen. Not a cowboy hat. The kind of hat with a brim that extended in an enormous circle. A hat you'd see in a magazine, by a fancy swimming pool, on the coiffed head of gracefully lounging woman.

Grandma waved to the big-hat woman again. "Here we are, Monique!"

Monique tottered toward them in high wedge sandals. She wore black cotton capris and a red-checked blouse tied at her waist. "There you are, Lillian. And Maya! I'm glad I found you."

What was Monique doing here? Maya glanced at Grandma suspiciously. Her smile was completely bland, which meant she was definitely up to something.

"There you all are!" Annie strode up in her usual faded jeans and cowboy hat. "Oh hi, Trisha."

Annie was here too? "Grandma…" Maya started to say, but Annie interrupted.

"I almost forgot this, Lillian. Had to go back for it." She tossed a folded green table-cloth onto Maya's plastic table.

"Oh good, I found you!"

They all turned to see Kathy stumping to-ward them across the rough grass in a bright yellow tracksuit.

"I was worried you wouldn't get here on time," Grandma said.

"Traffic was terrible and parking is worse." Kathy gestured to the crowded booths around them. "I think our little rodeo has been dis-covered by tourists."

Annie nodded. "At least we still have a rodeo. So many places have let theirs go."

Maya stared from one Book Biddy to an-other, trying to figure out what they were all doing here. Finally she leaned down to help

Grandma smooth the cloth across the table and whispered, "Grandma, what is going on? What are you up to?"

"Helping," Grandma whispered back with a wink. "There." She gave the cloth one last gentle shake and stepped back. "Now that looks official."

"Good thing we have you, Lillian, to think of this kind of stuff." Annie surveyed the table appreciatively. "I would have shown up just like you, Maya. Plastic table, a few fliers, the bare bones."

"That's why you have friends like us." Monique reached into her vast purse, pulled out a mason jar and plunked it in the center of the table. Next she brought out a small bouquet of daisies, wrapped in paper. She unwrapped the daisies, popped them in the jar, then filled it from a water bottle she'd brought along. "There." She looked up at her silent audience. "What? We said we were going to pretty up her display."

"Your purse is like one of those clown cars," Annie said.

"They're lovely," Maya added quickly. "It's just not something I would ever have thought of, but it looks great!" It was so sweet, really,

Annie's green tablecloth, these flowers… It looked like they were all going to sit down and have a nice picnic.

"Now, doesn't this look lovely?" Mrs. Axel came bustling up, carrying a tote bag with something brown sticking out the top. It looked like a…stuffed animal?

"Hi, Mrs. Axel." This was beyond sweet. The Biddies had promised moral support, and here they were, true to their word.

"I hope I'm not too late! I brought the photos!"

Maya turned to see Eva, dressed in black leggings and some kind of wearable art tunic made from different pieces of brightly colored fabric. She pulled out three photographs, framed in black-and-white, and set them on the table. "Here you go, Maya. And nice to see you, by the way."

"Nice to see you too." Maya suddenly recognized the pictures. "I took these!" She stared, a sense of wonder almost overwhelming her. Eva had made her photos look professional, with white mats and simple black frames.

Maya glanced at Grandma. "You gave her my photos?" She'd taken this one on her second day here, in the early morning, when she'd finally gotten close enough to catch the mountain lion she'd tracked in the long lens of her camera. The puma had draped himself on the lower branch of an oak tree, and in this photo, he was leisurely licking one of his paws.

"The wonders of email." Grandma looked proud, like she'd invented the internet herself. "You sent them to me, and I forwarded them to Eva. And no, Maya, I'm not apologizing. They're gorgeous and the world should see them."

It was an overstatement, but Maya couldn't argue with Grandma. Not when she was trying so hard to help.

Kathy pointed to another photo, of the puma sprawled asleep on an oak branch. "He's pretty adorable." She turned to the group, bringing her hands together in a brisk clap. "So, I think we're all here now."

"We?" Maya put her hands on her hips and looked at the six women assembled around her information table. "Is someone going to explain to me what is going on? And why does Mrs. Axel—I mean Priscilla—have a stuffed animal?"

Mrs. Axel pulled the creature from her bag.

"It's a mountain lion. Her name is Uma. Uma the Puma. I found her in a nature shop in San Francisco, when I was there visiting my niece yesterday. Isn't she adorable? I figured people should be reminded that mountain lions aren't just these big scary predators. They're beautiful. And this one is cuddly too. Go on, give her a squeeze."

This wasn't exactly what Maya had planned for her table here at the rodeo. She'd thought to keep things professional. Scientific. So that ranchers would listen to her ideas and take them seriously.

Maya glanced around to make sure no one was looking, and then gave Uma a small squeeze. The lion was soft and squishy, and she resisted the urge to pull the stuffy in for a bigger cuddle.

Instead she set Uma on the table. It did look cute there. Maybe The Biddies were right. Uma and the photos could be a reminder of all the things people liked about mountain lions.

But Maya also couldn't see herself trying to talk seriously about wildlife management with The Book Biddies clustered around, chiming in at odd moments.

"I really appreciate your support," she told

them. "But don't you all want to go watch the rodeo?"

"Seen it a million times," Annie said, waving her hand toward the arena dismissively. "Though I'll make sure to watch the barrel racing. See how the young ones are doing."

"Annie was quite a barrel racer in her day," Grandma Lillian told the group.

"Well, I might take a look at a few of these cowboys," Monique said, casting an appraising eye at a handsome, middle-aged guy headed for the arena. "But mostly, today we have a higher purpose."

"And what exactly is that?" Maya tried to keep the trepidation out of her voice. It was hard to know what would happen next when it came to The Biddies.

Monique reached into her never-ending purse and pulled out something bright blue, which she shook out with a flourish. "Ta-da!"

It was a T-shirt. And written across the chest, in big white cursive letters, were the words Cougars for Cougars. Maya stared, caught somewhere between laughter and shock. They really were serious about helping her. Except they weren't serious; they were totally, ridiculously silly.

"They came out great!" Mrs. Axel reached eagerly for the shirt. "Did you get extra large?"

"Of course," Monique assured her.

"Cougars for Cougars." Annie's mouth flattened into a thin line. "Monique, this is *not* the slogan we discussed."

"Oh come on now, Annie. It's much more catchy than Biddies for Big Cats. Or Readers for Predators. Or whatever it was you suggested."

"Well, I'm not sure I want to be viewed as some kind of cougar." Annie folded her arms across her chest with a huff that really did make her look like an indignant biddy. "We're not all here to drool over the young cowboys."

"Are you sure?" Monique dropped her fake eyelashes in a lascivious wink. "Give it a try. You might like it."

"*I* like it," Kathy chimed in. "The slogan, I mean. It's funny. And if we make people laugh, maybe they'll be more likely to listen to us when we talk to them about Maya's work."

It really was a great name. But Maya wasn't sure the Cougars for Cougars were the wildlife ambassadors she needed. When she'd decided to take this job, she'd envisioned herself impressing the citizens of her hometown with her scientific knowledge and her professionalism. Maybe it was shallow, but she wanted them to see that she'd done well, that she wasn't like her parents, or the wild teenager they'd all assumed her to be when she'd crashed the car.

Plus was it really okay for Maya to be silly, to use a funny name on a T-shirt and a goofy stuffed puma when Julie Dunne's scholarship booth was just down the way? Maya glanced at Trisha, but she seemed oblivious to any worries. She'd just accepted a T-shirt from Monique and was tugging it over her head.

"You all can't spend your entire day helping me. You should go enjoy the rodeo."

"Oh don't worry. We'll enjoy it," Grandma said. She rummaged through one of Maya's tote bags and pulled out a stack of fliers. "Living with Mountain Lions," she read. "These will be perfect. We'll hand some out for you. And we can direct people to your table, if they have any questions."

There was clearly no use arguing with their plans, and deep down Maya didn't really want to. It was love and support for her in action, it was The Biddies having her back, and that was too precious to squash. "Okay, put on your T-shirts, ladies. I want to get a photo of this."

Monique handed out the shirts, and The Biddies pulled them on over their clothing. Trisha glanced shyly at Maya. "I have other volunteers taking over Julie's booth for the next couple of hours. Handing out fliers will be fun."

"Technically you're a little young to be a cougar," Maya teased.

"You're just kittens, both of you." Eva looked thoughtful. "Or is it cubs?"

"It's actually both. Both words are used."

"See?" Grandma elbowed Maya gently. "You're a natural at this education thing."

Monique clapped her hands. "Cougars, line up, please. Priscilla, you hold Uma."

Maya raised her camera and took the shot. Then they all wanted to hold Uma, and there was an incident with Monique's hat brim and Eva's eye, but finally they had enough photos, and the Cougars for Cougars and Trisha wandered off, with fliers in hand, to educate the public about mountain lions.

Watching them go, Maya noticed that Trisha walked with a slight limp. Guilt surged through her system in a familiar murky tide. Maya had escaped the accident with a broken shoulder and a mild concussion. Trisha's leg had never totally healed. But this time, as the guilt threatened to rise up, to flood everything, a thought surfaced like a life preserver. *Trisha says you're not at fault.*

Hands shaking, Maya laid out her fliers and fact sheets, and rearranged the framed mountain lion photos and Uma the Puma. She opened the binder she'd filled with ideas and examples for predator management. And slowly, the guilt subsided, as if Trisha's kind words were a full moon, shining like a beacon and shifting the current.

Maya absentmindedly scratched Uma the Puma's fuzzy ears. Grandma and her friends' astounding and unfamiliar generosity had thrown her off balance. So had Trisha's easy forgiveness. Maya was so used to managing everything in her life alone, it was tempting to push away all of their help. To retreat to her comfortable solitude.

Solitude was safe. She knew what to expect when she was on her own. Friendship, love, family—it was all so risky. Maya knew too well how those things could disappear so easily.

But maybe that possibility of loss was another fear to face, just like public speaking and coming home.

Maya picked up Uma and gave her a quick, comforting squeeze. Facing her fears was clearly the theme of the summer, whether she liked it or not. Luckily for her, the The Book Biddies wouldn't let her push them away. As promised, they had her back. And surprisingly that was a pretty good feeling.

# CHAPTER TEN

CALEB'S LEG ACHED with every step toward the rodeo parking lot. He needed to get home and start on the chores waiting for him. With his leg like this, it would probably take him longer than usual to get them done. He was such a fool thinking he could relive his high school glory days with shrapnel still stuck inside his calf—a little souvenir from the Taliban.

Doctor Upshaw at the VA had said it was close to the bone, and had to work its own way out. It wasn't easy to live with, but in some ways Caleb didn't mind the pain. It helped him remember that he'd gotten off easy, compared to so many others.

The doctor would probably have something to say about Caleb's decision to ride a bull, next time they met. Though maybe the doc would be okay with it if he knew how much it had helped him. Dr. Upshaw wanted Caleb to slow down his drinking, attend support groups, go to therapy and get in touch with his emotions.

Well, for the last couple of weeks Caleb had stayed off the booze, so that would make the good doctor happy. And as for therapy, Caleb was pretty sure that riding a bull just now had done more for him than any shrink could. The huge animal's attempts to shake him off brought on the adrenaline rush Caleb's body needed. The laser focus required to anticipate the bull's next move had swept all the clutter out of his brain. And the way he could still bring it home, land on his feet, even... that had helped his self-esteem, for sure.

And just being here at the rodeo had to be therapeutic too. His first rodeo without his mom working the concession stand for the PTA, and his dad standing around, talking with all the other ranchers. His first rodeo without Julie racing around the ring with her drill team, then racing the barrels later on. It had been hard to be here without them, but he'd done it. And that was something.

Lost in his thoughts, Caleb heard Maya before he saw her, like her voice was coming right out of his conscience, reminding him of what a jerk he'd been on his ranch a couple weeks ago. And how rude his aunt had been after the town meeting.

Glancing around the field circled by vendors' booths, he spotted her just a few yards away. She was standing next to a table covered in green cloth, her hands on her hips, her booted feet planted apart in a defiant stance he recognized. With all of her five-feet-and-change drawn up high, she still looked tiny compared to the man looming over her.

Caleb squinted and recognized the guy, despite the years that had carved changes into his features. Fred Corrigan. An ornery old rancher who owned a large dairy farm south of town. He was always arguing with someone. Mom used to say that the only reason Fred showed up to town events was because he was hoping for some conflict.

Looked like not much had changed.

Caleb would know Maya's voice anywhere. Only right now it was raised just a little, and her tone was sharp.

He hadn't realized she was at the rodeo today. Maybe that was better. If he'd known, he'd have been looking for her in the crowd, hoping she was watching when he rode that bull.

He shook his head, annoyed at the old memories rising up. Why would he hope for that? He'd made his choice about Maya after Julie had died. And even though at first he'd broken things off out of rage and grief, over the years he'd tried to accept that breaking up made sense. How could they be together after a tragedy like that? How could he love the girl whose mistake had killed his sister?

Though she was a whole different person now. A grown woman, tough as nails and fiercely independent, strong and brilliant. Not the kind of woman who'd even be interested in a guy like him.

Still he wanted to see her, to talk to her, to just be around her. Outside that town hall meeting, witnessing the compassionate way she'd handled his aunt, something in him had unwound. Her calm spirit, her quiet determination, soothed him like nothing else.

He owed her an apology and had wanted to deliver it then and there, but he'd been afraid that his aunt would step in to twist his words with her bitterness.

It didn't matter what he wanted though. Maya wouldn't want to see him right now. Not after the way he'd mistreated her on that still-drunk morning. She was working, and she didn't need him to mess up her day. But her words cut through the background rumble of the crowd and he couldn't resist the chance to hear her voice. He paused to listen.

"I understand that you're upset, Mr. Corrigan. But my job is to help manage the wildlife in this region. So you'll need to check with me if you're having problems with predation."

Caleb took a few steps closer, even though now it was pretty obvious he was eavesdropping.

Fred Corrigan grimaced at Maya with a squinty smile on his face, as if he was looking forward to putting Maya in her place. "Well, it's real sweet that you want to save the animals, little lady, but I have a ranch to run. And seeing as I've been running it longer than you've been alive, I think it's safe to say that I know what I'm doing."

Caleb's hands went into fists and he jammed them into his thighs to keep from using them. Corrigan was talking down to her in the worst way.

Like a punch to the gut, he realized he'd

done the same thing. Had he sounded this mean? This stupid?

But Maya was tough. He'd experienced that toughness firsthand. She'd want to handle Fred on her own.

Still, he didn't like the way the old rancher was moving so close to her. Looming over her. It wasn't right, that kind of physical intimidation. Someone needed to step in. Caleb glanced around but no one else seemed to have noticed. So that left him. He approached the table, stopping just a few feet behind Maya, listening to her answer back.

"First of all, Mr. Corrigan, please don't call me 'little lady.' My name is Maya Burton."

The old rancher fixed her with an appraising glance. "Oh trust me, I know who you are. Everyone in this town knows about that."

What was it with people bringing up her past like this? Caleb realized suddenly how protected he'd been. Since it was his sister who'd died, people treaded lightly, didn't mention it or, if they did, it was to offer a kind word.

But what kind of experience had Maya had? If people like his aunt and Fred Corrigan were making insinuations about the accident now, so many years after, what had they said to her right after it had happened? Back then, in his own youth and grief, he'd never thought about it. Now he realized he was getting a tiny window into all that she'd experienced.

And he'd been the first to point a finger at her. Knowing that she'd been injured, terrified and full of grief because she'd loved Julie too.

Caleb remembered, suddenly, her heated words when she'd let him have it on his ranch. *You acted like you believed those rumors around town. That I was drunk. And since you seemed to hate me, a lot of people assumed those rumors were true.*

He couldn't change what he'd done then, but he could learn from his mistakes now. He moved to stand next to Maya. "Is there a problem here?"

Maya paled at the sight of him. "No. Everything's fine."

He didn't believe her. He might not know her anymore, but he knew how to read her face, still. He recognized the stress tightening the corners of her mouth. The frustration adding a shrill note to her voice. "It didn't seem fine from where I was standing. I couldn't help overhearing what Fred here was saying."

Maya took him by the arm and turned them both away from Fred. "Caleb," she hissed. "I don't know what you're doing here, but I don't need your help."

"I know that you don't need it. But I *can* help, I think. Let me? Please?" He'd go if she made him, but he hated that she had to take flak from people like Fred because of their shared past.

Her brows creased in confusion as she studied him for a long moment. Well, that made two of them confused. The need to put himself between her and Fred came from some deep protective instinct he hadn't encountered since his last time in combat. That it was rearing up now, with Maya of all people, was something he'd have to think about later.

"Fine." Her whisper was sullen and Caleb knew that as much as she hated to admit it, she was having a hard time with the old rancher. They both turned back to face Fred.

Maya took the lead. "Caleb, I was just explaining to Mr. Corrigan here that if he's having problems with mountain lions on his land, or coyotes, I can give him some ideas to help deter them."

"Sounds reasonable." Caleb flushed when he caught Maya's surprised look. They both knew that he hadn't been reasonable when she had tried to do the same thing for him. Caleb reached out and shook Fred's hand. "Good to see you, by the way," he lied.

Fred might be a jerk but he wasn't going to snub someone so soon back from war, and that was exactly what Caleb was counting on. "Good to see you too, son," Fred said, gripping Caleb's hand briefly in his own. "Glad you made it home safe from Afghanistan."

Caleb nodded. "Me too. Thanks."

Fred looked delighted to have a larger audience. "I was just saying to Maya that we wouldn't have so many problems with these vermin if tree huggers in Sacramento weren't making all these rules, telling folks like me that we can't defend our livestock. I don't see why we're protecting these mountain lions anyway. As far as I can see, they're nothing but trouble."

"Well, apex predators' right to exist is a philosophical issue that I'm sure you and I could debate for a long time," Maya told him, and Caleb almost smiled at the way she used scientific language as a weapon.

"I just want to debate why I can't shoot a mountain lion if it comes after my sheep."

Caleb cringed, hearing his own stubborn self in Fred's words. Had he sounded as pompous and pigheaded? Probably.

"Well, we've been over that a couple of times now." Maya picked up a pamphlet off the table. "Why don't you read about the latest methods of predator management, and then contact me if I can be of assistance."

She was trying to dismiss him—doing a pretty good job of it too—but the thing was, Fred Corrigan was a bully. He had been even when Caleb was a kid. And as long as he had someone like Maya stuck here at her information table, he'd just keep going.

"What I do on my own property is none of your business."

Yup, there he went. And he'd keep running his mouth until this rodeo was packed up and done, unless someone put a stop to it.

So Caleb would have to try. "I was saying the same thing as you, Fred, just last week."

Fred's face lit up with satisfaction, while

Maya glared at him, clearly sensing betrayal was on the way.

"But, Fred, what Maya explained to me is that if you kill off one of these predators without a permit, you can get fined a lot of money."

"Maybe. If anyone found out."

Caleb figured he'd just ignore that particular comment. "Like you, I was skeptical at first. I've had some of the worst lion problems in the area, and I figured I'd solve them all by shooting the predator. But I've realized that shooting won't solve my problems for long."

Maya's eyes were wide brown pools of shock. Then the corners crinkled with humor as dry as dust in drought. "You were listening at the town hall meeting. I'm glad you learned something."

He couldn't look away from her, from the smile in her eyes that didn't reach her mouth, like a secret, meant just for him. "It was a good presentation."

"Huh?" Fred peered at him from under the brim of his brown felt hat. "Seems like shooting can solve a lot."

Caleb figured he'd better let Maya take

over from here. He glanced her way and she nodded slightly. They were tag-teaming Fred and it was kind of fun to be on the same side for once.

"Killing off the predators in this area could make many other issues worse," Maya said. "It will give you an overpopulation of deer, rabbits, raccoons, skunks and other smaller animals. Mountain lions even kill off coyotes, and I'm sure you don't enjoy having *them* on your ranch."

Caleb turned to Fred. "The way I see it, that makes mountain lions pretty useful. Because I don't know about you, Fred, but I've never actually laid eyes on one of our local lions. But I see coyotes running around all over the place."

Maya was studying him intently, like she wasn't quite sure if maybe he'd gone crazy or been drinking again or something.

Caleb gave her a wink to try to jolt her out of her stupor. "Right, Maya?"

"Oh yes," she stammered. "Absolutely."

Fred was about to reply when a crisp voice had them all turning.

"Is that Fred Corrigan?" It was Annie Brooks, hustling up in a bright blue shirt with

Cougars for Cougars written across the front. Caleb tried not to laugh as Annie's friends came tromping up behind her, all in the same hilarious T-shirts.

Fred turned to greet Annie and his entire demeanor changed. Annie ran things in the ranching community and had the respect of all of her peers, even Fred. "Annie, how are you? Good to see you." He peered at her more closely. "Cougars for Cougars?"

Caleb had never seen Annie look so flustered. Her normally stoic face turned bright pink. "It's just a thing we're doing for today, my friends and I, to help Maya get the word out about the good work she's doing for the ranching community."

"Hi, Fred!" Maya's grandmother, Lillian, came up next to Annie and shook Fred's hand. "How's your lovely Irma doing? I dropped some soup by for her the other day. I'd heard her hip was bothering her again."

"Why, thank you, Lillian. That was very kind." Fred looked from one woman to the other, and then at Caleb with a pleading look in his eyes. They were drowning him in kindness and the old codger didn't know what to do about it.

Caleb turned to the women. "Great shirts," he told them.

A woman he didn't know, in an enormous hat, tottered over to him in high heels. "Thank you. I designed them myself. I'm Monique, owner of Monique's Miracles. Come on by if you ever need a haircut, cowboy."

"Will do," he said, liking her immediately, even though out of all the ladies here, she might actually be the cougar that their shirts professed them to be. But she was also a leader, he could tell right away, and this group she was a part of had shown up for Maya today.

Like he should have shown up for her, a long time ago.

"Well, I guess I'll get going." Fred was already backing away from the group of women, who'd surrounded Maya and her table.

"Oh hang on." Caleb recognized Mrs. Axel, his third-grade teacher, waving a flier at Fred. "Take one of these pamphlets with you. It sounds like you'd really benefit from Maya's expertise."

"That's right," Annie chimed in. "Did Caleb mention that he's thinking of working with Maya? Isn't that right, Caleb?"

All the ladies turned to stare at Caleb. *Thank you for that, Annie.* And Maya was staring too, first at him, then at Annie, her brow creasing in suspicion.

Caleb saw Fred looking on with interest and he realized this was his chance to make a difference. To do what he hadn't been able to do when Julie had died. To stand up for Maya in public and show her he believed in her.

"Yeah, I am. Maya, I haven't mentioned it yet, but I could use your advice around my ranch."

Maya's face went from pale to pink to pale again. "You *want* my advice?" Then she glanced at Fred and cleared her throat. "I mean, yes, that sounds good. I'm looking forward to working with you, Caleb."

The relief on her face was the final straw. He'd do this, not just for Fred's benefit, but his own. Annie had made it clear, when she visited his ranch, that he needed help. And, for starters, he needed to make sure he didn't lose any more sheep. So he'd learn whatever Maya could teach him. "Would Monday morning fit with your schedule?"

"Monday would be fine." Her mouth twitched at the corner, like she was trying not to laugh. And it did feel good to be sticking it to Fred, after he'd been so rude to her. But he suspected it was more. Even if it was only for a few minutes, they were on the same side, and an echo of their old connection rippled between them. She had to feel it too.

"Oh Caleb, I'm so glad you're taking advantage of Maya's expertise," Mrs. Axel exclaimed. She looked at Fred and there was steel behind her kind eyes. "Did you know Maya is one of our country's leading experts on predator interaction? Her work has been written up in several magazines and many scholarly journals."

"Mrs. Axel!" Maya's face went an adorable tomato red.

"What? I can't follow the career of one of my most beloved students? You should take advantage of her knowledge, Fred. She'll only be in town for a few more weeks."

Her words hit Caleb in the chest. A reminder that Maya wasn't here to stay. Which was a good thing. They both had their own lives to lead.

But maybe if they worked together while she was here, Caleb could finally get some closure. Because Maya took up this space inside him, not in his heart exactly, but maybe in his soul, and it didn't leave much room for anyone else.

When he'd been in the service, his lack of a romantic life hadn't been much of a problem. But now that he was home, he figured at some point he'd want to try to meet someone. But it was hard to imagine it when Maya's face, her smile, all that they'd had and all that he'd destroyed was always there. Like a mess he could not figure out how to clean up.

If they spent some time together, and he got to know who she was now, maybe his heart would accept that the girl he'd loved had grown up into this tough, successful scientist, who had no room for a broke rancher like him in her life. And then maybe he could finally let that girl go.

"So, what do you think, Fred?" Mrs. Axel pressed. "Are you going to work with Maya?"

Caleb glanced at Fred Corrigan, wondering how he would protest. But no one could resist Mrs. Axel. She'd taught every child in this town. Fred's kids too, Caleb reckoned.

Sure enough, Fred fell like a tree in a windstorm. "I'll consider it," he told Mrs. Axel. He must have realized it was a good moment to make his escape. "Well, I'll see you all later." He hustled away across the field, glancing back a time or two as if he was worried about being followed.

"You'd think he was being chased off by a pack of cougars or something," Monique drawled, and the other women started laughing. Caleb took in the group, surprised to see Trisha had joined them. She had on the same blue T-shirt as the other women.

"Aren't you a little young to be a cougar?" he asked.

She grinned. "I think it's more of an honorary thing." Then her smile faded a little. "Thank you again for the other night," she said softly. "At the bar."

"Hey, it's ancient history," he assured her. "Don't even mention it. Plus didn't you thank me about a hundred times already?"

She flushed. "Yes, probably. But it's the kind of thing there aren't really enough words for."

"Well, you'll have to keep the rest of them to yourself, or I'm going to get a big head."

Maya, who'd been looking at Trisha, and then him, gave a small snort. She flushed when they both glanced her way, and turned to gather up her pamphlets.

"Perhaps someone thinks your head is already large enough." Trisha winked at Caleb and put a hand on Maya's shoulder. "Can I help you pack up? I think your grandmother is having us all over for drinks at her house now."

"Oh no, I'm fine. I don't need any help," Maya answered.

It was Caleb's turn to make a derisive sound. It was classic Maya. Fiercely independent.

"What?" Maya looked from one of them to the other.

"I don't know you that well, Maya," Trisha said. "But I get the feeling that's your standard answer to any offer of help." She grabbed a tote bag from under Maya's table and started loading fact sheets into it. "I'm helping. Get used to it, lady."

Caleb listened to them laugh and tried to absorb this new information. Trisha and Maya were becoming friends? He'd never have expected that these two would put the past behind them and choose to spend time together.

If they could do it, then maybe he and Maya could do it too.

Annie interrupted his thoughts with a hand to his elbow. "I've had an idea, Caleb, and I don't want you to say no right away. Just listen to me, and think about it for a while, okay?"

Uh-oh. Whatever it was, Annie looked like she had the bit in her teeth and was ready to run. Keeping her hand firmly on his elbow, she led him closer to her fellow Cougars for Cougars. "What do you all think about throwing Caleb a good old-fashioned barn raising?"

"That's a great idea!" Maya's grandmother, Lillian, clapped her hands together. "How fun! Caleb...you've agreed to this?"

Caleb stared. "Um..."

"It's just the kick in the pants his ranch needs to get on its feet again," Annie explained.

Caleb felt like she was giving him a kick in *his* pants. One he wasn't at all ready for.

"Wouldn't it be fun to get the whole community out to your ranch for a project like that?" Mrs. Axel beamed at him. "We could feed everyone, and maybe even have a barn dance afterward? We'll make it a party."

Caleb was about to protest when Lillian put a soft, warm hand on his arm. "I would love to help organize it, Caleb, if you're all right with the idea."

"I'm…" He didn't know what he was, but whatever the feeling, he couldn't voice it because of the lump stuck in his throat. Grandma Lillian had felt like his own grandmother growing up. He'd spent so many evenings at her house with Maya, watching old movies, eating popcorn, drinking lemonade, listening to her stories about living in Shelter Creek when she was young.

He'd lost her when he'd lost Maya. Yet here she was, despite the way he'd treated her granddaughter, offering help.

"I think he means yes." Monique, the owner of the salon, gave him a wink.

Grandma Lillian clapped her hands together gently and gave Caleb a smile with her twinkling eyes. "Well, that's settled then." She turned to her friends. "Cougars? Who here is up for planning a barn raising?"

Every hand shot up, and pretty soon the group was clustered together at one end of Maya's information table, making to-do lists on their phones.

Maya was still busy packing up. When Caleb moved a couple of bags off the table so she could remove the cloth, she gave him a small smile and tilted her head to the other women. "They're a force of nature." She picked up a stuffed mountain lion from the table and waved it at him. "They showed up this morning and decorated my table. They passed out fliers all afternoon. They're all in Grandma's book club, The Book Biddies, but now they're also Cougars for Cougars."

"They're trying to help you out."

"Well, now they're helping *us* out, because you're getting a barn raising, whether you like it or not." She folded the tablecloth, not meeting his eyes. "I'm surprised you accepted their help."

"It's the second offer of help from Annie. It feels rude to keep saying no. And your grandmother was always kind to me. I couldn't say no to her either."

"And now you want to work with me?" She glanced at him, her brown eyes clouded with questions, like redwoods in fog. "What changed your mind?"

Emotion rose and scattered his words, but this time Caleb took a deep breath, and then another, and found them. "I was such a jerk when you came to my ranch. I was embarrassed, about my drinking, about how bad the place looks. And all that stuff you said about the accident—it was hard to hear. But you're right. Especially about me not taking my share of the blame. I'm not making excuses for my behavior...for any of it. But I am sorry. Really sorry."

She nodded, but stayed silent. So he plowed ahead.

"Then there was that scene with my aunt the other night, and then Fred here." He cleared his throat, forcing himself to continue. "I don't want to hold on to the past the way they are."

She studied him for a moment, with a look that reminded him of the coyote he'd run into on his ranch early this morning. A long, assessing look, as if she was wondering whether to run, attack or just wait for him to go on his way. "Okay," she finally said. "I'll come by Monday, in the morning, like we said."

"Thank you. I'll be sober. And ready to listen."

"That would be helpful." The press of her lips might be holding back a smile. Fair enough. He deserved her derision and more. She was going to give him another chance. She was willing to help him. That's what mattered.

He turned to go, feeling like he wanted to

stay, to be the guy who packed up her fliers, took down her table and carried it all to his truck. Which was ridiculous. He'd lost the right to be that guy over a decade ago. It was just old memories, an old way of being with her showing up because they hadn't yet figured out who they were, now that their paths had crossed again.

"Caleb?"

He turned back. She was as still as that coyote, her eyes just as unfathomable. "I'm sorry too."

He nodded, not quite sure what she was apologizing for. But he was grateful that she was reaching out, when he'd given her so many reasons to push him away. "Thanks. See you soon."

Caleb said a quick goodbye to the Cougars for Cougars and headed for his truck.

As he moved through the rodeo crowd, a few people stopped to congratulate him on his ride earlier today and to thank him for his service. Others waved and smiled. Caleb flexed his rusty muscles into some semblance of a return smile until his mouth hurt. But he didn't mind the discomfort so much.

He'd been back in Shelter Creek for over two months now, but he'd spent so much of that time feeling lost. Today he felt like maybe, just maybe, he'd finally made it home.

# CHAPTER ELEVEN

MAYA HANDED KATHY and Eva the cocktails Grandma was whipping up in the kitchen. "Cougaritas," Grandma called them, in honor of their successful day at the rodeo. Really they were margaritas with some grenadine added to tint them pink.

"This looks amazing," Eva said, taking an appreciative sip.

Trisha walked in with two more glasses and a pitcher on a tray. "Here, Annie, take this one. And Mrs. Ax—Priscilla, this is yours."

"You girls just can't get used to calling me anything but my teacher name, can you?" Mrs. Axel asked.

Maya glanced at Trisha and they both laughed.

"You're right," Maya said. "Once someone's teacher, always their teacher, I guess. But we love you, no matter what we call you."

Trisha sat down on Grandma's sofa, next

to Mrs. Axel, and gave her a hug. "You were the best teacher. Maybe that's why we can't think of you any other way."

Mrs. Axel wiped at her eyes. "Oh that is the sweetest thing you could say to me."

Maya realized that Trisha had no glass in her hand. "Can I get you a cougarita?"

A shadow of something—worry maybe?— flitted across Trisha's pretty face.

"No, thanks. I'm going to stick with water. I think I got a little dehydrated out there at the rodeo today."

"That was a great event." Monique came in with a couple more glasses on a tray. "We must have distributed a hundred of your fliers, Maya. Most people seemed excited to have some information about mountain lions. I'll bet your phone will be ringing off the hook with people wanting your advice."

"I hope so." Maya sank into one of Grandma's big fluffy armchairs. Einstein, who'd been lying out of the way behind the sofa, came over and flopped down at her feet.

"That dog knows where his bread is buttered," Kathy said.

"He's lucky Maya found him." Annie left her seat by the piano and knelt by Einstein, who raised his head and regarded Annie with his big brown eyes.

"I swear, the stories this creature would tell if he could talk." Annie caressed the big dog's rough coat. "Where'd you lose that leg, Einstein? How did you end up by the side of the road?"

"He's gained weight," Eva said. "He was skin and bones when you brought him home."

"Grandma's been fattening him up," Maya said. "Slipping him extra treats all the time. He's gotten very spoiled."

"He deserves to be spoiled," Trisha said. "How could someone abandon this sweet dog? Emily, the vet, thinks he's only about five years old. His gray hair came in early because he's had such a hard life."

"Here." Monique filled Maya's half-empty glass back to the top. "You probably need this more than any of us. What a nuisance that rancher was. Fred Corrigan? I just wanted to smack that man."

"You could have taken him out with that hat of yours." Annie gave Einstein one last pat and returned to her seat.

"Hey, I like that hat." Monique set the tray down on the coffee table. "It protects my complexion. I always tell my clients that blocking the sun is the number one way to prevent aging. And skin cancer."

Annie ran a hand over her own weather-beaten cheeks. "Oh well. Guess I'm a little late for that."

"It's never too late," Monique assured her. "You should come by the salon this week. I've got some great products to even out your skin tone. And you know, if we put some dark lowlights in that gorgeous gray hair of yours, it would be even more dramatic."

Annie eyed Monique thoughtfully. "You know, I might just do that."

"Annie!" Kathy stared at her friend in shock. "I've never, in our whole lives, known you to go to a salon."

"Well, maybe there's a first time for everything." The pink of Annie's drink matched the pink of her cheeks.

"Oh Annie, does this mean you are finally going to go out with Juan Alvaro?" Everyone turned to stare at Grandma Lillian, who was bustling in with another pitcher. "Oh come on," Grandma said. "Didn't you all know? That rancher has been sweet on Annie for years."

"You come by my salon, date or no date," Monique told Annie. "I'll fix you up."

"Speaking of being sweet on someone," Trisha said, "Caleb Dunne certainly came to your rescue today, Maya. I couldn't believe it when he showed up at your rodeo table to stop old Fred from going on one of his tirades. I was way over by the arena, and I saw Fred start in. Just when I was trying to decide if I was brave enough to come to your rescue myself, there was Caleb, striding over. So I figured you'd be okay."

"I was pretty shocked too," Maya said. "He's the last person I thought would help."

"He seems to have a thing for damsels in distress," Trisha said. "He rescued me a couple of weeks ago. I'd finally worked up the courage to try online dating and I met this guy at Dex's. He slipped something in my drink while I was at the bathroom."

"What?" Maya put her drink down in shock.

"That is horrible." Grandma's face was pale. "Trisha, I'm so sorry."

"It's scary to think about," Trisha said. "But nothing happened to me, thanks to Caleb. He saw it happen and went ballistic. He threw the guy out of the bar. People had to restrain him from ripping him to shreds in the parking lot."

"So that's what the fight in the bar was about." Monique regarded Trisha thoughtfully over the rim of her glass. "I heard about it, but I had no idea it was all in your defense."

"I came back from the bathroom and my date was already getting arrested. I'd missed the entire thing. I thanked Caleb when he came back in, but he just kind of grunted and went to play pool with Jace."

"Well, Caleb has always had a bit of a temper," Grandma Lillian said. "But maybe it was put to good use that night."

Maya was staring from one to the other, trying to take in all that was being said. "What happened to the guy?" she asked Trisha.

"I pressed charges," Trisha said. "They had the whole thing on Dex's security footage, and the bartender saved my glass, so there's evidence against him. I don't want him trying that on anyone else."

"What a creep," Eva said. "I'm so glad you're okay."

Trisha shuddered. "Me too. I'm telling you,

it is brutal out in the dating world. Every time I try to date anyone, it's a disaster. And now I don't think I'll have the nerve to go out with anyone for a long time." She looked at Annie and smiled. "Maybe when I'm your age, Annie. And I've been friends with the guy for decades. Juan sounds perfect."

Annie grimaced. "I sure hope so. It's a different universe from when we were young. Right, ladies?"

All of The Biddies nodded sagely.

"I'm glad I put those days behind me," Kathy said. "Annie, you're brave, thinking about having a man in your life again."

"Well, not just any man. But Juan and I… well, we have a lot to talk about. I don't even know if it's a date, but he did suggest that we get dinner next week."

"Whoo-hoo!" Mrs. Axel raised her glass. "Annie has a date!"

It was amazing how girlish The Biddies seemed, giggling into their pink drinks. Maya raised her glass to Annie, along with the rest of them, and sipped her cougarita. It was so refreshing after the long, stressful day.

"But," Trisha said brightly, "let's change the subject back to Maya and Caleb. Because

I saw you two talking even after we got Fred out of there. And now he wants your help on his ranch. Is it possible that an old flame is rekindling?"

"Oh gosh no." The words burst from Maya's lips before she'd even given thought to her answer.

"That's not what I saw." Kathy wagged a finger. "That man can't take his eyes off you."

"The rest of us might as well not have existed," Mrs. Axel said. "He still has feelings for you."

"Yes, he does. Feelings of hatred, resentment and anger." When they all stared, probably startled by her vehemence, she added, "It didn't go so well, the first time I went out to his ranch."

"Well, there's a lot of hurt between you," Kathy said. "But hurt can heal."

Maya reached down to pet Einstein's floppy ears, not wanting to go too far down this road. There was no way she and Caleb could ever fall in love again. Julie's accident was a chasm they'd never be able to cross back over. And they had gone on to have very different lives, in different states. "I think Trisha is right. He likes to swoop in and be the rescuer. Maybe it's an ex-Marine thing." He was probably already regretting his super-hero impulses, since they'd gotten him stuck working with her.

But hey, if Caleb's need to rescue women helped Maya rescue a few mountain lions, then that was a good thing.

There was silence in the room, and then Monique broke it with her worldly drawl. "Stop by the salon tomorrow, ladies. I'll be taking bets. And my money is on Maya and Caleb figuring out this mess between them before the summer is over."

"You all have had too much cougarita," Maya admonished. "If Caleb and I can figure out how to work together for one day without yelling at each other, it will be a miracle. Maybe bet on that."

It was easier to think of it that way. Safer too. He'd broken her heart—no, exploded it into fragments so tiny, she was still trying to find pieces, so many years later.

But today at the rodeo, there'd been this moment when it had felt so good to be taking on Fred together. To be on the same side again. Maybe that was them, healing their old wounds, just a little. It would be nice to have that healing. When this job was over, she'd be able to leave Shelter Creek knowing that her history with Caleb was truly in the past. That they'd done their best to make amends and move on.

And then she could get back to her simple, straightforward life in Boulder. Where she could think and work, and focus on her research again. It might seem boring to some people, but it was all she needed.

Maya reached for her cougarita and raised it to the group. "I want to thank you all for joining me at the rodeo today. I had no idea you had planned all that—the decorations for my table, Uma the Puma, the amazing T-shirts, all of it. Let's raise a glass to Cougars for Cougars, and all of their hard work at the Shelter Creek Rodeo."

They clinked glasses, and there was a moment of relaxed silence while everyone drank. Trisha sipped water, but even she looked relaxed, leaning back on the sofa, her eyes closed.

Eva was the first to break the peaceful mood. "Speaking of cougars, I want to run something by all of you."

"Hang on." Monique hopped out of her seat and started refilling everyone's glass. It was going to be a legendary Booze Biddy meeting for sure.

"So, I've never really mentioned this." Eva set her glass down and folded her hands, looking uncharacteristically uncertain. "But I actually have quite a bit of money set aside. I've been holding on to it while I figured out a use for it. I want to do something that will help make a difference in the world. And I think I've found what that something is."

"A donation to The Biddies' retirement fund?" Kathy quipped.

"Well, I'm happy to pay for the cougaritas." Eva smiled and patted her friend on the knee. "But no, this is something a bit bigger than that. It is actually inspired by Maya here."

Maya sat up a little straighter. Einstein lifted his head too, as if he recognized Maya's name when Eva said it.

"When I moved to Shelter Creek a few years ago, one of the things that drew me here was all of the beautiful nature around us. Listening to Maya talk about her work, I've realized that we need someplace right here in town where we can educate people about our local wildlife. I'm picturing a nature center, but one that would also offer services such as wildlife rescue and consulting, like what Maya is doing now." Then she skewered Maya with a shrewd look. "And we'd need biologists like you on staff."

The room was silent for a long moment.

"That is a brilliant idea," Grandma Lillian said.

"I love it," Mrs. Axel added. "Can I volunteer?"

"Of course," Eva nodded. "If I can ever figure out how to really make it happen. I'll need investors, donors, grants—my nest egg isn't big enough to cover everything. But it's seed money. Maya, what do you think of the idea?"

It was tough to figure out a way to answer. Maya didn't want to dampen Eva's enthusiasm, but what she was proposing was a huge project, and Maya had no room for it in her life. Finally she managed to assemble a few sentences. "I think it's an amazing idea. Truly. This area is so rich in wildlife, and what you're describing would be great for the ranchers, for tourists, for everyone. I'd be happy to advise you however I can. But I won't be here to help. I have a grant for a research project in Colorado in the fall. I'll be studying the interactions of mountain lions and mountain goats and doing a lot of research out in the field. That's the kind of work I enjoy the most."

Despite Fred Corrigan's unfriendly visit, talking with people at the rodeo today had actually been fun. Most people had great questions and truly wanted to learn. Maya had been surprised at how quickly the time went by, and how many people had made her laugh and smile.

But she couldn't stay here in Shelter Creek. She'd worked so hard to establish herself in Colorado and her new research grant was waiting. Her colleagues respected her, and, more than that, she was peaceful there. She wasn't faced with her past every day, the way she was in Shelter Creek.

Plus how could she stay here and watch Caleb's life go on without her? Which it would, eventually. He'd find someone to love. He'd get married. He'd have children. And of course she wanted him to find that happiness. But she couldn't be a witness to it. Not when it had been her dream for them. Not when she could barely meet his eyes, or stand near him, without feeling all that old longing start to rise in her veins. She'd worked so hard to banish it, to ignore the way she missed him.

Yet it had all come rushing back today at the rodeo.

But they were different people now. With different lives, in different places. And even if they could find common ground, they'd probably caused each other too much pain to find happiness together again. But that didn't mean she wanted to stay here and watch him find it with someone else.

She tried to ignore the disappointment in everyone's eyes. Especially Grandma's.

"Any advice you could give me would be very helpful." Eva was watching her carefully, and Maya got the feeling she'd read every one of her thoughts. Then Eva looked around at the group. "What do you think, Cougars? Do you want to help me start the Shelter Creek Wildlife Center?"

The Biddies raised their cougaritas in unison.

Maya raised her glass too. The wildlife center seemed like a great idea. And the fact that her love of wildlife had inspired it was something she'd remember with pride.

But it was bittersweet because it was hitting her just how short this summer was. That she would be leaving in a few weeks. And not just leaving Grandma, but leaving The Biddies, and now Trisha.

Maya had worked hard to create a self-reliant life, where she couldn't hurt or disappoint anyone, and they couldn't let her down either. It was a lonely life sometimes, but at least it was free of heartbreak. But these amazing women had somehow gotten past her armor, and she already knew it was going to be really hard to leave them behind.

## CHAPTER TWELVE

CALEB TRIED TO slide the halter over Amos's nose, but the big black gelding tossed his head and backed into the corner of the stall.

Caleb reached into his pocket for the grain he'd stashed there and held a handful out to the worried horse. He'd picked Amos up from a rescue organization about a month ago, which meant the quarter horse mix had probably been abused. Whatever his history, he clearly still had a few mental issues to work out.

Which made two of them.

Caleb hadn't ever believed in things like ghosts, but now he wondered. He'd had the dream again last night. He closed his eyes at night and the boy was there. Running toward him out of the dark. The bulky shape around his chest.

And then the bang and flash of Caleb's gun and the still form down in the dust, and Caleb awoke in the dark, his heart banging on his ribs like it was trying to escape.

He'd struggled out of the covers, desperate to get outside, into the cool foggy air, so he could pull in all that clean oxygen and remind himself that he wasn't there anymore. He wasn't in Afghanistan, he wasn't on guard and he wasn't trying to make impossible life-and-death choices in split-second intervals.

Hobo had followed him outside, weaving his soft and strangely comforting form around Caleb's ankles, until Caleb scooped him up and cuddled him to his chest.

He'd brought his blankets outside and slept the rest of the night out on the porch, with the cat cuddled close. At least he hadn't brought a bottle with him this time. Maya was coming to visit this morning. And Caleb was glad to have another day of sobriety under his belt, for both their sakes.

Caleb stretched out his hand to get the grain closer. "Come on, Amos. It's me. You know me."

Amos reached his nose as far forward as he could, trying to reach the grain without moving his hooves. Finally, Caleb turned his back on the horse and held out his hand to his side. There was a soft shuffling of hooves on wood shavings as Amos came toward him. A light snuffling of lips on Caleb's palm. A small victory.

"See? That wasn't so bad." Amos was funny in the mornings. Like he had bad dreams too. But once he got out into the fresh air, he seemed happier. No wonder he and Caleb seemed to understand each other so well.

Amos finished the grain and nuzzled Caleb's pockets for more. "Once your halter is on." This time Amos obliged, letting Caleb slide the halter over his nose and buckle it behind his ears.

Caleb rewarded him with another handful of grain and ran a hand under the horse's thick, black mane. Amos was a lot of work right now, but he had potential if he could just learn to trust Caleb.

The big horse already liked Hobo. The nutty cat had followed Caleb into the stall and was perched on the old wooden manger. When Amos finished his grain, he brought his nose down to the scraggly orange fur ball and snuffed him, allowing the cat to rub his back along his nose.

"Hobo, you've got to end this lovefest. Amos and I have to get ready." Caleb wanted to be organized when Maya arrived. So she'd see that he wasn't that same drunk guy she'd found on the porch that morning.

Caleb swore the cat gave him a grumpy, disappointed look. Like a kid who'd been told he had to stop playing and start his homework. He shook his head at the ridiculous thought. Jace was right. He was spending way too much time with that cat.

He led Amos out of the barn and tied him to the corral fence, leaving the knot pretty loose in case Amos had one of his panic attacks. Luckily they were getting more rare. Six weeks into his stay at the Bar D, and Amos had finally seemed to realize that Caleb meant him no harm. In fact Caleb was starting to wonder if Amos's skittish haltering behavior wasn't just an act to get a little extra grain.

But even if Amos was warming up to Caleb and Hobo, he still treated the rest of the world with suspicion.

"Hey, Caleb." Maya's voice came softly from several yards away, and Caleb turned to see her standing there, as if she'd been watching him for a moment already. "What a gorgeous horse."

She came forward and held out her hand. Amos instantly did his giraffe imitation, head up as high as the rope would allow, eyes rolled back as he glared down at the stranger in their midst.

"Easy, Amos. You're fine." Caleb ran a hand down the horse's neck. He turned to Maya. "Maybe take a step back. He's not too sure about other people yet."

Maya stepped away but still held out her knuckles, standing quietly, patiently, like she had all the time in the world.

Amos huffed out a few sharp breaths but lowered his head, stuck out his nose, tentative at first but growing more confident as Maya stood unwavering. He nuzzled her hand, then jerked away, as if waiting for a blow to fall.

Maya didn't react; she just kept waiting, until he nuzzled her again. And again. Until finally Amos huffed his horsey breath all over her face and shoulders as he checked her out more thoroughly. When he nuzzled her ear, she laughed and Amos didn't startle.

"You've got a way with him." It had taken a

couple of weeks for Caleb to get to that point with the horse.

"If there's one thing my career has taught me, it's how to stand still and wait for an animal to do whatever it's going to do." Maya ran her hand down Amos's neck, a shy smile tilting the corners of her mouth. "It may be one of my few real talents." She gave Amos a last pat and stepped back. "Nice to meet you, Amos."

Caleb took her in: torn jeans, old cowboy boots, a pink T-shirt with Rocky Mountain National Park printed across the front. Her baseball cap was so faded, it really didn't have a color anymore. But it didn't matter what she wore. Her hair hung down in two long braids, and her deep brown eyes were smiling at him.

She was beautiful. Like no one else he'd ever seen. A hollow feeling in his chest had him swallowing hard. "Are you ready to ride? It's the easiest way to see the area where the lion showed up."

"That would be great."

"You remember how?"

"I've ridden a lot over the years." She had the quiet confidence he was beginning to recognize. Not much rattled her. And because of it, he felt more rattled around her. Or maybe it was because she was Maya and she was here, smiling at him, forgiving him.

She'd ridden a lot. Another reminder that she'd had a whole life elsewhere, full of all kinds of people, places and experiences he knew nothing about. A sudden sadness tugged at him. He'd missed it all. Because of the accident, his hurt and his anger.

"You'll have to take Newt today."

There was her real smile, full and dimpled and lighting up her eyes just like he'd tried not to remember all these years. "You still have him? How old is he now?"

"Seventeen. He's pretty mellow these days. Jace's kids came by to ride him a few days ago, and he was perfect with them."

"Newton's Bright Flash." Maya's voice was almost dreamy. "I always thought we should have called him Flash."

Caleb couldn't help but smile at the memory. He'd raised Newt from birth, and had been grateful that his dad had hung on to him, even when he'd sold off all the other livestock.

"Don't blame me. You're the one who said

he wasn't very flashy. Kind of brown, like a newt. You called him Cute Newt. And it stuck." He remembered it all so clearly. And he was letting it affect him way too much.

Maybe the bad night had left him lonely, made it easy to forget all that was impossible between them. "I'll go get Newt," he told her.

She nodded absently, studying his barn, probably noticing the places where he'd patched rotting wood with plywood. She didn't say anything, but she bit her lower lip, as if she was considering the evidence of his changed circumstances.

He got Newt's halter and led the big quarter horse outside, tying him to the rail, a good distance away from unpredictable Amos. Maya fussed over her old friend, letting him snuffle her hands and face.

"I think he knows me." She laughed softly as Newt nibbled at one of her pigtails.

"Horses have long memories." Caleb handed her a brush and went to groom Amos, not wanting her close, because he could feel her laugh like a warm breeze, feel all of her movements when she was near, like the air she moved in somehow moved him.

She turned to Newt and began at his neck,

brushing in long strokes over his rusty brown withers. Time twisted and Caleb could see her when they were young, so similar to how she looked now, reaching up on tiptoe to give him a kiss, thanking him for taking her riding, looking at him with such admiration and feeling in her eyes. He missed that Maya with a sharpness that startled him.

What would it be like to be loved that way now?

Nope. Bad idea. They'd agreed to put the past behind them today, yet here he was already dredging it up. He should focus on Amos, on brushing the horse's dark hair, on rewarding his patience with another nibble of grain.

Amos had probably known how to do this at one point. How to stand still and be groomed. But all that had been disrupted by whatever trauma he'd gone through. Now he was learning how to be someone's horse all over again.

Just like Caleb was learning to be a civil person again. And he'd practice today, by offering Maya friendship, respect and professionalism.

He went to get his saddle and the only other one that Dad had left here. Caleb had no idea what happened to all of the others, Mom's and Julie's saddles, all tooled leather and laced in silver. His dad had probably pawned them when money had gotten tight. The one Caleb found for Maya had probably been too old and plain to sell.

Putting his saddle on the fence for now, he handed Maya a saddle pad, nodding when she put it in just the right spot. He swung her saddle up and cinched it around Newt's belly. "He could use the exercise," he told her, patting Newt's round stomach. "Mostly he just hangs out and eats."

"I'm glad your family kept him." Her eyes darted again to the patched barn.

"I know. I was surprised Dad held on to him, when he let everything else fall apart."

"The ranch must have been really hard to come home to." She ran her hand over Newt's mane and Caleb was grateful she wasn't looking at him, that she was giving him space to say what was tough to speak of.

"It was. My mom moved to New York years ago and Dad stayed here on the ranch. I guess he was pretty depressed for a long time, but I didn't realize it. We emailed pretty often and talked on the phone when we could, but he never mentioned any problems."

She glanced his way, her teeth worrying her lower lip. "I'm so sorry."

"Not your fault. I should have come home, I should have checked on him. I was selfish, protecting myself instead of looking out for him."

She nodded. "I did the same, with my grandmother." Her quiet understanding made it okay to tell her the rest.

"When I got home from the Marines, I discovered that he'd given up on the ranch, and sold everything off to get by. I found all kinds of mail that he'd never even opened, including a letter from the state. It said they were going to take possession of the ranch because he hadn't paid his taxes in years.

"They'd given him a month to respond, but when I found the notice, the deadline was two weeks away. I've been negotiating with the state ever since, paying what I can so they won't take the property. I hired a lawyer to help me." He gestured to the barn, the fences, the disaster that was now the Bar D. "I don't have money for much else."

She looked stricken. "I'm so sorry that happened. Annie's barn raising will help, right? And there is grant money available, if you want it. From this mountain lion advocacy group. They'll pay for all kinds of improvements here, to help control predation. In exchange, you'd give tours to other ranchers, so they could learn from you."

"No," he said quickly. "I'm already feeling like a charity case thanks to Annie's plans. I don't want anything else."

"It's not charity—it's getting involved in a cause. And it could help you fix up the ranch. You could have state-of-the-art technology to prevent predators. I really think you should consider it."

She sounded almost frantic, and it hit him suddenly why. "You're not responsible for my dad not paying his bills. You don't have to try to fix everything."

He saw the words hit her, saw their impact, and knew he'd been right.

"I *feel* responsible. I was driving the car that night. Then, after the accident, your dad got depressed and stopped paying bills."

"No, Maya, don't." He put a hand to her arm, as if he could stop her mind from racing off in the wrong direction. "You were right about something, the last time you were here. I'm responsible for that accident too. I was the one Julie called for a ride that night. I passed that duty on to you. That's a regret I have to live with.

"And that same logic extends to my parents. They were stern with us. Not the kind of folks you wanted to admit a mistake to. If they'd been more understanding, maybe Julie would have called them that night. Please stop carrying this on your shoulders. I was so wrong, to put that burden on you."

Her eyes welled, and she went back to petting Newt's neck. Caleb fought the urge to pull her to him, to hold her and assure her that he meant what he said, but he had no right to touch her, no matter how much he wanted to.

They couldn't be close, so he pushed them apart. "I don't need you to come around here, trying to make things better. That's my responsibility." He glanced around at the myriad of repairs he still had to make. "It's going to be a long road, but I'll get there."

She was quiet for a moment, and finally turned to face him with an audible, shaky breath. "Sometimes the long roads are the ones worth walking."

Years ago he'd have known exactly what she meant. Because he'd known her, all her layers and nuances. Now she was a mystery. But clearly she'd walked long roads of her own. He still couldn't quite believe that they'd led her back here, to him.

"Speaking of long roads," she said, sounding a little more cheerful. "I've got a friend who's had a bumpy one. Can I introduce you to my dog, Einstein? I left him sleeping in the back of my truck but I'm sure he's ready to say hello."

"Of course. Just keep him leashed around Amos at first."

She left for her truck and came back with one of the coolest-looking dogs Caleb had ever seen.

"He's got eyebrows." He knelt down, and Einstein sat and offered a paw. Caleb shook it, then ran his fingers over the dog's rough coat and his enormous ears. "What a good guy." He watched Einstein head back to Maya on his three legs. "He gets along pretty well, doesn't he?"

"Can he ride with us? He's good around livestock. He's been going out to different ranches with me and he always behaves."

Caleb glanced at Amos, but the skittish gelding didn't seem to care much about the dog. It was probably only humans who got him worried. "Sure."

Einstein sat where Maya told him to wait by the fence, and they finished getting the horses ready. Caleb tried to hold Newt for Maya while she mounted, but she met his eyes with a soft, "I've got it," and swung up like she'd been riding every day since he'd last seen her.

Another good reminder that they were strangers now.

He wasn't nearly so graceful getting up on Amos, thanks to the shrapnel in his calf that stabbed him when he moved like this.

It took a minute for Amos to settle, but finally the worried horse stood quietly. Caleb looked at Maya to find her watching him with a slight smile. "You're good with him. Patient."

"He's still figuring stuff out." Caleb saw Hobo wending his way along the fence, toward him. If they didn't get out of here, the cat would probably try to ride Amos too. Maybe it was vanity but Caleb wouldn't mind maintaining a few shreds of dignity while he rode with the woman he'd once loved so much. "You ready to go?"

"Lead the way." She patted Newt on the neck. "I can't believe I'm riding this guy again. Come on, Einstein." The big dog trotted behind them, keeping a safe distance from Newt's hooves.

Caleb moved Amos forward, heading for the dirt road that wound out through the ranch toward the hills. He couldn't believe it either. It was like time travel, her on Newt. Them riding together. It was nice. It seemed like they'd repaired a little of the hurt between them. And when they finished working together, and she went back to Colorado, maybe they could each go forward with a little more peace of mind.

Except now, with this tenuous connection between them, he wasn't sure how he felt about her leaving. Even during all the years they'd been apart, when he'd assumed they'd never see each other again, he'd missed her. Missed them and the way they'd been. And now that they were talking a little, he caught glimpses of what he'd missed, and it was like seeing something so precious in a fancy jewelry store window and knowing that he'd never get to have it. She'd made a whole new life for herself in Colorado, thanks to him. So he had to respect that.

Maybe the connection he felt with her was really just because she'd showed up on his porch that drunken morning like an angry angel, to show him just how messed up he was. How far he'd gone in his pursuit of oblivion. She'd woken him up, brought him back to life. Made him face his past. It would be easy to mistake his gratitude for something more.

Caleb urged Amos into a brisk walk, let the big horse pull ahead of Newt, let the wide-open trail ahead act as his own personal metaphor. He had a whole life ahead of him and so did she. He listened to the steady beat of hooves, felt the weight of his legs in the stirrups, worked on keeping flighty Amos in check. His horse, his ranch, his path, his life here on the Bar D.

Maya was just here to advise him about mountain lions. And he'd best remember that.

## CHAPTER THIRTEEN

NEWT'S HOOVES HIT the ground in a relaxing rhythm and Maya wished they could stay like this, ambling evenly through the wide-open field, Caleb and Amos a good distance ahead, Einstein trotting just behind. She needed this time to think about all that Caleb had said, and all he'd encountered, coming home to such devastation. He'd almost lost the ranch. He was still fighting for it, every day.

And even though he told her otherwise, she had played a part in his crisis. So whether Caleb liked it or not, she was going to try to help him. Maybe she needed to make amends, and maybe she was just absolving her own guilt, but that grant he didn't want could change his life. She had to find a way to show him that. To make him understand that it wasn't charity. He'd pay back the money tenfold by showing other ranchers how to keep predators away.

Funny how she'd thought she was coming home to help Grandma. But really it was Grandma helping *her*, by getting her to come home and finally deal with the accident and its aftermath. And now here she was, trying to help Caleb. And Caleb had helped Trisha, who'd then turned around to help Maya. The four of them were a circle that might just have the power to repair the past.

The hills were closer now and Maya studied their contours. The gullies made by winter runoff traced vein-like patterns in the ground where the hills came together. She could see the coyote brush and coastal sage clumping at the base of the hills, creating perfect hiding places for predators.

In the distance Maya could see the fluffy backs of about a half dozen sheep. A big oak tree. And a fence that was a recipe for disaster. "Caleb," she called and pointed. "Can we go over there?"

He nodded. "You want to go a little faster?"

She glanced back at Einstein. The dog might be missing a leg but he hadn't lost his love of running. "Let's try it."

He nudged Amos into a lope, and she asked Newt to follow. It was like riding a rocking horse. Maya didn't even try to keep up with Amos's mad dash, content with Newt's easy gait, which Einstein could match, and her view of Caleb's denim-clad back, his posture upright as he and Amos covered the ground to the fence, then stopped to wait for them.

He was iconic, in that tilted hat, his ease in the saddle, his dark eyes and his slight smile as he watched her ride toward him. He might actually look happy, though she didn't know, anymore, what happiness looked like on him.

But if not happy, he definitely seemed more clearheaded and she wondered if he'd quit drinking. Hoped he had. But she knew how easily hopes got crushed by one bad night and a bottle.

She pulled her gaze away from Caleb to study the grass along the fence line ahead of them. When she and Newt came up alongside him, she asked, "Is this where the lion killed your sheep?"

He looked surprised. "Just up there, a couple hundred yards. How did you know?" There was a different note in his voice. It sounded a little like respect.

Maya dismounted and handed Newt's reins to Caleb. She pointed to a path of slightly broken grass. "That's where the puma dragged its kill away. It probably cached it in those bushes on the other side of the fence. Most likely it came back to feed on it for the next few nights."

Caleb ran a hand along the stubbled line of his jaw, staring where she pointed. "So, you're saying I didn't need to go hunting for it up in those hills the night we met? I could have gotten it right here?"

She glanced up at him, not sure if she should be amused or dismayed. "Just to be clear, I'm glad you didn't kill it, wherever it was. But yes, pumas like to kill larger animals and eat them over time, rather than go hunting every single night. So they hide their kill and return to it to eat."

She looked around, picturing exactly how the slaughter might have happened. "How many sheep did it kill out here?"

"I found two, but I was missing three." He tilted his chin in the direction of the bushes she'd pointed out. "Now I know where that third one probably was."

"It killed more than it needed." Maya studied the fence. It turned sharply inward, to make its way around the far side of a few oaks. "I think the sheep got trapped here, in this corner of the fence under the tree, and panicked. The mountain lion may have picked up on their fear. When livestock panic, it can cause a mountain lion to kill more than one animal."

"Like I said, the thing was killing for fun." His voice was almost as hard as it had been the night they first ran into each other on the trail.

"Not fun," she corrected. "It's all instinct. Their vision isn't like ours. They sense motion and follow that. When sheep panic, they're in constant motion. When a mountain lion panics, it kills until all the motion stops."

"But why would the lion panic?" Caleb protested. "It was in charge here."

"If the prey felt trapped, and ran back and forth in this little space, the lion might have felt trapped too."

Caleb stared at her warily, like he thought she'd lost her mind. "If you're trying to make me feel sympathy for a claustrophobic lion, you're wasting your time."

She bit back a sudden urge to smile. Was he trying to be funny? "I'm not trying to make you sympathetic. But I suspect that if the fence was straight here, instead of making this corner, the sheep would have run off and the lion would have only taken one of them."

"So, you're saying I should get rid of corners."

"It will help. There isn't one perfect solution to stop predators."

He stared at her and she looked right back up at him. This wasn't the first time she'd had to stare down a stubborn rancher, though it was different because it was Caleb, and if she stared too long, she felt kind of dizzy. Like she'd been looking too long at a bright light.

A slow, unexpected tilt to his mouth hinted at humor. "You know what they say about cutting corners."

"You're laughing about this?"

"Laugh or cry, I guess. And depressing as this is, it's kind of nice to see you in full-blown science mode."

She had no idea what to say to that. "It's what I do. And at least we've solved this mystery. As you're rebuilding the fences around the property, just keep this situation in mind. No sharp corners."

"And what else?"

"I think the best way to learn about it is

to visit a ranch that's already made these changes. If you're willing to go on a road trip with me, that is."

"How long of a road trip?" He looked so worried that she almost laughed.

"A couple of hours. You can go on your own if you'd rather. There's a guy up north near Willits. Aidan Ford. A couple of years ago he accepted some of that grant money I mentioned before. He's had a lot of luck deterring predators. You can see how he's doing it."

"You're still trying to get me to take that money."

"I'm trying to show you the best practices for managing your livestock and wildlife. How you pay for it is your business. Though, yes, I think you should take the grant."

His jaw set in a hard stubborn line. "I'll think about it."

She wanted to smack him with frustration. The grant money could turn things around for him, and it was only his pride keeping him from seeing that. "Look, why don't I get in touch with Aidan. You can visit his ranch and then see what you think about the grant."

He looked relieved. "Okay."

Maya took Newt's reins back from him and led the horse along the fence, looking for more signs of mountain lions. Einstein trailed alongside, stopping to sniff various interesting items along the way.

Caleb was talking to Amos in a low, soothing voice, and Maya glanced back to see the big black horse jogging restlessly, not wanting to slow to Newt's relaxed walk. It was such a contrast: the big man in the dark cowboy hat, with his broad shoulders and tattooed arms, and those sweet, calming words.

Maya forced her gaze forward again. It wouldn't help her to notice things like that. Caleb wasn't for her. She had a few more weeks in Shelter Creek and then she'd get back to her own life. Moments like this, when she noticed how handsome Caleb was, how compelling—well, these were the moments when she realized she couldn't get back to Colorado fast enough. She could not let her heart get hung up on him again.

She scanned the trail in front of her. "Hang on." She stopped Newt and crouched down to examine the droppings left by a mountain lion and a couple paw prints, left in the dust.

"What did you find?" Caleb had caught up with her and was sliding off Amos.

"Scat."

"Was it something I said?"

She blanked for a moment, then got the joke and couldn't help the laugh that escaped. She'd forgotten he was funny. It was one of the things that had drawn her to him when they were in high school. His goofy murmured jokes were such a contrast to his big frame and his serious good looks.

His eyes, bright with humor, had deep lines creasing the corners, and she couldn't look away, couldn't remember what she'd been so interested in, because she just wanted to study these new lines, the worry etched between his eyes, the unfamiliar scar along his cheekbone, the way his dimple still carved an arc into his cheek.

She pointed to the ground. "Be serious. This is important. It's from a mountain lion and it's fresh."

"And you look like Christmas just came early. So I guess I know what to get you come December."

Ugh. "No scat in my stocking, please. But listen. This could be really exciting. These tracks are fresh too. I'd bet this lion is still in the area, waiting for dusk."

"That's not exciting—it's nerve-racking. At dusk it's going to try to eat my sheep."

Maya took a deep breath, hoping this new ease between them would carry over into what she wanted to ask him. "Actually, at dusk I'd like to try to get a radio collar on it, if I can."

His eyes widened. "You want to catch this mountain lion?"

"Yes." She stood, trying to find the words that would make him see why this mattered. She pointed at the track. At the scat. "This is pure luck."

To her surprise, he started laughing. "That's *not* what most people would consider lucky."

She grinned, trying to concentrate, because his face, lit up with laughter, was a sight to behold. "Hey, I have long since accepted that I'm not like most people. But seriously, we have an opportunity here. If we can catch this mountain lion, we can learn all about it. Whether it's male or female, how old, in what state of health. If it's related to any of the pumas already in the Department's database." She had to make him see how much this mattered. "With a radio collar, we can track it, learn where it roams, including if and when it comes near your ranch."

"How are you going to catch it?" Caleb gestured to her vaguely. "You're not exactly a match for it."

This was good. If he was making short jokes, he wasn't going to say no. "Don't worry, I'm not going to wrestle it." Excitement had her pacing back and forth, staring at the hillside by the trail. "You know, in this situation, I think a cage trap might work. And the vet, Emily, said she'd like to help me if an opportunity like this came up. I'll give her a call."

"Emily Fielding? When did you meet her?"

"I took Einstein in for a checkup when I found him. Emily asked about my work. She said that if I trapped any lions, she'd love to help assess their health."

He looked at her doubtfully. "So, tonight, you and Emily will sit out here, in the dark, waiting for this lion to show up?"

"Something like that."

"And you'll use my livestock as bait."

So that was his worry. "I'd never do that.

I'll pick up a nice hunk of meat from the butcher for bait."

"How do you know this lion doesn't want its meat nice and fresh? I can't risk losing another animal."

She cast around for some way to assuage his fears. "Can't you lock your sheep in the barn? It's huge. It should hold them all, with tons of room to spare."

He looked chagrined. "The doors don't exactly shut."

This was ridiculous. "Okay, that's it. You are having that barn raising sooner rather than later. I am texting Grandma when I get back to my car, and letting her know that The Biddies should go full speed ahead with planning."

His voice came out rough. "Please don't."

She tried to reassure him. "It's not charity. It's neighbors helping neighbors."

"It *feels* like charity. And it's not just that." His jaw tightened into that familiar, stubborn line. "It's privacy. It's everyone knowing my business."

She knew what he was trying to describe. "I felt that way a lot, growing up."

"What do you mean? You weren't a charity case."

Did he know her so little? Or had he forgotten? "I was in foster care until Grandma took me in." The memories came flooding back. "When I moved here, everyone in town knew my story. About my parents and their drugs. People tried to be kind, but each time a new rumor went around, about their arrests, or whatever trouble they were in, I could feel people looking at me differently. All that pity. Ugh."

Maya stopped, horrified. She rarely talked about her parents. She tried not to think about them too much either. They were one more thing in life that was impossible to understand. "I'm sorry—this isn't about me."

"I didn't ever know you felt that way. You always seemed so strong, so focused and calm." Caleb reached out his hand, then stopped himself, and she felt the loss of what hadn't happened. What she hadn't known she wanted. The touch of his hand on hers.

She took a step back so she wouldn't reach for him. "It's in the past. But the point is, let The Biddies help you. They are so happy to do it."

Then she turned away and scanned the hillside to get her mind back on the task at hand. And away from that intimate moment. Because the more of those they had, the harder it would be to keep Caleb neatly filed in the work category of her mind. She needed him to stay there. He'd made a choice to cut her off all those years ago, and he could do it again in a moment.

She had no time to think about any of this. She didn't even live here, and wasn't going to move back, so even if there was something between them, it was a nonstarter.

Plus about a million things needed to happen between now and tonight if this crazy idea was going to work. It was time for facts, details, tasks. Which were far more comfortable than thinking about Caleb. "I'll need to round up all of my gear and call Emily, and I hope I can get a trap in time."

Then it occurred to her. He hadn't said yes. "So, is it okay if I hang out here tonight and trap a mountain lion?"

He nodded. "On one condition. I get to hang out here and trap the lion with you."

"You want to help?"

"I don't want you to get hurt."

There was that rescue complex again. "I have been trapping mountain lions and bears and wolves and coyotes for years, Caleb Dunne. And I didn't have some man's protection for most of that." She rolled her eyes dramatically. "It's a miracle I survived without you."

"Okay, okay." He held up his hands in mock self-defense. "I apologize. I never meant to suggest you weren't capable. Clearly you can accomplish anything you set your mind to, all on your own. But I'd still like to help out, if you'll let me."

"Thank you." She was still suspicious of his motives. She didn't want him there if he thought her weak. If he had some misguided idea that she needed him. "I thought you hated mountain lions."

He shrugged. "Well, they're causing me so much trouble, I may as well meet one if I have the chance."

That she could accept. Maybe if they trapped one, if he could see one up close, she could help him understand why the big cats mattered. Why it was so important to find ways to coexist with them.

"Just one thing though." She made her

voice stern. "If we catch a lion, you have to listen to me. No arguing. No trying to take over."

"You're the expert. I'll just be there to help."

"Help is good." Maya went to get Newt, pulling the sweet boy's head gently out of a yummy patch of grass. "We should go back. I've got to get things ready. It's going to be a busy day and a long night." She climbed into the saddle and gathered her reins. "Come on, Einstein."

The big dog looked up from the clump of sage he'd been investigating. His eyes held so much intelligence that sometimes it seemed like he was part human. He trotted over to fall into step beside Newt.

Caleb motioned toward the sheep, still grazing peacefully, farther out in the pasture, oblivious to the mountain lion that might be lurking close by. "Want to help me bring them into the barn? I'll figure out a way to barricade them in there for the night."

"Yes." Maya's heart warmed as she remembered days when they'd done this before. Happier times, when she'd helped him with his chores around the ranch.

Caleb swung up on Amos and set off at a jog toward the sheep. The small flock instantly turned away from him and headed back toward the barn. Maya flanked them so they'd stay on course. When she glanced at Caleb, he waved, a big grin on his face. It was almost like they were a team. It was almost like the life she'd imagined for them. A brief glimpse of what might have been possible, once upon a time.

# CHAPTER FOURTEEN

MAYA PUT ANOTHER branch on top of the wire-cage trap and glanced at Caleb. "What do you think?"

"It's getting hard to see it." The sun was almost down, barely peeping over the ridgeline.

"That's the idea."

He laughed. "I was referring to the fact that it's almost dark. Not our amazing camouflage." He came forward with the last piece of brush they'd cut and handed it to her ceremoniously. "Would you like to do the honors?"

"Why, thank you." She set the branch across the top of the doorway. "I'm glad you're here with me. I don't know how I'd have gotten this trap out of the truck and up this hill by myself."

"Happy to help." She'd made it clear she didn't need his protection, but no way was he going to let her do this alone, even though she'd been trapping wild animals for years.

While they'd packed the truck to come out here, she'd told him stories. Grizzlies. Wolves. She'd worked with them all. It was amazing to realize how rugged so much of her life had been. How tough she was to live the way she did.

He glanced down the dirt road for Emily, who'd had to close up her clinic before she could meet them. No sign of her yet. Hopefully she understood the directions he'd given her. They were on a remote corner of his ranch and it hadn't been easy to explain how to find them.

Maya picked up a canvas tarp from the pile they'd brought and spread it out in the bottom of the cage, careful not to touch the plate at the entrance that triggered the door to close. Caleb squinted at the contraption through the dimming light. They'd wedged the cage halfway in the bushes, and covered the rest with brush. "You know, if this mountain lion is dumb enough to walk into this crazy-looking trap, it deserves to get caught and collared."

Maya laughed. "It does look kind of crazy. Hopefully the lion will be too excited to eat the meat I brought to notice our mediocre camouflage."

"Do you think this will work?" It was hard to believe that an elusive animal like a mountain lion would just show up here and walk inside.

"I have no idea. There are plenty of reasons why it might not. The lion could have moved on. It might not be interested in eating lamb. Maybe it came by your ranch to look for deer."

"Well, overall I'd prefer that."

"Let's hope that, just for tonight, it really, really wants lamb." Maya went to the cooler chest Caleb had carried up the hill. "Time for bait." She pulled out two huge legs of lamb and tossed them into the back of the trap. "Hopefully that will tempt our mountain lion friend. And hopefully it won't tempt anyone else."

"You think we might catch something else?"

She grinned at him. "You never know what's out and about at night. Skunks, of course. Maybe a bobcat or a fox. The pressure plate on the floor of the trap is so sensitive, any of them could trigger it."

"So all of this work, hauling this gear, sleeping out here, it could all be for nothing."

"Welcome to the world of field biology, my friend. Some days it all works out, and other days you get a skunk in your trap."

She was funny. She always had been. He'd smiled more today than he had in a decade. "There has to be another way."

"We usually use dogs to track and tree the lions. It works much better. But I can't get trackers on such short notice."

"You use them in Colorado?"

"All the time."

He was staring, and maybe it was rude, but he was trying to imagine her pelting through the woods with a couple of hound dogs, chasing a mountain lion up a tree.

"Why are you looking at me that way?" Maya asked. "I know it's not your average job but it's what I do."

"Why do you do it? Why did you decide to study predators?" He wanted to try to understand what she got out of this life, which seemed so solitary and even scary to him. Anything could happen to her out in the backcountry, including one of the animals she studied deciding to make her its next meal.

She caught her lower lip in her teeth as if not sure how to answer at first. "They're beautiful and fascinating and they're misunderstood, you know? Everyone thinks they're these vicious killers—that they deliberately want to hurt other animals. But they don't. They're just hungry, and finding food the only way they know how."

"You mean it's not their fault that they are who they are."

Maya nodded. "They aren't out to cause harm. It's just what happens."

Caleb remembered what she'd told him about the attack on his ranch. The panicked sheep in constant motion. The panicked puma trying to make that motion stop. And then it dawned on him, the deeper meaning, perhaps, behind her choice of careers. "There is no fault," he said softly. "Like an accident."

"Yes." Maya's eyes searched his, as if seeking his understanding. "Like an accident."

He nodded, looked away and swallowed hard. "Thanks for telling me," he said. "I've wondered." And now he knew. That the very thing that had broken them apart, that had set him off to the military, to hide from the pain, that had dissolved his parents' marriage, had also set her life in motion, along a unique path she might not have pursued otherwise.

"And spending so much time in the wilderness? Do you like living like that?"

The sigh she gave was so small, most people might not have caught it. But he was listening hard.

"It's easier. To be alone. To work alone. Being around people is kind of uncomfortable. If I make friends, they want to know about my past. Then I have to make a choice. I can tell them about the accident, but then they'll always see me differently. I can avoid mentioning it, but then no one really knows me. When I first started doing fieldwork, I realized I didn't have to worry about any of that in the wilderness. And it felt like a relief." She stopped, clapped her hands to her cheeks. "Oh my gosh. I'm going on and on. You must think I'm insane."

"I don't." It was the opposite. Like she'd put into words something he couldn't. "I felt the same way. That's why I reenlisted. In combat, you're entirely focused on the mission. You don't have to think about anything else. And guys in the military—well, it's not like they want to have a lot of heart-to-heart talks about the past. You work hard, you joke around a little and that's enough for everyone. I liked that. It was a shock to come back here, where everyone knows my history. And I imagine it was even harder for you."

"Well, most people have been kind. But sometimes I feel a little bit like prey. Like I could get ambushed by someone who still believes the rumors about me, at any time."

"I'm sorry it's like that. I imagine that if you stayed here, you'd eventually get all the ambushes over with, and then you could feel more at ease."

"Well, I won't be here long enough to find out, I suspect," she said.

He wished he could do more to keep her safe. To make her feel like this town was still her home. Of course she wouldn't want to stay here—she had a far more interesting life waiting back in Colorado—but he hated that his actions had been a big part of what made her feel unwelcome here for so many years. "I promise you, if anyone says anything to me, I will set them straight."

She shot him a shy smile. "Thanks."

Maybe it was the dusk that made everything shadowed and a little unreal. Maybe the dim light gave him courage. Whatever the reason, Caleb said what was on his mind.

"Telling you to go, telling you that we were done—it was one of the biggest mistakes I've made. I didn't want you gone. And I missed you, once you were."

Maya froze. Turned. Her eyes were wide, her lips slightly parted, but she didn't say anything. Instead she walked away, and he watched her hands ball into fists at her sides, then release, like flowers closing and opening again. At their pile of gear, she picked up her duffel bag of clothing, fiddled with the zipper, then dropped it abruptly and plunked right down to sit on it, like his words had knocked her legs right out from under her.

He sat next to her. "I'm so sorry, Maya."

"Me too." She hit him, suddenly, hard on the shoulder.

"Ow. I guess I deserve that though."

"All these years," she said, tears audible in her words. "All these years I thought you hated me. That you blamed me. And that made me blame myself even worse than I already did. Why didn't you write? Or call? Why didn't you let me know, somehow, that you hadn't meant everything you said?"

She was furious and he wanted to wrap his arms around her, to make it all okay, but he couldn't be the person to fix this. He'd broken it too badly already.

But he could be honest. "I think it's easier to try to stay angry. Anger is simple. Way simpler than other feelings. Stuff like fear and regret. Or sadness. Or love." He blew out a breath. "All that other stuff is so hard to figure out."

"And maybe anger made you feel stronger," Maya said.

He looked at her in surprise. She still saw right into him. She always had.

"It might feel like strength in the moment, but it isn't. It's just pushing people away, until you're sitting on your porch, drinking by yourself, wondering what the hell happened."

She nudged him with her elbow. "Hey, at least you have that cat."

His laughter surprised him. Again. She kept doing that. Taking all of the knots inside them and gently untying. "Yeah, I'm glad there's Hobo."

"But your drinking..." Her voice was serious again. "It scares me."

Her honestly hit like a blow to the sternum. He drew in a breath to steady his head. "I stopped drinking after that morning you came by. I plan to stay stopped."

She was silent, staring at the trap for a long moment before she looked his way, her eyes dark and troubled. "I'm glad of that. I really am."

He remembered then how she'd seen drinking go from bad to worse. How it must feel to know your parents chose booze and drugs over a life with you.

She bumped her shoulder gently into his. "Let's finish getting set up. Then hopefully Emily will get here and we can eat. And then we have to sit, really, really quietly, without all of this chatting. Think you can do that, cowboy?"

"I dunno. I just can't seem to keep my mouth shut around you."

The look she gave him was a little shy. "I like that we're talking."

That smile. Her lips curved just so. The softness of them, the sweetness of her—it had him leaning in, just a breath of a movement, before he realized what he'd almost done.

He couldn't kiss her. She didn't want that from him, and he couldn't have it from her.

She was here for a few weeks, to do a job. That was all.

"Come on." He stood, offered a hand and then pulled her up. "Let's make sure we're ready for your lion."

The sound of an engine had them both turning to where Emily's truck bumped and rattled across the field and parked at the foot of the hill.

It was just as well she was here. They needed a break. A chaperone, to keep things simple between them for the night.

Emily, tall and athletic, ready for their campout in a parka and knit cap, clambered up the hill toward them. "How's it going?" she asked. "I brought pizza."

"Hallelujah," Maya said with a reverence that had them all laughing.

Emily switched on her flashlight and studied them both for a moment in the dim light. "You two look a little worn out. Come on, Caleb. Help me get my gear out of the truck and you can have an extra slice."

His stomach growled. He'd been so busy getting the chores done around the ranch and getting his gear together for camping out tonight, that he'd forgotten to eat. He followed her down the hill. "Emily, you're an angel."

"Nah," she said, shoving the pizza boxes into his arms, still warm, and smelling like heaven. "But we need to keep our strength up if we're going to catch a puma."

# CHAPTER FIFTEEN

CALEB HAD BEEN dreaming of Afghanistan again. Of the night they camped in a dry desert canyon, between some jagged rocks, and hoped like hell they hadn't been seen on the way in.

The snap of metal hitting metal had Caleb reaching for his gun. But instead of a rifle, his hand found something warm and soft. Slowly awareness crept in. Damp fog misting his face, the smell of sagebrush and Maya, still asleep, curled up against his shoulder.

He was awake, on his ranch, with the woman he'd always loved right there with him, like some kind of miracle.

That metallic sound must have been the trap. Something must have triggered it. He glanced down at Maya. The moon was up there beyond the fog, and in the faint glow, he could see Maya's shoulders rise and fall with her breathing, the small smile that played on her lips as she nuzzled closer to his shoulder. Through the sleeping bags, he could feel the heat of her body along his, and he closed his eyes, relishing that small contact, wondering how he would ever find the strength to wake her, if it meant ending this.

So he lay for a moment longer, letting her warmth seep into him and wake something all the way down in his bones, in the very marrow of him, that had been frozen, stuck and lifeless for so long.

A rustling from the trap reminded him that it wasn't fair to wait. The animal might be frightened, might be panicking to find itself caged.

"Maya," he whispered, and she popped her head up, peering at him through wisps of hair that had escaped her ponytail.

"Did anything happen?" She whispered too, and sat up, peering through the dark in the direction of the trap.

"I heard a noise. I think we caught something."

"I can't believe I even fell asleep." She was up and out of her sleeping bag and reaching for her hiking boots in one fluid motion. "Did it sound like a big something? Or a small something?"

"I have no idea," he admitted.

Emily sat up from the other side of Maya. "What's going on?" she whispered.

"We might have something."

"Oh wow." Emily reached for her jacket and boots. She and Maya could have been Marines, they were so efficient.

For a moment the only sound was the rustle of clothing. When they were dressed, Maya pulled out a flashlight. "This one is really dim but I'd like to use it when we go over there. So we startle our animal as little as possible."

"Especially if we caught a skunk," Emily murmured, and Caleb grinned. Maya pressed her hand to her mouth to suppress a giggle.

"Okay, let's bring the bags of gear." She held up a long, flat, zippered case. "Emily, I have the tranquilizer gun in here. If it's a mountain lion, let's get the dose loaded quickly so we don't have to stress it out for more than a moment."

Emily reached for the case, and Maya grabbed a folded tarp from next to where they'd slept. "When we get close to the trap, we'll set everything down on this. Let's go."

Caleb picked up the two heavy duffel bags that Maya pointed to, and let Maya and Emily lead the way to the trap. It felt like a military operation, with Maya as their squad leader. He didn't mind following behind. He smiled to himself in the dark. If it was a skunk, he'd also be farthest out of spraying range.

He was enjoying this, and he had no idea why. Any mountain lion that showed up here was a threat to his livestock. He should be angry at it. He should hate it.

But anger and hate didn't fit here. Like Maya had said earlier, predators weren't wrong; they just existed, following the only instincts they had. They'd never asked to play the role they did.

Plus he was with Maya, and as much as he didn't get it, being with her was the only thing that had given him any peace since he had left the Marines. Maybe it was only because they were constantly butting heads. Arguing with her was a good distraction from his worries.

Or maybe it was because she brought solutions. The grant. The barn raising. Trapping this mountain lion so they could collar and track it. Though of course the chances of this being a mountain lion—

"Oh my gosh." Maya turned, eyes wide, to face him and Emily. "We got it."

What were the chances? For a moment, they just stared at each other, stunned. Then they all turned to look at the trap.

Caleb had expected any mountain lion they caught to be panicked, thrashing in the crate. But when Maya turned her light on it, keeping the beam pointed at the ground and to the side to protect the big cat's eyes, there it was, lying on its stomach, paws out in front, just like Hobo did when Caleb gave him a treat. Except this was a mountain lion, with an entire leg of lamb between its paws.

They were just a few yards away. The big cat's eyes glinted green and glassy in the flashlight's dim glow.

"Let's back up a few paces," Caleb said, suddenly wanting to give the proud animal space. Its ears were round and alert. Its pale nose was rimmed in black, a white patch at its throat.

"It's so beautiful," Emily murmured.

Caleb moved a few yards farther away. "Should we put our stuff down here?"

Maya quietly unfolded the tarp. "Okay, let's not waste a minute. Caleb, will you open up those two duffel bags? And Emily, will you measure out the tranquilizer? I'm assuming that puma is about a hundred pounds."

Maya held the light while the vet picked up a vial and filled a large syringe with liquid.

"Okay, we're ready." Emily slipped the syringe into the gun and held it out to Caleb. "As ex-military, I suspect you're the best shot among us. Can you do it? Aim for the center of the thigh muscle, below the hip, above the knee."

Caleb took the gun, acutely aware that the last time he'd carried one, he'd wanted to kill a lion. And had almost shot Maya. His hands shook at the memory.

"I can do it if you'd rather." Maya held out her hand, and in the dim glow he could see the concern in her eyes. She'd noticed his shaking. "I've done it a bunch. Watch and learn, soldier."

He gave her the gun. She handed him the flashlight.

"Emily, can you grab a brighter light?" she asked the vet.

Emily rummaged through the duffel and pulled out a light almost as big as the ones that military police carry on base.

"So, here's the plan," Maya told them, keeping her voice low. "We need to be quick and quiet. We'll walk up to the crate. Emily, when we get close, turn your light on. The lion will focus on you, and that should let me get close enough to fire the dart through the bars."

Emily nodded.

"Caleb, you'll stick with me and try to shine your flashlight right on the lion's haunches so I can see where I'm shooting."

Maya was a natural leader, giving them their mission. She double-checked the tranquilizer gun, seemingly in her element, fulfilling this calling that was so uniquely hers.

Caleb glanced back toward the cage, invisible in the darkness. The puma was silent, either wary and listening to them, or still enthralled by its easy meal.

"Let's go," Maya whispered, and Emily led them close to the cage. A low growl erupted from the darkness as they approached. "Now," Maya said, and Emily flipped on the big light, revealing the cougar crouched, teeth bared, staring at the light, ready to take on the threat it perceived.

Caleb followed Maya through the shadows. When they were just a few feet away from the trap, Maya tapped him on the arm, and he switched on his light, aiming the beam right at the big cat's hind end.

In one sure movement, Maya shot the tranquilizer dart through the bars, and the cat let out a yowl of shock.

"That must have hurt," Caleb said as she backed up to stand at his side. His light revealed the poor cougar turning in circles, disoriented, already swaying with the effects of the drug. "Is it okay?"

"Yes." Emily came to join them. "It's not in pain—just a little woozy. And it doesn't like the crate. But at least it's safe in there."

Almost on cue the puma let out a loud sigh and lay down on its side, surrendering to the medication.

"Let's go." Maya reached up to unhook the side of the crate. Caleb helped and they lowered the panel down to the ground. "Emily, Caleb, can you each grab one corner of the tarp? We need to work quickly, to get everything done before it starts to wake up."

The three of them tugged on the tarp, heavy with the big cat's weight, freeing it from the trap. The puma's front paws twitched and Caleb started.

"It's okay," Maya told him, reaching right past those paws to slip a soft cloth over the puma's head. "This will protect its eyes."

Caleb tried to remain as calm as the women were, but it was a mountain lion, and his instincts, the caveman ones that had kept his ancestors safe from saber-toothed tigers at the dawn of time, showed up and sent his heart pounding. He was grateful when Maya sent him to find the scale so they could weigh the animal.

When he was ready, Maya and Emily took hold of the tarp and carried the puma a few yards, carefully setting it, tarp and all, on the canvas portion of the scale.

"We need to weigh it. Which means it's time for Muscles Dunne." Emily shot him a teasing smile. "Can you lift it?"

Grommets on the canvas attached to metal hooks on the scale. Caleb slid them into place and then pulled the scale up to chest height so the canvas made a sling. Maya and Emily made sure the lion was comfortably arranged.

Maya glanced up at him with a grin. "Ready to prove just how tough you are?"

He gave a short, nervous laugh. "Ready as I'll ever be." He took hold of the metal circle at the top of the scale.

"Okay." Emily grasped the canvas to keep it steady. "Ready, set, go!"

Caleb lifted the puma-filled sling in the air while Maya and Emily tried to read the number on the scale. His arm and chest muscles were screaming in protest at the awkward angle.

"One-hundred-eleven pounds," Maya read. Emily helped Caleb set the cougar carefully down and unhook the scale. "Take five pounds off for the tarp."

"What a beautiful boy." Emily dropped to her knees next to the lion and pulled a clipboard out of the bag. "A little skinny for his size, don't you think? I bet it's a young male, looking for territory. Caleb, will you please hold the light?"

Caleb kept the light fixed on the puma as Emily recorded the weight and Maya grabbed a measuring tape out of the duffel. She climbed around the big cat's body, measuring carefully and efficiently, while Emily took down notes like the two of them had worked together for years.

Caleb stood, mesmerized by the powerful mountain lion, so limp on the ground. It was big. Maya said it was eighty-three inches from head to tail. Twenty-five inches from its paws to the top of its shoulder.

It was beautiful, with thick fur the color of earth and branches and shadows, exactly designed for camouflage.

"You can touch it, gently," Maya said, as if reading his thoughts. "It's probably the only time you'll get to pet a cat this big."

Caleb knelt and ran a shaky hand over the lion's surprisingly thick, smooth coat. It was automatic to keep petting, to feel this incredible animal that most people never got to approach. He took in the thick paws and the lean muscle underneath his hands. "I never did think I was a cat person. But I've sure had a lot of them in my life since I came back to Shelter Creek."

"Hobo won't know what to think when he smells this kind of cat on you," Maya said.

It was surreal, to be here, in the dark, right before dawn, petting a lion. Every moment seemed to stand out as more crisp, more meaningful, because this mysterious predator was in their care.

Lying there asleep and utterly helpless, the mountain lion seemed so vulnerable. It wasn't a huge animal. In fact, it was almost delicate, with its lean stomach, long legs and streamlined body. And it was here on his land because it was trying to survive. Trying to find a few acres of its own in a territory crowded with other mountain lions, and fragmented by freeways and vineyards and more and more housing developments.

Until tonight, lions had lurked in Caleb's psyche as a shadowy threat to be eliminated. Enemies, out to get his livestock. But here in the dark, feeling the big cat breathe beneath his palm, he realized that Maya was right. This lion was just being who it was born to be. It had never asked to be a predator. It was just trying to get by.

The thought had him smiling to himself, there in the dark. Maybe he had more in common with mountain lions than he'd realized. He'd spent over a decade now just trying to get by.

Maya nodded her head toward the bag. "There's a camera in there. Do you want to snap some photos?"

Caleb reluctantly took his hand away from

the mountain lion and pulled the camera out. Maya gently lifted the fabric from the puma's face, then carefully revealed its fangs. Caleb snapped the photo and then Maya measured the teeth.

Emily peered into the big cat's mouth. "It has good oral health."

"What else do you notice?" Maya asked, taking the clipboard from the vet.

Emily looked in the lion's ears, and then ran her hands over its belly. "It's got a fair amount of ticks. We'd better do a count."

"Let's get a blood sample first," Maya said. "In case it wakes up. I'd rather check for diseases and get some genetic material if I have to make a choice."

Emily drew a vial of blood from the inside of the cat's leg, and then started counting ticks. Maya quickly put the equipment away and handed Caleb a full duffel bag."

"Can you set this by our sleeping bags?"

When he got back, Maya was holding something that looked like an enormous stapler against the cat's ear. When she squeezed, a tag popped on.

"You're piercing its ear?" Caleb peered closer. The tag read Department of Wildlife.

"Yes. If anyone finds it, they'll know to contact us."

He didn't want to think about that. How this amazing animal might die. From a rancher like him with a gun. Or cars on a freeway.

They counted the ticks. Seven, which seemed like a lot to Caleb, but Maya said it wasn't that bad at all. Emily plucked a few hairs off its belly and put them in a vial. Then Maya pulled out a collar with a wide band and a flat box on it. She set it carefully around the lion's neck, fastening the clasp with a screwdriver. When she'd finished, she double-checked that it wasn't too tight. "I think that's it."

Caleb couldn't take his eyes off the collar. It looked really big, taking up most of the mountain lion's neck, and it changed it. Made the lion seem a little less wild. It seemed unfair, to make it carry this contraption wherever it went, for the rest of its life. He swallowed hard, surprised by the lump in his throat.

"It's difficult, isn't it?" Maya must have read his thoughts, because she pointed to the collar. "But it could save its life. People are less likely to shoot a collared animal. And we'll be able to keep track of it. Learn from it. And figure out how to better protect its habitat as a result."

"But you won't be here," Emily said. "Who will track it?"

"I'll turn its information over to the crew in the Sacramento office. They'll keep an eye on it. And I'll be able to access the data as well. But I'm also going to try to get one of the California universities interested in this region. Hopefully they can get some graduate students out here to continue this work."

The entire time she'd been talking, she'd been working. Carefully removing the hood from the puma's face, and throwing the rest of her equipment back into its duffel bag.

"Okay, let's move away from here."

Caleb took a last look at the majestic mountain lion, so still on the tarp. "What do we do now?"

"We watch it until it wakes up, to make sure it doesn't get hurt." For one moment Maya dropped her busy professional demeanor and stroked the cat's shoulder. "Hey, big guy," she murmured. "You might feel a little weird when you wake up. But you'll be all better, very soon. Good luck out there."

Then she rose, grabbed the duffel and led the way toward their sleeping bags.

Then there was nothing more to do but wait. Dawn was turning shadows to gray. The chill fog had left a layer of moisture on everything, so they loaded Caleb's and Emily's trucks with damp sleeping bags and all the equipment. Then they dismantled the trap and put that into the truck too, stepping carefully around the sleeping puma.

"Can we leave the lamb for it?" Caleb figured the poor lion deserved it after being shot with a dart, measured, tagged and collared. But Maya told him no. That the lion would wake up woozy and wander away to sleep the drug off in a den or tree. The last thing they wanted was to invite it back and get it used to snacking on lamb at Caleb's ranch.

It made sense. But seeing the lion lying on the tarp, with the big collar around its neck, Caleb felt like they owed it something. Because with that collar, they'd taken some of its freedom. Its ability to go undetected, to truly be the wild animal, free of human interaction and contact, that it was born to be.

Maybe the collar would be the lion's salvation. People like Maya could intervene to try to save it if it got too close to a ranch or town. But that salvation came with a sacrifice.

Emily plunked down in the grass where she could see the lion and put her hands to her mouth to stifle an enormous yawn. "What I wouldn't give for some coffee," she murmured.

They hadn't slept much. They were seeing the dawn in. But Caleb felt the opposite of tired. His mind buzzed with awe and wonder, and the kind of gratitude he felt when he'd been part of something important. Like he'd felt once, in Afghanistan, when they'd made a connection with locals and helped them build a much-needed medical clinic.

He glanced at Maya, sitting to the other side of him. She must have felt him looking, because their gazes met, lingered for a moment, hers sparkling with satisfaction and excitement that matched his own. And no wonder. She'd spent the night doing what she was meant to do.

"Look," she whispered, and he pulled his eyes away from hers to see the mountain lion rising from the tarp.

The big cat shook himself, staggered sideways and stood, swaying. Then it looked their way, and for a moment Caleb's blood chilled in a primal reaction. Prey in the sights of a predator.

But this predator was sleepy and confused. It regarded them with mild interest, then turned and started up the hill, a little wobbly but moving slowly away, its fur blending into the tall dry grass, until Caleb had to squint to see it. Until it reached the top of the hill and disappeared from view.

He felt the loss of it. The return to the ordinary after something so unique.

"Okay, then." Emily rose to her feet. "Caleb, do me a favor. Take that crazy horse of yours for a ride up this hill later today, just to make sure our lion doesn't get into any trouble. If all is well, it should be nowhere in sight."

"Will do."

"I'm heading home for a shower and a pot of coffee before I have to go back into work. Thanks, Maya, for inviting me to help. That was pretty incredible."

"I'm so grateful for your help. This would have been a lot more difficult with just me and Caleb."

"You two would have been fine. You're a

good team." She waved and jogged down the hill, to her truck.

Maya turned to Caleb. "So, what did you think?"

All his awe and amazement spilled out in a flood. "What an incredible animal. I had no idea they were so...so..." He didn't have the words. But he knew that he'd witnessed something special, that most people would never get to see. "I can't believe how small it was... I mean, it wasn't small, really, but I guess I was expecting this huge animal, since they can do so much damage."

"Small but mighty," she said.

"Like someone else I know." It came out automatically, and for a moment he worried that she might be offended by it.

But instead she smiled up at him, and it was like the sun had come out, even though the dim morning was still thick with fog.

"Thank you," he said. "For showing me the lion. For letting me help. It's something I'll never forget."

"Just doing my job." She shrugged shyly. "Sometimes it works out. I'm just glad we didn't spend the night out here only to end up with a skunk or a raccoon in the trap."

"Me too. Though it still would have been a good adventure." *And I still would have been with you.* He couldn't say it. He might think it, but there was no point going down that road.

Even if she did enjoy his company, she was leaving. She'd made it very clear she had work that mattered that she was eager to go back to. He'd heard her tell Emily last night that she'd be studying mountain goats and mountain lions next. So he assumed she'd be living up in the Rocky Mountains for quite some time.

At least he'd have these next few weeks with her. Because he'd made a decision while he was watching that mountain lion wake up and wander off.

"I'd like to take that grant you mentioned," he told Maya. "If the offer still stands."

He was gratified when she turned toward him with a megawatt smile. "Really? You want to be a demonstration ranch? Caleb, that's fantastic!" She threw her arms around his neck in a hug that jolted them both.

"Oh I'm so sorry." She scrambled back, beet red. "I guess that was an old reaction, from another decade."

"Don't worry about it." He'd loved it. Wished he could figure out how to make that a regular thing between them.

Maya stood up and started pacing back and forth, clasping her hands in front of her with a huge smile on her face. "Okay, so I'll give the organization a call today, and we have to write up a proposal with the type of equipment you want to install, the changes to fencing..." She paused for a quick breath. "Remember that ranch I mentioned? The man who used this same grant? Let's go see him this week."

It was impossible to say no to such sheer joy. It was as if he'd given her some kind of gift and she was so excited, she could barely keep still. As they walked back to the truck, and then drove back to the barn, she was pointing out things they could change, questioning him about his water supply, in case they wanted to install sprinklers, and asking so many other questions that, by the time she left, Caleb watched her drive away from his ranch with relief.

He needed to be alone with his thoughts, to process what he'd realized during his night trapping a mountain lion.

That he wanted to protect mountain lions.

That he was willing to try to teach other ranchers how to protect them too.

That he was ready to put pride aside and accept help with his ranch.

And that he was pretty sure he was falling in love with Maya Burton, all over again.

# CHAPTER SIXTEEN

MAYA TRIED NOT to be nervous as Caleb pulled his truck in front of Aidan's house at Bell-weather Ranch. She'd dragged him all this way, a two-hour drive north of Shelter Creek, and she just hoped that Aidan was as success-ful a rancher as she'd heard he was.

It had been an awkward drive. Now that she and Caleb were getting along so much better, she was nervous around him. The things he'd said earlier this week, when they'd caught the lion, still spun around her head like some kind of science experiment in a centrifuge. Her emotions whirled and whirled, and she couldn't find a way to switch the machine off and let the contents settle.

He regretted blaming her. Regretted driv-ing her away. He'd missed her over all these years.

In a way it was good news. She'd lived with his blame for so long, and now it was gone. But it was also infuriating. He'd never reached out to tell her that he'd been wrong. He'd let her suffer, let her struggle under the burden of his blame, when just her own guilt threatened to drag her under.

But he'd thought he was doing the right thing, letting her go. And maybe he had been right. His blame had set her on a difficult but amazing journey. Had led her to seek out the wilderness and its wildest creatures. Had given her work that mattered and a career she was proud of.

And then she'd hugged him. And that had been a mistake. Just that brief contact, the hint of his solid, muscled shoulders, threatened to destroy her common sense. He was beautiful, of course. He always had been. But now, hardened and honed by the tough path he'd walked, he was more than that. Compelling. Intimidating. Magnetic. As soon as she'd pulled away, she'd missed the instant connection she'd felt.

It was too much to think about, and much too tangled to make sense of. But thankfully they'd had Einstein the dog sitting like a big furry, panting buffer between them the whole drive, so it hadn't been just the two of them in the cab.

And Maya had pulled up a country-music playlist on her smartphone, so they'd listened to that and hadn't had to talk much at all, except when she let Caleb know that she'd been tracking their mountain lion via data from the GPS tracker on his radio collar and it had headed northwest, toward the section of his ranch closest to the coast. It seemed like a promising choice. Caleb had no livestock out there. At least not yet.

"So, here we are," Maya said brightly. "Bellweather Ranch. What do you think?" There were chickens strutting all over the lawn in front of the big white farmhouse. Farther off Maya could see two big weathered gray barns.

"I think this guy lives out in the middle of nowhere."

Caleb was right about that. The barely paved road to the ranch had wound up and down hill after hill, west of the town of Willits, taking them way out into the coast ranges.

The ranch sat on the top of a ridge, with even higher hills behind it. Maya gestured to the pastures sloping up behind the house, tinged gold from the summer sun. "But isn't it gorgeous?"

"Yeah, it's pretty nice."

It didn't sound like high praise but Maya could see it in Caleb's eyes and the appreciative curve of his mouth. He was a rancher, and Aidan's ranch was truly beautiful.

Aidan appeared, striding around the side of the house. Maya's first thought was that he was very tall and very blond. He looked like a Viking whose ship had somehow run aground in this remote corner of California.

Aidan's shaggy hair curled from under his baseball cap, but it was his piercing eyes that startled Maya. They were an odd greenish-brown color and he seemed to look right into her as he reached out his hand.

"You must be Maya. Thanks for making the trip out here."

His grip was firm and strong as they shook. "Great to meet you, Aidan. Thanks for making time for us today."

"My pleasure. And you must be Caleb. It's great to meet you."

When they shook hands, Caleb, who always seemed so big to Maya, looked small in comparison. He also seemed a little stunned as he retrieved his hand from Aidan's, flexing his fingers a time or two. Good. Caleb was such a tough guy, he might be more likely to take advice from someone even stronger than him.

"I appreciate you taking the time to show me around." Caleb gestured to the hills around them. "You've got a great piece of property out here."

"Thanks." Aidan waved an arm toward the nearest barn, a few hundred yards away. "You ready to check it out?"

"Sure." Caleb gestured for Aidan to go first. "Lead the way."

Einstein meandered up from where he'd been sniffing at a gopher hole.

"Hang on." Aidan crouched down. "Who is this?"

"This is Einstein." Maya watched with pride as Einstein offered a paw for Aidan to shake. The dog had put on some weight and his coat was getting shiny. "I found him a couple of weeks ago."

"Nice to meet you, Einstein." Aidan straightened and turned his attention back to Caleb. "Let's start over near the first barn." They walked down the lane, and Aidan led them to a high wooden fence that ran right up to the barn wall. Aidan pointed over the fence, a slightly self-conscious smile tugging at his mouth. "Caleb, meet my flerd."

Maya bit back a snort of laughter when she saw the surprise on Caleb's face. Yes, it was good they'd come here today. He'd never be willing to learn about flerds from her.

Caleb shot her a questioning look.

"Yes, you heard him right," she said. "Flerd."

Aidan waved Caleb closer. Maya joined them and even Einstein put his front paws on one of the lower boards and peeked through at the big pasture beyond. In the distance they could see white specks of sheep mixed in with larger, darker blotches of cattle.

Aidan pointed to the animals. "It might sound a little crazy, Caleb, but a flerd is the way to go. It's a combination of a flock and a herd. You put your cattle and sheep in the same pasture. It works great. Look how happy these guys are."

"Why?" Caleb sounded a little stuffy. As if Aidan had just suggested he start a petting zoo.

Maya put a hand briefly on his arm to get his attention. "Keep an open mind," she murmured.

"Sheep and cattle forage differently, so you'll get better use from the land," Aidan explained. "And cattle are tough. Once they bond with the sheep, they'll circle up around them if a predator shows. They'll try to protect them."

"I'm not sure how this would work on my ranch. Will all kinds of cattle protect the, um…flerd?"

He glanced at Maya as he struggled to say the word and she couldn't help it. A laugh escaped. "Try it three times fast," she advised. "Flerd, flerd, flerd."

Aidan smiled at her joke, but answered Caleb's question. "Yep. I've been doing it for three years now, and never had a problem. I've also started leaving the horns on my cattle. Pumas and coyotes don't want to mess with that."

"But don't the horns create a lot of trouble?" Caleb frowned. "We've always dehorned cattle on my family's ranch."

"Well, horned cattle surely need more space and better supervision. It can be trickier when you bring them in for vetting too. But it's also easier to guide them along." Aidan grinned. "Natural handles. Steering."

Maya smiled at the image of Caleb, guiding a cow along by its horns.

"I guess so." It came out as more of a grunt, but at least Caleb was still listening. She'd been right to bring him out here. It was hard to argue with Aidan. The guy looked like he could fell a tree with his bare hands.

"There's a lot you can do to discourage predators," Aidan said to Caleb. "I switched to fall lambing, for example."

Caleb looked astounded. "What? That makes no sense."

"I know in this area we usually lamb in the spring to get all that good green grass. But mountain lions also give birth in early spring, so they're hunting a lot of food for their young at that time."

"But in the fall you have to buy feed. The grass is all dried out." Caleb's brows were drawn together, and Maya could practically see the numbers crunching in his brain.

"Yup." Aidan shrugged. "It's a trade-off. You've got to calculate it all against the price of lamb. If you're worried, you could also lamb in spring but keep the ewes and lambs in your barn for a while."

Caleb looked at Maya and she mouthed the words *barn raising* at him. He was still protesting about charity, but it hadn't stopped The Biddies from going ahead with the planning. They'd already picked a date, two weeks from this Saturday.

Aidan was describing his lighting system and sprinklers, which were both on solar-powered motion sensors that activated at night when predators came near. "And besides all that, I've also got my dogs."

"Dogs?" Caleb asked.

"Thor and Odin. My guard dogs."

"You named them after Norse gods?" It was so perfect that Maya had to suppress a giggle. Maybe he really was a Viking.

"Well, I figured they're out there, dealing with life and death. I'd better give them names to match."

"What kind of dogs can take on a mountain lion?" Caleb asked.

"You can use a few different kinds," Aidan said. "Some ranchers like Great Pyrenees, but they have really thick coats and it can get pretty hot out in these hills. So I've got short-coated Anatolian shepherds."

"And tell him how many animals you've lost since you made all of these changes," Maya prompted, remembering the conversation she'd had with him on the phone earlier in the week.

"None."

Caleb gaped at Aidan. Then at Maya. Then back at Aidan. "You've lost *no* livestock? Living out here in the middle of nowhere? This ranch looks like mountain lion paradise."

"Pretty awesome, right?" Aidan's smile was part triumph, part relief. "No losses for the last two years. Not just because of the dogs though. The flerd, the lambing, good fencing, technology—it all helps."

Maya elbowed Caleb, because she knew him. Knew how he loved animals and how much he'd love Aidan's dogs. "Did you hear that part? You have to combine a lot of different preventative measures. Not just dogs."

His wide smile took her back in time to the boy she'd loved. "Yes, ma'am. But can I meet the dogs?"

She laughed, trying to ignore the way her heart seemed to flip over when he looked at her this way. "I knew you'd like that part best." He'd already fallen for Einstein, chatting with the big mutt as they drove up and scratching his floppy ears any chance he got. He may have been adopted by Hobo the cat, but Caleb was a dog person at heart.

"The dogs are pretty far out on the edge of my property right now. Want to take a ride?" Aidan nodded toward the battered pickup parked next to the barn. "You guys can ride in the back. Take in the view."

"That would be great." Maya felt like a kid again at the prospect of a ride in a pickup across this amazing property. It was refreshing to be out of Shelter Creek. So good to be somewhere else, with Caleb and Einstein, hearing all of Aidan's exciting ideas. She lifted Einstein up onto the tailgate and climbed up after him.

Caleb just stood there, looking at her with an odd, bemused expression on his face.

Maya plunked herself down on the side of the truck bed. "Are you coming?"

"You're welcome in the cab too," Aidan assured him.

"No." He shook his head just a little and climbed up after Maya. "Back here is fine."

"All right. Let's get going." Aidan climbed into the cab.

Maya looked at Caleb, who'd sat down on the side of the truck opposite hers. "Everything okay?"

"You reminded me so much, just now, of how you were in high school." He looked away for a minute and tugged the brim of his cowboy hat down a little lower. "I still think you're beautiful."

"Oh." She didn't know how to answer. Didn't know what to do with his words or the way they washed like warm sunlight over her skin. *He* was the beautiful one, and maybe it was that, or the reverent way he'd treated the mountain lion the other night, or the fact that he was finally willing to work with her, but all of her old feelings for him seemed to be waking up and emerging from wherever she'd stashed them all these years.

"I'm sorry. I probably shouldn't have said it."

"It's very kind of you." She sounded oddly formal, but she was rusty at this and he was looking at her all heavy-lidded and handsome, the way he used to, when they'd loved each other. Maybe it was shallow, and it was certainly foolish, but she wanted him to notice her, to see her as attractive.

But that's all this could be. A temporary attraction. She was only in Shelter Creek for a few more weeks. And when she left this time, she wanted it to be on a positive note. No heartache. No tears. "I'm glad we can work together." She could feel the distance her neutral words created and a part of her wanted to bridge it again immediately. But she couldn't. She had a life to go back to, work to do. She had to stay strong. She'd ignored her feelings for Caleb for over a decade now. She could keep it up for a couple weeks.

And after that? Well, then she'd be in Colorado, too busy to think of him much.

It was better this way. Caleb was heartache and trouble. She was smart enough not to need to be taught that same lesson twice.

Caleb reached for Einstein, giving the big dog a few pets as Aidan started the truck, bouncing them along a rutted road. Maya searched for a new topic. "What do you think of all this?" She waved her hand to encompass the pastures around them. The air up here, so far from any big city, was clean and full of the scents of summer—hay and sage and dry earth.

"I like it. How could I not? Aidan has a great piece of property."

"And some good ideas?" She couldn't help but gloat a little.

"Yes." He winked. "Especially if your grant is going to pay for them." He looked ahead, his expression eager. "I sure am curious about these dogs."

"You always used to have sheepdogs around the ranch, way back when."

"Yeah, we did. But when the last one passed on, my dad decided he didn't want another dog. Said it was like losing another family member and he didn't want to go through that again."

His words hit her in the stomach and it must have shown on her face, because his eyes went wide.

"I'm sorry. Dumb thing to say. I wasn't thinking."

"No." She reached for Einstein, rubbing the dog's ears for comfort. "It is what it is. What happened that night—it's like when you drop a rock in a lake and all those ripples go out from that one event. Your dad giving up on dogs and the ranch. Your parents' divorce. Probably even you joining the Marines."

"You can't blame yourself for all of that." Caleb pulled off his hat and twisted it in his hands. The sun caught on his dark hair, decorating it with flecks of light. "Maybe my parents would have divorced anyway. Maybe I'd still have wanted to enlist."

"Maybe." She wasn't sure she believed him, and busied herself folding and unfolding Einstein's ears. All this old hurt was one good reason she needed to keep her distance from him. It would always be there, waiting to trip them up.

"I understand, more than you realize."

She looked at him, surprised.

Caleb pressed his lips together, like he was trying to decide what to say. When he spoke again his voice was a little hoarse. "In Afghanistan, I was on guard duty one night. And I heard this noise and I looked up, and someone was running toward me, out of the darkness. I called out, but he didn't answer. I couldn't see his features, but I could tell that he had this vest on, and all I could think was *suicide bomber.* So I shot him. He died there in the dirt, right in front of me."

Maya's heart hurt, as if it had suddenly grown too large for her chest. "Oh no. Caleb, how horrible." She couldn't imagine having to make a decision to kill. Her instinct was to take him in her arms, to hold him, but she couldn't do that. They couldn't be like that. So she waited.

"When I got to him, I saw that he was just a kid, barely a teenager, and the vest, that damn vest, was a fishing vest. I still don't know where he got it, or why he was wearing it. Just this old fishing vest with every pocket empty." He ran a hand over the stubble on his jaw. "Who wears a fishing vest in Afghanistan? They don't even have any water." He looked down at the floor of the truck, swallowing hard.

Einstein, sensing his distress, laid his big head in Caleb's lap. Caleb pet the dog's ears absentmindedly.

"I had no idea," Maya finally said when she got her voice under control. "Does anyone know? Does Jace know?"

He shook his head. "How do you bring it up? I mean, even right now, it's random. By the way, Maya, I killed an innocent kid."

She understood that dilemma all too well.

"Did you ever find out who he was? Why he was running at you like that?"

"It turned out he was the son of one of our interpreters. Coming to tell us his father had been taken by the Taliban." He cleared his throat and when he met her eyes, his face was stark with pain. "So I know what it's like to live with your kind of regret."

Maya couldn't keep her distance any longer. She reached across the truck, took Caleb's cold hands and wrapped them in her own, wishing he'd told her about this somewhere else. Somewhere other than on a short ride in the back of a truck. This was no place for tears, or for the outpouring of sympathy that he deserved.

And then it struck her that, consciously or not, he'd picked this spot for a reason. Because he didn't want all of that emotion. He didn't want her pity. He just wanted her to know.

So she'd respect that, even while her soul ached for what he'd been living with, all by himself. "Thank you for telling me." She resisted the urge to wipe the single tear she saw on his cheek.

They'd reached the steepest hill yet and Aidan downshifted so suddenly that they both crashed down into the truck bed. It was the comic relief they needed.

"Ouch." Caleb rubbed an elbow, then pushed himself back so he was leaning against the cab.

Maya grabbed for Einstein's harness, but missed. The dog wasn't in any danger, but she wasn't sure how he'd handle the jolting, sloping truck with just three legs. She shouldn't have worried. The good boy sat calmly while he slowly slid downhill toward the closed tailgate. With his ear flopped over, he looked surprised, mildly alarmed, but still somehow dignified.

Maya realized she was laughing through tears. Caleb's story was so tragic, and Einstein was so ridiculously cute.

She scooted back to join Caleb and he put an arm around her, his strength keeping her steady as they rocked up the last part of the rutted slope. The old truck managed the climb, and they evened out on a flat hilltop covered in sun-bleached grass. They were at the top of the ranch, the top of the world, with grassy hills and wooded ravines rolling out in every direction.

Maya allowed herself a few more moments to savor the feeling of Caleb holding her. Then she slid out from under his arm and perched on the side of the truck again. Leaning on him was too comfortable, and too comforting. She couldn't let herself get used to that.

But she wasn't ready to drop the subject he'd broached. Maybe that boy's death caused the pain Caleb had been trying to drink away. He seemed so much healthier now, a completely different man than the one she'd found passed out on his porch a few weeks ago. But she didn't want him to fall back into that pit. "Caleb, you couldn't have known about that boy. Anyone would have panicked, seeing him dressed like that, running toward your camp in the middle of the night."

"My buddies all said the same thing." He moved to sit opposite her again. "But I go over those moments in my mind, wondering if I could have done something different. Wishing I'd taken one more second to observe and think before I reacted."

She offered him the only wisdom she had. "You have to accept that you did the best you could in that moment." Easier said than done, of course. How many times had she questioned her reactions behind the wheel the night Julie died?

The truck stopped with a jolt and Aidan hopped out, tugging the brim of his baseball cap down as he came around to open the tailgate. "Did you all survive back there? It's kind of a rough road."

"Yeah, it was rough, for sure." Caleb's eyes met hers and he smiled bleakly at the double meaning.

Maya reached for Caleb's free hand and clasped it in both of hers, hoping to reassure. The gratitude in his dark gaze, told her she'd succeeded. "It was bumpy but we're tough," she told Aidan. "We're hanging in there."

# CHAPTER SEVENTEEN

CALEB DIDN'T WANT to let go of Maya's hand. Her warm skin and small fingers were the comfort he needed. He knew just how well she understood what he'd told her. How she was one of the few who could truly understand what that kind of mistake felt like.

But there was no time to savor this moment. Aidan opened the tailgate and Maya scooted out of the truck, and then turned around to help Einstein. With the big dog sprawled in her arms, she glanced at him with a small smile, like she was trying to reassure him.

He tried to smile back but it came out kind of creaky. Probably looked weird. Because as soon as her hand was gone from his, he wondered if he'd said way too much. She didn't need his confessions. She had enough to live with, without carrying his burdens too.

But still, it felt good to finally tell someone. As if, by sharing his horrible secret, he'd made it just a fraction lighter and a bit more bearable.

Though if he was being honest, it was more than that. He was falling for her, and any contact, any time with her, was shelter from the storms inside.

Ever since their adventure trapping the mountain lion a few nights ago, he'd been thinking hard, hoping he'd find some way to convince her to stick around Shelter Creek and give him a chance that he absolutely didn't deserve. He hadn't had any brilliant ideas yet, but he knew that before he asked her to consider him as anything more than a client, and maybe an old friend, he owed her the truth about his own mistakes. And the memories that haunted his sleep.

Well, now she knew, and if by some miracle she decided to give them a chance, she'd go in with full knowledge that she'd be getting the raw end of the deal.

Though he was stupid to think confessing his past to her would change anything. She'd made it clear, when he'd blurted out that compliment, that she did not want to go down that road with him. He didn't blame her, really, considering where it had left them last time.

But still, they were good together. Two serious people who made each other laugh, who understood each other. Everything was more intense and vivid when he was with her, but somehow also so comfortable. And maybe he was reading her all wrong, but it seemed like maybe she felt the same things.

Caleb realized Aidan was waiting for him and jumped down from the truck. The rancher shaded his eyes to look out over the ridge. "Let's meet the dogs," he said. "Though Einstein may have to stay here. Herding dogs are likely to attack strange dogs who come near their sheep."

Maya tied Einstein's leash to the bumper, where he'd have the truck's shadow to shade him. "Stay here, good boy," she told him, giving his soft ears a caress. "We won't be gone long."

Einstein whined, and even his floppy ear rose up straight in a plea to go with them.

"He's a great dog," Caleb said. "He's got character."

Maya leaned down as if she was listening to something the dog said. Then she straightened. "Einstein says thank you. He thinks you have character too."

It wasn't a gushing assessment, and it apparently came from the dog and not her, but he'd take it.

They followed Aidan through the grass. The trail was narrow here, so Maya slowed, letting Caleb go in front of her.

They were near the sheep, and the closest animals shifted nervously, still grazing but walking a few steps away. Suddenly two brown-and-black heads popped up from the middle of the flock.

The sudden motion surprised him and inspired a laugh from Maya. "They're like doggy periscopes," she explained when Caleb glanced back at her.

The dogs' narrow faces and long necks peeping over the dusty backs of the sheep were comical. But when they stepped out of the flock, they were all business. Tan fur bristled, floppy ears perked up and keen dark eyes zeroed in on them. The dogs walked toward them with wary steps when Aidan called out their names.

They were handsome. Like Labs on steroids: big, broad-chested, long-necked, thick-furred. They were domestic dogs, to be sure, but there was a wariness and a wildness about them too.

Caleb realized his mouth was slightly open. He wanted dogs like this on his ranch. They were just so cool.

"So, like I mentioned earlier, these guys are short-coated Anatolian shepherds," Aidan explained. "I was worried rough-coated dogs would be too hot up here in summer. But if you're near the coast, rough coats might be better in all that fog. It's something to consider if you choose this breed."

"Which is which?" Maya asked.

"Thor has the darker face," Aidan explained. "Thor, come!"

The bigger of the two dogs broke into a trot, and Caleb held out his hand. Thor slowed as he got within a couple of feet of Caleb, stretching his nose to snuff the outstretched knuckles. His lighter-colored buddy followed suit.

"That must be Odin." Maya held out her hand and Odin gave her a passing nuzzle. Then both dogs went to Aidan, snuffling him, tails wagging with dignified affection. The rancher ran his hands over them, checking for injuries or ticks, said a few kind words to each and then pointed to the sheep. The two dogs trotted back to their flock. "They're looking good but I'll have the vet out soon to make sure they're healthy."

"So, they just live out here?" Caleb watched as the dogs circled the sheep and then disappeared into the moving mass of grazing animals.

"Yup. They're basically a part of the flock. They consider the sheep their pack and they'll do anything to protect them. They've got a massive bark, so usually that's enough to scare predators away. I hear them bark a lot. Which is something to consider."

"It won't bother me if I know they're barking to keep my sheep alive," Caleb said. It would be incredible having dogs like this to help out. It would bring peace of mind, for sure.

"Exactly." Aidan nodded. "I figure it's a small price to pay. But if you have neighbors…"

"No neighbors," Caleb told him. "My place is a few miles from town."

"Well, they're a great breed for this work. Loyal, not aggressive with people, but plenty willing to fend off anything that bothers the flock."

"Do you bring them food?" Caleb asked.

"Twice a day. I just keep their food and bowls in a container in the truck. I usually bring the sheep down the hill at night, so I'll feed the dogs then."

"How do you train them?" Maya asked.

"A lot of it is just instinct. They don't need a ton of training." Aidan motioned to the flock. "You want them to bond with the sheep. Not with you. So they sleep in the barn, with the sheep, from the very beginning."

Caleb had so many questions, he didn't know where to start. "What about if you did have to take them to the vet or something? Wouldn't they be upset to leave their flock?"

"When I come out here, I bring a leash and I take them on walks away from the flock and away from each other, so they'll at least be somewhat used to some separation."

"I don't know if I could do it," Maya said. "I'd want to play with them. Especially when they were puppies."

Aidan looked a little grim. "Maybe it's different when you need them so badly. I'd lost enough livestock by the time I got these two that it was pretty easy to keep in mind what they were here for."

Caleb knew they had to let Aidan get back

to work soon, but he was still trying to understand how this all worked. "So, you raise them with the sheep, but how do they know what to do out here?"

"As long as they're bonded with the livestock, they'll bark like crazy if anything comes to bother them."

"It's that simple?" Caleb looked at Aidan in disbelief. Nothing was that simple.

"Yup." Aidan gave an offhand shrug. "Unless you get a dud."

"A dud?" Maya looked at Aidan. "How do you know it's a dud?"

"Once in a while a dog won't have the protective instinct. Then you'll need to rehome them as a companion animal."

Caleb watched Odin emerge from between a couple of sheep, sniffing at them as if to make sure they were all right. One of the sheep lifted its nose from the grass and nuzzled him back.

"He looks pretty happy," Maya said as Odin flopped down in the grass next to his sheep-buddy. She sat down in the grass too, breaking off a blade to fidget with. "And I don't blame them for liking it out here. It's a great place to be."

"It is. I'm a lucky guy." Aidan smiled but it didn't quite reach his eyes, and Caleb wondered what his story was. Aidan was friendly, and clearly his ranch was a success, but there was something about him, kind of a lost feeling, that Caleb recognized. Maybe because he'd felt lost for a long time too.

Until Maya showed up and slowly but surely drove that feeling away.

"I'm just going to look over the sheep while we're here." Aidan turned and wandered off.

Caleb looked down at Maya, who was sitting totally relaxed in the grass, with a slight smile on her face. "You're like these dogs. Totally at home living outdoors."

She eyed him. "Are you trying to say I'm uncivilized?"

"Nah. I'm saying you're independent. And you seem pretty happy out here in the big wide-open."

"Well, you're a rancher. You're independent and pretty happy out here in the big wide-open too, right?"

His smile turned to a grin. "Yeah, I guess we're alike that way." He sat down next to her. "It's really good to be around you again."

"It's good to be around you too."

Caleb wanted to say more, to ask for more times like this, but it would ruin the moment. And she'd made it clear that moments like this were all they were going to get. So they sat in silence, watching the dogs and the sheep.

"What do you think?" she asked after a while. "Are there Anatolian shepherds in your future?"

"Absolutely. I want to get the name of the breeder Aidan used and call them when we get home."

"That's great news. And of course you have to try a flerd," she teased him.

Flerd. Just the name was nuts. "Well, I'll try pretty much anything, I guess."

She looked at him with mock alarm, and then reached up to put a palm to his forehead, as if checking to see if he was ill. "Is this the same Caleb I met a few weeks ago?"

He grinned at her, happy, so damn happy, to be joking around in this field with her. "No. It's not. You've changed me. And I truly appreciate that." His gaze met hers and he couldn't resist. He leaned forward and brushed a kiss on the soft skin of her forehead. He heard her breath catch in her throat, and she tipped her head up to look at him, her brown eyes so solemn. And there was that bond, those ties that had never really broken, tugging at him, pulling him down until his lips met hers in the sweetest touch, his mouth on hers for one perfect second.

And then she pulled back, her cheeks flushed, her glance shy, her words barely there. "Glad I could help." She stood up, as if needing some distance between them. "I'll just check and see if Aidan is ready to go." And she was off, walking down the path to find their host.

He got up too and watched her go, pressing his lips together to memorize the feel of her. Wanting so much more of what they'd just had, but knowing he didn't have the right to push her. He wandered back to the truck, to check on Einstein and give Maya the space she obviously wanted.

The big dog was asleep in the shade when Caleb approached, but he popped his head up and wagged his tail in greeting. Caleb knelt down and rubbed the dog's ears and the thick ruff around his neck. "Help me out," he told the mutt. "Help me talk her into staying."

Einstein watched him carefully, ears up, as if he was truly trying to understand Caleb's words. "And if she won't stay, then take care of her for me. Okay, big guy?"

The dog sat up and offered a paw, as if he wanted to shake on it. So Caleb shook. And hoped he and Einstein could find a way to convince Maya to stay in Shelter Creek.

## CHAPTER EIGHTEEN

CALEB STEPPED AWAY from the old lambing shed to take it all in. There were people everywhere on his ranch. It wasn't a barn raising; it was an entire ranch raising, and all morning he'd had to take breaks, take deep breaths, because he was worried that he might just start bawling like a baby.

Annie, Maya's grandmother Lillian and all of their friends must have worked some kind of magic. Half of Shelter Creek was here—maybe more—all giving up their Saturday to rebuild his ranch.

So many people had shown up that Annie had divided them into crews. Most were here, rebuilding his lambing shed. Supervised by Jed Hurley, a local contractor, they'd already put up a new frame. And it was only ten o'clock in the morning.

Another group of locals had gone off to fix fences. Others were replacing the patched siding on the main barn. The entire crew of Shelter Creek Plumbing had shown up to repair his water pipes, so he could easily get water out to all the pastures. An electrician, Cory Prine, his former high school buddy and owner of Coast Light Electrical, was climbing all over the barn with his assistant, replacing the wiring.

Even Jace was here with his nieces and nephew, painting the new barn doors that he and Caleb had hung the other day.

Caleb couldn't believe all these people had turned up for him. He hadn't exactly been a social butterfly around Shelter Creek since he'd moved back to the ranch.

He wished his dad could be here to see all of this. Caleb had tried to call him, but his aunt had said he was out on the golf course. Golf? Since when had his dad played golf? But hey, if Dad had taken an interest in something, Caleb figured that was progress.

He'd tried Mom too. But she was in a meeting with an interior-design client, so after making sure nothing terrible had happened, she'd said she was happy for him and ended their chat.

As she'd hung up, Caleb had heard her say

something to her client about chintz. He'd have to look up that word later. It was surreal that his mom lived in a world so different from his, so different from the world that they'd shared together, here on the ranch, that she had an entirely new vocabulary.

He should get back to work. He bent to pick up Hobo, who'd been his shadow today, concerned about all of the commotion around the normally silent ranch. The cat snuggled under his chin. "It's okay, buddy," Caleb told him. "Everyone is here to help us today."

"Talking to your cat again?" Maya was walking toward him through the dry grass, with her jeans and shirt covered in sawdust, and Einstein hopping at her side.

Caleb grinned at the sight of them. The odd couple. Maya was tiny, contained, graceful and efficient. Einstein, propelling his huge body along on three legs, smiling his goofy, flop-eared doggy grin, was her gangly opposite. Yet somehow they fit together, because this was Maya, the champion of predators, the underdogs of the animal world. It made sense that she'd find the most underdog of all dogs and make it hers.

Einstein looked so happy, accompanying

his mistress across the ranch. The mutt knew he'd struck gold when he'd met Maya. She was the human angel in his doggy heaven, and no way was the stray going to let her out of his sight.

Caleb knew just how he felt.

Watching Maya approach, with her faded, dusty jeans rolled up to reveal cute tan hiking boots, and her hair in a ponytail beneath her ball cap, the disconnected feeling he'd had after phoning his parents vanished. Because somehow *she* felt like home now. She felt like family. He was a fool to think it. Clutching on to her was like trying to grab on to the wind or one of the swallows that was circling indignantly above the barn. She was a free spirit, moving on soon. But she *felt* like his. His other half, that he'd lost for so long.

They were meant to be together. He just needed to find a way for her to see that too.

Hobo jumped down and growled at Einstein, a sharp grating sound. Einstein immediately sat, wagged his tail and whimpered, like he was desperate to make friends.

Maya laughed. "These two remind me a little bit of us six weeks ago. You all huffy and grumpy, and me trying to make it all okay."

Caleb grimaced, remembering how rude and sullen he'd been. "Thanks for having patience with me. I'm glad you didn't just give up."

Maya's cheeks seemed to flush a little pinker and she knelt down to give Einstein a hug. "It's okay, buddy. Hobo will come around. He's just feeling insecure."

He smiled at the indirect jab. "I guess you could call it that. Insecure, and a whole bunch of other things."

She looked up at him, cheek-to-cheek with the old dog. "But we're doing better now. Right?"

"Seems like." They were friends, so that was certainly better than how they'd been when Maya first came back to Shelter Creek. But ever since that kiss on Aidan's ranch two weeks ago, he'd wanted so much more than friendship.

They'd spent a lot of time together over the past two weeks, getting the solar-powered lights set up, making plans to reroute fences and researching changes to his lambing schedule. They'd even started mixing Caleb's cattle in with his sheep, trying to get them to bond into a flerd, though Caleb still had trouble saying the ridiculous word.

He'd helped Maya install a couple of wild-life cameras around the ranch so he could see who was visiting at night. No mountain lions had shown up so far, but he'd been amazed to see how many coyotes, skunks, foxes and bobcats lived on his property.

But every time he'd tried to talk about that kiss, or how he felt, she'd change the subject and focus them right back on work again. She was always ready to help, but seemed intent on keeping him at a distance.

But then he'd catch her watching him, with this expression in her eyes that seemed like part admiration, part want, and part misery, and then he was sure she felt the same way he did.

Well, if she wanted to just be friends, he could do that, for now. But not for much longer. Just a few weeks ago he'd been numbing himself with drink so he wouldn't have to feel anything. Now, thanks to Maya, he knew his feelings well. A few weeks ago, he couldn't find words to share much of anything. Now his words were ready and just waiting to be spoken. That he loved her. That he wanted to be with her. He knew he couldn't hold them back much longer.

Caleb glanced toward the lambing shed, and saw Jed waving at him. "Hey, since you're already covered in sawdust, want to help me hang some plywood?"

She glanced down at her dusty clothes. "Sure. Don kicked me off the saw. Apparently Trisha's cuts are way straighter than mine, so she's his favorite now."

Caleb laughed. "Don's a character, all right."

"How do you know him?"

"I don't. He runs a lumber mill outside of Santa Rosa somewhere and he's part of a veterans' group there. Someone told him about the barn raising and mentioned that I'm a veteran too. So Don offered to come out with a truckload of wood."

"Wow. He donated all that wood?"

Caleb nodded, still unable to believe the generosity. "Yeah."

Maya laughed. "I can see you cringing when you say that. But the guy wants to help. I'm glad you're letting him."

"I felt like I didn't have a choice. He pulled me aside this morning and told me he'd been injured in the first Gulf War. Went home, got better and volunteered to go back to Iraq again after 9/11. No way could I argue with a guy as brave as that. If he wants to donate wood, he can donate it. Hell, if he wanted to move into the barn, I probably wouldn't say no."

Maya rubbed Einstein's ears, suddenly thoughtful. "It's amazing how many people we see every day have done such incredible things. But you wouldn't know it, just seeing them around town or driving next to them on the road."

"You're one of them. You've changed everything for me." He took a step forward, hoping for the chance to reach for her hand, to tell her what was in his heart.

"We've changed things together," she said briskly. "Come on. Let's go build some walls."

She started for the shed, and he didn't have much choice but to fall in step beside her and keep things light. "Let's just hope you're better with a hammer than that saw."

"Hey, I was decent with the saw! Just not as good as Trisha."

"I've seen you trap and tranquilize a mountain lion. You don't have to be the best with the saw. If you were, the rest of us would get intimidated."

She glanced back at him skeptically. "You're just trying to butter me up so I'll do a good job on your lambing shed."

He played along. "Yeah, that's the reason."

Maya smiled at him for a brief golden instant and then started running ahead down the sloping trail. "Come on, cowboy," she called over her shoulder. Einstein broke into a three-legged gallop and raced to her side. Hobo took off like a streak of orange fire and Caleb knew. Tonight at the party to celebrate the barn raising, he'd tell her how he felt. That he was in love with her. That there had to be a way they could be together. Maybe he'd follow her, just like Hobo and Einstein, even if it meant selling this ranch and buying a new one in Colorado.

Maybe he could make her see that she belonged here with him.

Either way, he had to say something. He'd destroyed them once by lashing out and saying way too much. He wouldn't lose her this time because he was too cowardly to say enough.

THE SUN WAS setting and the ranch was transformed. The lambing shed was completely rebuilt. All it needed was a coat of paint, and Jed said he knew a painter who owed him a favor. The siding on the barn was patched, and the doors and windows fixed. The driveway had been graded, and the barbed-wire fences along it replaced with fancy-looking wooden rails. There was plumbing and wiring and more generosity than Caleb had realized existed in the world.

Caleb hadn't even known that there were so many people living in Shelter Creek, but all day long, as word of the barn raising spread through town and beyond, people kept showing up. They'd had to come up with new projects to accommodate all of the volunteers.

And now it was party time. The Book Biddies had strung lights between Caleb's rewired barn and the oak trees that stood between the barn and the lane. Somehow they'd found a whole bunch of tables, which they'd decorated with colorful tablecloths and jugs of flowers.

People were arriving with dishes of food, bottles of wine and folding chairs. Several members of a local cooking club had brought gas grills, and the smell of barbecue rose, mouthwatering and smoky, from their make-shift kitchen area.

Caleb had been helping the band set up—and how he'd ended up with a band at his barn raising, he had no idea—and now they started into a classic country hit. People gathered around, turning the trampled grass in front of the musicians into a makeshift dance floor.

Maya's grandmother, Lillian, came up to Caleb and pressed a cold beer into his hand. "You look like you could use this," she said quietly.

He hesitated a moment. He hadn't had a drink since the night before Maya had found him on his porch. But it was kindly meant, so he took it, relishing the icy bottle against his sore palms, blistered from a day of hammering. "I don't know how to thank you and your friends," he said. "I don't know why you did it. After the way I treated Maya. After the way I blamed her. The way I let other people blame her."

"Caleb!" Lillian looked a little startled by his blunt honesty. "You can't be held responsible for what you did or said when you were seventeen, right after your sister died."

She was being too kind. "Don't they say that the real measure of who you are comes out in the hard times?"

"That seems a little harsh. What about all the stuff you've done between now and then? What about the years of service to our country? What about the way you've come back here and tried to turn this ranch around?" She reached out and patted his shoulder. "What about the way you've made my granddaughter smile again?"

"I'm not sure I can take credit for that."

She gave him a conspiratorial smile. "Oh I think you can."

Was she matchmaking? He hoped she was, hoped it was a sign that Maya shared his feelings. "Thank you. For all of this." He waved his hand at the party. "You and The Biddies transformed my life today."

"Well, we can all use a little transformation sometimes." She pointed to where Maya stood, talking to Trisha and Emily under the oaks. "You should ask her to dance, you know."

Yep. She was matchmaking. And Caleb's hopes rose in his chest as Lillian bustled off toward her fellow Biddies.

Caleb took a long, slow breath to steady his heart and studied beautiful Maya. She'd changed from her dusty jeans into a knee-length dress that she wore with tan cowgirl boots. Her hair fell down her back in a waterfall of rich brown, except she had braided the pieces in front so they stayed off her face. When she smiled at something Emily said, she chased away the last of the shadows that lurked in the corners of his heart.

He set his beer on a fence post, wiped the damp from his palms and started across the space between them.

## CHAPTER NINETEEN

MAYA LISTENED TO Emily tell Trisha about their night with the mountain lion. It had happened over two weeks ago, but it felt like yesterday, the memories were so vivid.

It was one of the best parts of the job, those brief moments when she got to be close to such an incredible animal.

"Hey." Caleb stood before her. He'd changed into clean jeans and a pale blue button-up shirt. He'd washed the dust of the day from his hair and it was slicked back from his face, one lock falling over his forehead, and she realized she hadn't seen him cleaned up, without his beat-up old cowboy hat, since she'd run into him after the town hall meeting. And that night she'd been flustered. Distracted.

She wasn't prepared for him like this. So handsome, so purposeful, his dark eyes intent on hers, his rolled-up sleeves revealing the tattoos on his forearms, mysterious and compelling, as he held out his hand. "Will you dance with me?"

Maya glanced at her friends and was met with raised eyebrows and big smiles.

"Hi, Caleb," Emily said.

He flushed, like he realized he'd been rude. "Hi, Emily. Hi, Trisha."

"Nice to see you, Caleb." Trisha bit her lip, clearly trying not to laugh.

They were teasing him, teasing her, and it all felt like they were back in high school again. Back when being asked to dance was the biggest thing that happened to any of them.

Actually, considering how little Maya had dated since then, this was still a big deal.

"Have fun!" Emily waved them off.

Maya put her hand in Caleb's, and there was that warmth, that comfort, that sensation of everything falling into place, that came whenever his skin met hers. She resisted the urge to skip as they walked toward the band. Happiness fizzed like champagne beneath her skin. And a sense of recklessness too. She couldn't have Caleb long-term. But what was wrong with enjoying a dance with the most attractive man she'd ever met?

As long as she didn't let herself think their dance meant something more than just a two-step in the dust, she'd be fine. She was already getting emails about her new project in Colorado. A few grad students from the University wanted to assist with her research. Their professor, someone Maya was acquainted with, was even interested in joining them in the field. All this collaboration would be new to Maya. She'd always tried, as much as possible, to work alone.

But maybe one thing this summer in Shelter Creek had taught her was that she had better people skills than she'd realized. So she'd told the professor a tentative yes. They were going to meet up and talk details as soon as she got home.

But thinking about leaving was starting to hurt. She tried to lighten her mood with a lame joke. "Why do I feel like we're leaving for a date?"

Caleb laughed. "And Emily and Trisha are the parents telling you to get home by ten?"

"Something like that. But I doubt they'll ground me if I stay out after curfew."

"That's good to know." His deep voice added a touch of innuendo that rippled over her skin, leaving heat behind. She was already in trouble with Caleb. She'd tried to keep her distance but the truth was, she'd fallen hard. Again. Handed her whole heart to the man who'd shattered it years ago. She was a smart person. So why was she so stupid when it came to Caleb Dunne?

On the makeshift dance floor, he pulled her in close for the slow song the band was playing. Maya really did feel like it was a first date—butterflies, goose bumps and all.

For a moment she closed her eyes, breathing in Caleb's salty, soapy scent, the warmth that seemed to roll off him in waves, making her want him close like this, every day of her life.

His arms were thick and strong around her back. What would it be like to finally give in to the impulse to run her hands over them? To trace his tattoos, to feel his muscles, the corded tendons she tried not to notice when they worked together.

This was ridiculous. She, Maya Burton, serious scientist, loner field biologist, was at a party in the hometown she'd avoided, dancing with the man whom she'd planned to never see again. Worse than that, spending time with Caleb on his ranch had become her favorite part of being home in Shelter Creek.

She'd fought hard against it, these past couple weeks. When they weren't together, she'd kept herself busy, visiting other ranches, doing classroom presentations with Mrs. Axel, building a website for Caleb's ranch, spending time with Grandma, Trisha and The Book Biddies and playing with Einstein. And she'd enjoyed that time a lot.

But Caleb was never far from her mind. She spent way too much time wondering what he was doing, and whether he missed her the same way she missed him.

Leaving him was going to hurt. Not the same kind of hurt she'd felt when they were young. That had been grief and betrayal and rejection and a shattered heart.

This time it would be different. It would be the ache of bad timing and potential unfulfilled. The ache of leaving the man she was falling in love with all over again.

Maybe she was a coward, but she was terrified of that hurt. She knew so well what heartbreak felt like. She'd lived with it for so long and she didn't want more of it, didn't want more loss.

"You're looking at me that way again."

Maya started. "What way?" She'd been so lost in her own frantic thoughts that she'd forgotten to talk with him, to laugh, to do all the things you were supposed to do when a man asked you to dance.

"Like you have some kind of secret that you're trying to keep. But somewhere inside, you really want to tell me what it is."

Why'd he have to be so darn observant?

"No secrets," she said lightly. "I'm just happy about today, and about your ranch. It's going to all work out, Caleb. You're going to make the Bar D a huge success."

"And you?" he asked. "What are you going to do?" His question was somber. Serious. He was requesting a real answer, not one of her silly quips.

"I'm going to finish up here in about a week and move on to my next project. Back to Colorado. In the fall. Brrrr." Oh why was she so lame, adding in weather sound effects? Especially when she could see the strain on his face that told her he hadn't liked her answer.

"What if you stayed?" He stopped dancing all of a sudden. "What if you stayed here with me?"

She stared, trying to take in what he was asking. The song ended and he stepped back, his mouth a tense line. "Can we talk somewhere else?"

Heart pounding in her ears, Maya followed him away from the crowds, until he stopped by the empty corral.

"What if you stayed?" he repeated. "What if we were together?"

"We can't be," she stammered.

"Why not?" He took her hands, so they stood facing each other. "We have so much between us. I liked that kiss on Aidan's ranch. I've wanted to kiss you ever since. I wanted to kiss you when we were dancing. I want to kiss you so badly, all the time."

She could swear she could feel each word like a spark on her skin. Of course she wanted to kiss him. It was almost all she thought about anymore. But kissing him again was a terrible idea. Because that kiss on Aidan's ranch hadn't been just a kiss. It had been the start of a bond that she knew she would never be able to break. "Kissing is just chemicals," she whispered breathlessly. "Pheromones. It's basic science."

He pulled on her hands, just enough to bring her a step closer. "But you like science."

"I do." The two breathy words were all she could manage because he was stealing her oxygen as he pulled her another small step closer.

"I like science too. And I have a hypothesis. That you're scared to kiss me. Because you know that once we start kissing, neither of us will want to stop. Ever."

Maya closed her eyes to avoid the intent in his. He must have leaned closer because she could feel his breath mixing with hers and his forehead gently touching her own.

"Some science just leads to destruction," she whispered. "Like the atomic bomb."

"But most of it makes life better. Inventions. Innovations. Healing."

She opened her eyes. His mouth was so close, only inches from hers. "And what kind are you offering?"

"The very best kind."

Of course it was, and she had to kiss him. It was science. Planets orbited the sun, predators hunted prey and she needed to kiss Caleb Dunne. It was just one more fact of life that wasn't good or bad— it just *was*.

Her heart was skipping, speeding, her blood rushing in her ears like water in a snowmelt river. She shouldn't do this. It would just make things harder.

But she was suddenly so tired of fear. She'd been paralyzed by it for so long. Protecting her heart also meant muffling it, smothering the joy out of it and missing out on what it felt like when Caleb took her gently by the shoulders, when he bent down because he was so tall and she was so ridiculously short, when he pushed her hair back from her face with careful fingertips. His lips brushed hers, just enough, as if he was trying to be sure that this was truly okay, as if he was still asking permission.

With a quick apology to her heart, to her soul, to everything that would break because of what she was about to do, Maya whispered *yes* to the question he hadn't asked out loud. Because wanting him, needing him, had been a part of her since they were young. It had never gone away, it just lived on quietly under the guilt and regret she carried. It had gone dormant, until she'd come back to face him again.

She slid her hands up around his neck,

which meant going on tiptoe, which meant acknowledging the breadth of him, the massive muscles that marked him as the complex man she'd come to know.

He'd been through so much she couldn't fathom. He'd been to war, killed, made mistakes he had to somehow carry, just as she carried her own. And the fact that he knew what that weight was like, what that burden meant, brought her heart even closer to his. When she pressed her lips to his, it was as if they blended into one being—strong, burdened, determined, worn down, but somehow still moving forward and still hanging on to hope.

He kissed her back, kissed her until her breath came in gasps, until she was clinging to him for support and balance, because his kisses could make her world spin, and make her forget who they were and who they'd been.

Tears stung in her eyes, because though she'd wished and wondered, she hadn't known it would be like this. That he would tilt her entire world, so when she pulled away, the twilight, the corral, everything looked different. Changed. Or maybe she was.

Caleb wrapped her in his arms and let out a breath that tickled her hair with what seemed like relief. Or maybe that was her, so grateful, so relieved that she wasn't alone with all of these feelings anymore. He was right here with her, feeling it all too.

She leaned into his chest, listening to the steady thud of his heart, giving her weight to his solid, strong frame.

"Maya." He straightened, brought his fingers to gently rest at her jaw. He kissed her hair, her forehead and the tip of her nose, and his dark gaze—eyes so brown they could be black—found and held hers. "I love you. You know that, right? I love you."

The miracle of words she'd never hoped to hear again had her wrapping her arms around his waist. As if by holding on tightly, she could hold on to those words, this feeling, this fantasy.

"Do you think it's possible?" He kissed her hair and put his cheek to it, and she could feel his heart speeding up, his arms wrapping around her back, holding her tighter. "Do you think we could be possible?"

Tears welled up, because there it was. They weren't possible.

She could be brave on the dance floor and by this corral, for a few moments. But Caleb was a risk. A huge risk. Until a few weeks ago he'd been drunk, angry and lost. And he could be that way again, so easily. An accident, an addiction, and he could turn around and tell her to get out of his life.

He'd done it before and she'd left this town broken and devastated. And she'd worked for years to build a life for herself that made her strong, so strong that she did what most people couldn't fathom. Hiked the highest peaks, worked in the most remote wilderness, studied the most dangerous animals. *That* was where she belonged. Not here, wondering if she was incentive enough for Caleb to overcome his demons.

She'd be forever grateful that she came home and helped him get on his feet again. That she had a chance to make some amends. And she'd never, ever forget that kiss.

Maya stepped back out of his arms, on legs that almost refused to obey, like her body wasn't willing to do what her mind knew she must. "It's not possible. I love you, Caleb. I don't know if I ever stopped loving you. But we are not possible."

His eyes narrowed, his gaze honed in on hers as if willing her to take those words back. "I get it. You're scared because I was a jerk. I'm the messed-up guy who was passed out on the porch that day. But you've shown me a different way to be. You've turned things around for me, and as part of that, I've changed. Can't you see that I've changed?"

His words only fueled her resolve. They were the evidence that supported all her fears. "That's the problem, Caleb. *I* turned things around for you. But that's not enough. I have to know that you can turn things around for yourself. That when things get hard, you aren't going to drink until you pass out, or tell me to get out of your life."

And there it was. The truth. It sounded hard and cold, and the words hung between them, sharp and stark in their honesty.

The hurt on his face was hard to witness.

"I should go." Maya walked backward a few steps. "Caleb, I'm sorry. I don't want to hurt you. But this is better, for both of us."

She'd only made it a few yards away, and already she wanted to run right back to him. To kiss the hurt off his face, to tell him she hadn't meant it. But as much as she loved him, had always love him, he was a risk she couldn't afford to take twice.

"Don't worry," she managed through the lump in her throat. "I'll still administer the grant. I'll finish the website for your ranch and I'll get someone from the Department of Wildlife to come by this area periodically, to check in about the pumas. But I think I'm going to go back to Colorado a little early. It makes the most sense, for both of us."

He finally spoke, his voice heavy with emotion. "Don't do this. Don't leave when we're just getting started."

"We shouldn't start. We lived without each other for years and we both did okay. We both made progress in our lives. We both accomplished things." She backed away from him as she spoke, needing space between them or she'd never be strong enough to do this. She was desperate to run into his arms, into that warmth, to try to reclaim that perfect kiss, that perfect moment that had made her feel so blissfully whole.

"Is that enough for you?" Caleb asked in a hollowed-out voice. "To do okay? To make progress? To accomplish things? Because to me that sounds like survival. And I'm tired of surviving. It's all I did, for years. You make me feel alive, Maya. I want to keep feeling that way."

Tears were coming now, rushing down her face in a silent river, coming too fast for sobbing, too fast to control. "Maybe that was what was meant to be. Me and you, coming together to finally heal this hurt between us. So we can go forward in our own lives."

"No." He shook his head and took a step toward her, one hand out in a plea. "That's not all it was."

She had to go now, or she wouldn't go at all. "I'll be in touch, Caleb. I promise I'll help you finish what we started on the ranch. But I'd better go."

His nod was barely there, but she took it as an agreement. He stood, hands balled into fists at his side, jaw rigid, eyes full of hurt. But she couldn't fix that for him. Couldn't fix anything more for him. It was time to get out, to save herself and her heart before she got in too deep.

She skirted the edge of the party to avoid seeing anyone, and surprised Einstein out of a nap when she climbed into her truck. Gunning the engine, she got them off the ranch before she could change her mind. Out on the main road, she slowed down and waited for relief to come. Relief that she'd kept her heart safe this time. That she was heading home to Colorado, where she belonged.

But relief didn't come. Not when she pulled into Grandma's driveway. Not as she let herself into the house and inhaled the sweet lavender smell. Not when she packed her bags, so she'd be ready to leave in the morning.

As she lay on her childhood bed, holding Einstein close, she understood. There was no relief to be found by walking away from the person who mattered most. But there was a strange peace, knowing that no one could ever hurt her as much as she'd just hurt herself.

Grandma Lillian's house had felt like such a comfortable refuge for these past six weeks. But tonight it was silent and strange, and there was no comfort to be had. And Maya wondered if her cottage in Boulder, or the mountains, or any place would ever feel like home again, now that she knew what it was like to be in Caleb's arms.

## CHAPTER TWENTY

CALEB DOWNED HIS whiskey in one gulp, trying not to remember Maya's words. *I have to know that you can turn things around for yourself. That when things get hard, you aren't going to drink until you pass out, or tell me to get out of your life.*

Well, he hadn't told her to get out of his life. She'd done that all by herself. And he wasn't drinking until he passed out tonight, or at least, not yet.

The power of low expectations. She'd expected him to drink again, and here he was. Though it wasn't really fair to blame her. He'd gotten to Dex's all by himself.

Of course he'd had to wait for the barn raising party to finish. He'd stood around, trying to talk with all of the folks who'd helped him today, to thank them again for their incredible gift of time and effort. And he thought maybe he'd pulled it off. That none of them had realized they were talking to an empty man. A man with no heart. Because the woman he loved had taken it with her and was currently tossing it in a suitcase to take to Colorado.

Maybe she'd put it on a shelf there, like a trophy.

Okay, his thinking was getting a little crazy, but a few glasses of JD would do that to a guy, especially a guy who hadn't drunk anything for about a month.

Dex was behind the bar tonight, watching Caleb with a worried crease between his thick brows. "Haven't seen you in here in a long time," the bar owner said. "I have to say I was kind of happy about that."

Caleb grunted a response.

"But now that you're here, you look like hell. Is there anything I can do?"

"Nah."

Dex went to fill a couple of pints at the other end of the bar and then came back. "Is this about your ranch? Seems like you should be celebrating. The whole town was out there, working on it today, I heard. I would have been there too, but Royce is off on some fishing trip, so I'm on my own here."

"That's very kind of you, Dex. Everyone has been very kind. I'm a lucky guy—I truly am."

He tried to feel it, the gratitude that should have him moved to tears right about now. Tears were close, but they were more about Maya than his ranch. And more about loss than gratitude.

But the gratitude was there too, and maybe that was one more thing Maya had taught him. That it was possible to have a lot of feelings at once. After Julie had died, he'd let grief take over, as the one emotion he felt. And it had shattered his love for Maya and their future together. Now he could feel it all. His heartache over her, and a profound sense of awe that his town had shown up for him the way they had today.

It was a whole lot of emotion, all jumbled and mismatched. And Caleb wanted to be numb enough to dull the jagged edges.

"Caleb, there you are." It was Jace, looking like he was still in dad mode, with a worried crease between his eyes. "I got your phone message just now—I couldn't hear it too well. Are you okay?"

The floor under Caleb's feet felt a little unsteady when he rose to clap his friend on the shoulder. "Thanks for coming. Let's celebrate my fancy, fixed-up ranch. Come on." Caleb walked across the floor that seemed suddenly uneven, and braced himself on the wall while he wrote his name on the chalkboard for a pool table. Jeez, he was drunk. His tolerance must have gone way down. Or maybe alcohol just affected you a lot worse when your hopes had crumbled into dust.

A hand came down on his shoulder. Jace was peering at him with worry and a touch of his usual humor. "You look like hell, my friend. What can I do? Bring you home?"

"No." That was the last thing he wanted, to go back to the ranch that had become his and Maya's, their project, their vision. "Grab us a couple beers."

"I think you've had plenty to drink," Jace said grimly. "I don't see you for a few hours, and now you're here looking like you got run down by a tractor or something. This has to be about Maya."

"She's leaving for Colorado. She doesn't want this." Caleb gestured around the bar as if it represented all of Shelter Creek. "She doesn't want us."

"I'm sorry."

Caleb had to keep moving. Keep busy. If he kept busy, maybe he wouldn't fall into the void where his heart used to be. A pool table was standing empty. It wasn't Caleb's turn yet; there was someone ahead of him on the list, but whoever that idiot was, he was forfeiting his spot. Caleb grabbed a cue and handed another to Jace. "Let's just play pool."

"Hey, dude, that's our table." This from a college-aged kid who was sitting with his buddies, well into the pitcher of beer in between them.

"It's not your table if you're not using it," Caleb said.

"My name is on the board." The young man stood up unsteadily. "Can't you read?"

"What, you think I look stupid?" Caleb stepped forward, the frustration that he could push himself so hard to become the man Maya deserved and she'd still walk away making him lash out.

Icy beer sluiced over him, washing off the last reason he should hold back. Caleb lunged and knocked the pitcher out of the kid's hand, and heard Jace shout somewhere through the buzzing adrenaline, "Caleb, don't!"

It was too late. He was swinging hard,

punching the guy who'd doused him in beer, wrestling off his buddy who'd jumped on his back. It was cathartic, going after this tangible problem, when there was so much he couldn't solve.

A blur of blows became his only issue. He took one to the gut, and another to the face. Jace jumped in to help him, but they were outnumbered. Still, they both kept swinging, kept going until the crowd parted and there were several sheriff's deputies, and one of them was Adam, shaking his head in disgust as he snapped handcuffs onto Caleb's wrists.

In moments he and Jace were in the parking lot, in the back of Adam's car, cuffed and bruised. Caleb's head was spinning—whether from the alcohol or the punches, he wasn't quite sure.

Jace slammed a shoulder into him.

"Hey!" Caleb turned, surprised to see his friend's face drawn with rage.

"Why can't you keep your cool, Caleb? What the hell?"

"He threw beer on me." Caleb stared at Jace a little disoriented, his thoughts booze-blurred. Shouldn't they be laughing about this right now? Plotting about how they were going to talk Adam into letting them go? "Why are you so mad?"

Jace made a strangled noise of sheer frustration. "I came out for one beer, one *damn* beer, because you sounded upset. And you lose it. You get in a fight. Now I'm sitting in the back of this cop car when I have kids at home, waiting for me."

Caleb had never seen his friend so angry. Jace's eyes were wide, his nostrils flared, and he rammed his shoulder into Caleb again.

In another time, another place, it would have been funny—Jace furious, trying to fight him with his arms cuffed behind his back. But Caleb could see real fear behind the fury in his buddy's eyes.

"I'm sorry, Jace. When that guy poured beer on me, I just lost it." Something in him crumpled. He was falling down into some dark Maya-less place. A chasm with no end he could foresee. But he hadn't meant to drag Jace down with him.

"Why are you so angry? Is it because of Julie? Because of whatever happened to you in Afghanistan? Because I'm *sick* of it, Caleb!"

Jace was yelling now, and Caleb had never seen him lose it like this.

"I'm *sick* of you being sorry for yourself. If you got messed up in the head in combat, go see a therapist. If you are sad about Julie, or Maya, cry. But stop trying to fix your problems with a bottle and a brawl." Jace ran out of steam and sat back in the seat. "Or at least do it far away from me."

Caleb stared out into the dark parking lot, at Adam's back, as the deputy wrote something on a tablet, probably some police form or another, getting ready to take them down to the jail.

Jace's words sat on his skin like a heated brand, stark and true. Here he was, drunk, acting like a sniveling victim. Again.

"I'm sorry." Jace's voice was quiet in the dark. "I've got a lot at stake here. I'm trying to take care of these kids and I've got social services breathing down my neck, telling me every five minutes that I'm doing it all wrong. Getting arrested tonight—well, it's not going to help my case."

Caleb's stomach churned. "Could you lose the kids?"

He'd never heard his friend's voice sound

so dull. "It's a very real possibility at this point. I was never going to win any dad-of-the-year prizes, but..." Jace's voice trailed off.

"I'm sorry. I didn't know. I'll do whatever I can to fix it." Caleb cast around his foggy brain, frantic to repair what he'd broken. "I'll tell them it was all my fault. I'll meet with the social worker, or whoever, and I'll explain." The drink in Caleb's stomach turned sour. He'd been so selfish, caught up in his own pain.

"If I need you, I'll let you know." Jace blew out a long, shaky breath. "For now just start dealing with your problems. And not here, at Dex's."

Shame was crushing Caleb down into the car seat. This was what Maya had predicted. One of the main reasons she'd left. She'd seen it too, this weakness in him. "I will. I'm really sorry, Jace."

They sat in silence for a long moment, and then Jace spoke again. "You're in love with Maya?"

"Yeah." It felt good to confess it. To be honest for once about what he was feeling.

"So, what the hell are you waiting for? Become the guy she deserves. Can't you see you need help? Do you need any more proof than this?"

Jace had nailed it. There was nothing like sitting in cuffs in the back of a cop car to tell you that something wasn't right in your world. Caleb started laughing softly, and when Jace looked at him with a raised eyebrow, he laughed harder. "I'm sorry," he gasped. "But you're right. It doesn't really get more pathetic than this."

And then Jace was laughing too, and that's how Adam found them when he finally opened the car door. Leaning on each other, laughing like a couple of hysterical, handcuffed fools.

Out in the open air, Adam unlocked their cuffs.

"Please don't cite Jace," Caleb said. "He wasn't down here, drinking. He just came in to check on me. This was all my fault. I started that fight."

"All your fault?" Adam eyed Jace sternly. "No one made you jump in, Jace."

"True," Jace admitted. "But he was outnumbered. What would you do?"

Adam shook his head. "Not answering that. I wrote you up a ticket for disturbing the peace. Just pay it and we'll call it quits." He handed Jace a slip of paper.

"Caleb, you'll get a notice to appear in court. You'll need to be there. Don't mess it up." Adam put a hand to Caleb's shoulder and gave him a quick shake. "Dude, you have got to get some therapy."

Jace snorted a laugh. "It's unanimous."

Adam looked from him to Caleb. "I'm not sure what's funny about this. All I know is that, Caleb, if you do anything like this ever again, even ten years from now, I'll lock you up and lose the key."

Caleb shoved his citation in his pocket. He thought he'd made progress. Thought he was growing up, making peace. Yet here he was, right back where he'd been when Maya first arrived in Shelter Creek.

Jace got in his truck and drove away. It killed Caleb to think that he'd put Jace's nieces and nephew at any kind of risk. Would they be sent to a different foster home because he'd messed up? It was almost too awful to think about.

"You're not driving," Adam said.

"Nope."

"You need a ride?"

"Thanks, but I'm going to walk." A long walk alone in the fog and the night. Because it was time he took a good look at himself. Maya was right. He had to find a way to face the hard times without blaming and drinking. Jace and Adam were right. He had to take responsibility and grow up.

He'd start right now. "I'm sorry, Adam. You've given me a lot of breaks since I got home, and I messed up again. This is the last fight. The last citation. I promise."

Adam clapped him on the back. "I'm holding you to that."

Caleb turned and started walking. He had five miles in front of him. Five dark, quiet, country miles to sober up and get his head together. He remembered suddenly what Maya had said a few weeks ago. *Sometimes the long roads are the ones worth walking.*

Tomorrow morning he'd call the VA and start on that road. He just hoped that if he worked hard enough, and walked long enough, his road would eventually lead him back to her.

## *CHAPTER TWENTY-ONE*

MAYA SAT IN her cottage in Boulder and studied her to-do list. Unfortunately she'd checked off most of the items already, and she wasn't scheduled to hike into the mountains and start her research for another week. Coming back early from Shelter Creek had given her a head start on all of her preparations. Her desperate need to stay busy, so she wouldn't think too much, or hurt too much, meant she was way ahead of schedule.

But with her to-do list done, she couldn't put off the inevitable any longer. She'd promised Caleb she'd still help with the grant and make sure he had everything he needed. But for the past couple of weeks, she hadn't been able to bring herself to open those files.

She'd work on that now, get it over with and then she wouldn't think about him ever again.

Ha. That was like saying she didn't need to eat or breathe. Thinking of him came naturally, every minute of every day. His rare smile, his dark eyes. The way he'd looked, awestruck and motivated, after they'd collared that lion. The way they'd kissed before she'd said goodbye.

She'd driven back to Colorado, wondering if she'd made a mistake. But one homesick day, when she'd gone on the website for the *Shelter Creek Sentinel*, she'd come across the police log. And there it was. Caleb Dunne. Arrested for drunk and disorderly conduct the night she'd said goodbye.

It had broken her heart all over again. And also made her think that she'd made the right decision about them. Caleb had a lot to figure out, and he had to do it on his own.

She opened her laptop and clicked on the financial spreadsheet for the grant money. It was a shared document, and Caleb had made some notes on expenses, including batteries for solar-powered lighting and improved fencing in the corrals by the lambing shed.

Seeing those impersonal notes felt personal. Footsteps he'd left behind as he walked through a life she couldn't be a part of anymore.

Her chat application pinged, and a window popped up. It was Grandma. They chatted every day, usually about her adventures with The Biddies. So much had already changed in the three weeks since Maya had left. Monique was a true cougar now, dating a younger man, a mechanic at Shelter Creek Auto. Annie and Juan Alvaro had been on a few very nice dates, and Grandma suspected they were falling in love. And The Book Biddies were reading a nonfiction book about powerful women in history. Grandma was inspired and thinking about running for a position on the town council.

Trisha hadn't been stopping by to visit as often lately, and Grandma was a bit concerned. And Einstein was doing well, but still slept near the door, as if he expected Maya to come home any minute. Maya had hated to leave her beloved dog. But she had decided, at the last moment, that he deserved a comfortable life. Not a life traipsing through the Rockies on three legs.

Plus knowing Grandma had Einstein for company made Maya feel a lot less guilty about leaving.

But oh my, she missed them both.

Grandma's next piece of news came through as if she'd written it in blinking neon.

Caleb is doing well. He's getting all kinds of help. He's getting sober.

That's great to hear.

But I know he misses you. He comes by with treats for Einstein and flowers for me, but it's all just an excuse to ask how you are.

Maya stared at the chat box. Coming back to Colorado had seemed like such an obvious choice when she'd made it. All she'd been able to think about was that falling in love with Caleb was dangerous. That coming home was safe, organized and planned.

Yet now that she was here, all the things that used to feel like they gave her life meaning—the science, the work—seemed like...not enough. It still mattered, it still felt important, but it didn't feel like enough.

She'd created a life here that was safe from emotion and insulated from risk. Yet now her carefully crafted world felt sterile. And empty. Because there was no love.

And not just love of Caleb. Maya typed to her grandmother again.

I miss you. I miss you and Trisha and Annie and Mrs. Axel and everyone.

Grandma wrote back.

We miss you too. Eva got a few grants for her wildlife center. Also several big private donors are on board. It's really going to happen. And she'd love it if you'd run it. Just saying.

Maya stared as the words opened doors. Eva had done it. She was making her dream of a wildlife center come true. And there would be work for Maya, meaningful work, in Shelter Creek. Not just a summer contract from an underfunded government agency, but private money. She could do real, meaningful research on the lions there. She could ask Mrs. Axel to help her create more educational programs.

And Caleb was getting help. She typed back to Grandma.

That sounds amazing. I'll think about it.

Oh and one more thing and then I have to go meet The Biddies for movie night. I ran

into Caleb today, and he asked me if you'd
checked the website recently. The one you
built for his ranch? I told him I'd remind you.

Thanks Grandma. Have fun tonight. Love you.

Grandma sent a few heart emojis and went
offline.

Maya typed in the web address for the Bar
D Ranch. She'd created this site for Caleb, so
interested ranchers could learn about all the
things he was doing to deter predators. She'd
also added a page where people could follow
the video feed from one of the most successful wildlife cameras she'd installed. She was
surprised to see that it already had a few hundred followers.

Although she'd taught Caleb how to post on
the blog page, she wasn't aware that he'd used
it yet. So she was surprised to see several
posts there. He'd blogged about the higher
fences he was installing near the lambing
shed. And he'd written about his flerd, with
photos of his sheep and cattle standing around
together, looking a little confused.

Pride and excitement mixed as Maya read
through all of his posts. The last one was a

video he'd uploaded two days ago. With a mix of anticipation and dread at seeing him and hearing his voice, she clicked on it.

He was standing by the newly painted barn wall, facing a camera he must have set up on a tripod, wearing his old battered brown cowboy hat and a self-conscious smile. "I'm Caleb Dunne," he said. "Owner of the Bar D Ranch in Shelter Creek, California."

An orange blur had Caleb staggering off camera, and then returning with a sheepish smile. "And this is Hobo the cat." Hobo looked at the camera and then nuzzled the brim of Caleb's hat, knocking it askew. "He makes sure I don't get too full of myself."

Maya smiled, tears rising as she took in his beloved face, his gruff voice, his ridiculous cat.

"I just wanted to explain to you all why I'm doing the work I am here at the Bar D. You see, besides being a working sheep-and-cattle ranch, the Bar D is becoming a demonstration ranch for wildlife management. People can visit and learn about methods to keep common predators, like coyotes and mountain lions, away from livestock.

"I didn't used to care much about preserving predators. I thought they were a problem best solved with a rifle and a bullet. But then I met someone."

Caleb stilled, as if he'd lost his train of thought for a moment. Then he reached up to scratch Hobo's ears and cleared his throat. "This person is a scientist, a wildlife biologist, and she taught me that predators like mountain lions don't kill because they want to mess with ranchers like me. They are simply animals acting on instinct, doing what they're meant to do.

"She taught me that sometimes people act on instinct too. Just like a mountain lion, we might attack or hide or go looking for new territory. But the thing is, unlike mountain lions, we have the power to think things through, to realize that we've made mistakes, to learn how to do things better."

His voice went a little hoarse. "Maya, if you're listening, please know that I'm trying to do better. A whole lot better. I just want you to know that."

Caleb and Hobo approached the camera and the video stopped.

Maya closed her computer and shoved it into her backpack. Then she started throwing things into a duffel bag. She had a week before her project started and her to-do list was done. So she'd catch a flight from Denver. She'd go home to Shelter Creek, to see Grandma and Einstein and Trisha and The Biddies. And Caleb. Because she wanted to try to do better too.

For years she'd craved the solitude of the wilderness, always looking for an excuse to avoid people, to avoid her memories and to avoid ever being hurt again. Like the solitary pumas she studied, hiding out alone was her instinct, her way of staying safe.

But like Caleb, she didn't want to act on instinct anymore. Maya wanted people, her people—Grandma, Trisha and The Biddies. She wanted to be a part of Shelter Creek and life with all of its unknowns. She wanted love. And she wanted Caleb Dunne.

## CHAPTER TWENTY-TWO

THE PUPPIES HAD arrived and Caleb was new-parent nervous. He checked the small notepad he kept in his pocket, where he'd written down everything the trainer he'd consulted had said about his two brand-new guard dogs, each just a few pounds of Anatolian shepherd fluff and a whole lot of energy.

"Okay, guys." He knelt down next to them in the stall full of clean wood shavings that he'd converted into a kennel. "For tonight, and the next week or so, you'll be in here. The sheep will be next door so you can get used to them. You'll meet them when you're bigger."

It was silly to talk to the puppies but the thing was, he'd gotten used to having someone to talk to during the couple of weeks that Maya had worked on the ranch with him. It was hard to go back to silence after that.

"Look at you. The proud puppy-daddy."

Caleb jumped up, startled. Maya was leaning on the stall door, her eyes bright with emotion. "They're so cute," she said. "May I come in?"

"Of course." His heart thudded hard on his ribs. He couldn't believe she was here. He wanted to reach out, to hold her, but he folded his arms across his chest instead.

Maya came around the stall door, dressed in her usual faded jeans, a flannel plaid shirt and that old ball cap. She flashed him a shy smile and went down on her knees, giggling as the puppies clambered all over her. "Hi, guys." She let them sniff her knuckles and reached out to pet the bolder of the two, smiling as his pink tongue popped out and slurped her fingers. "I love their black muzzles."

Caleb knelt next to her, trying to take in her presence. Was she visiting? Was it possible she'd changed her mind about him? About them?

"Hard to believe they're going to turn into giant dogs like Aidan's." Maya picked one up, gave it a quick kiss on the head and set it back down. Then she looked over at him, her smile wide and wondering. "It's so good to see you. How have you been?"

*Missing you*, he wanted to say. But he

didn't know what she was thinking, hadn't even known she was coming back to Shelter Creek. Hadn't even let himself hope she would. "I've been okay," he told her.

"I saw the video you posted on the blog. I loved it."

"I'm glad." His face felt hot. It had been a geeky thing to do. But he had to try something. And the thought of calling her, or emailing her, when she'd already told him *no*, made him feel like a stalker. So he'd figured he'd try the blog. Then she could just ignore it if it meant nothing to her.

"You said you were trying to do better."

He took a breath, bolstering himself, because admitting his troubles was still pretty new to him. "I've been doing some counseling and some support groups at the VA in Santa Rosa." On impulse, he reached into his pocket and pulled out his talisman. "My silver chip for my first twenty-four hours sober. I'll get a red one soon for thirty days."

"You're doing it." Tears welled in her eyes. "Caleb, I'm so proud of you."

He shoved the chip back in his pocket. "Well, one day at a time, right? But it hasn't been too hard. Maybe because I'd already stopped drinking for most of the time you were here in Shelter Creek. I slipped up for one night. The night you left. Then I got some help."

"I'm glad it hasn't felt hard. I hope it continues to be easy."

He knew there was more she could say. Her parents' legacy loomed. They'd chosen alcohol and drugs over her. He'd never do that; it was something he felt sure of. "I feel like, for me, maybe alcohol was a bandage over some big emotional scars. Now that I'm dealing with those, I don't feel the need for a drink. But I promise you, Maya, I'll keep working at my sobriety. Always."

She nodded, focused on the bigger puppy, holding out her fingers for the little guy to lick, and then pulling them away when he started nipping.

Caleb let a few more moments go by, and then couldn't wait any longer. He needed to know if this was a quick visit to check on his progress with the grant, or something more. "Do you want to tell me why you're here? I thought you'd be in Colorado, chasing lions."

She smiled but her eyes weren't full of their usual sparkle. "The lion chasing doesn't start until next week. But here's the thing. I don't really want to chase Colorado lions anymore. I think I'd prefer to chase the ones living around Shelter Creek."

Caleb tried not to move, tried not to scare her by whooping, jumping up into the air, dancing—any of the crazy things her words made him want to do. Instead he kept his gaze on the smaller puppy, tickling it with a piece of straw that the little guy pounced on and wrestled into submission. "What made you change your mind?"

"Well, Eva is actually making her dream of a Shelter Creek Wildlife Center come true. And she's hiring me to help make it happen. We're also looking for funding for a more extensive mountain lion study. There's still very little known about the mountain lions around here. We have a lot to learn."

Caleb turned to face her then. Her cheeks were pink and her eyes solemn as she studied him for his reaction. "What do you think about that?"

His voice was husky. She was coming home. He had a chance. *They* had a chance. "I think the Shelter Creek lions are pretty lucky to have you on their side."

"And I came home because I don't want to be away from Grandma anymore. Or Trisha or The Book Biddies or…" Her pink cheeks went pinker. "You."

It was the answer to his prayers. "I'm even luckier than those lions."

She stood then, held out a hand and hauled him up out of the wood chips. Small but mighty. Then she went on tiptoe, wrapped her arms around his neck and kissed him, her lips soft and warm and perfect against his.

He held her for a long moment, breathing in the sweet scent of her hair, overwhelmed by the risk she was taking, coming back here to start again with him, knowing he had troubles, that he was a work in progress. He might be the former soldier but she was the brave one. "What about your project in Colorado?"

"There's a professor who is really interested in the idea. He's taking over the grant and he's going to work on the project with a couple of his grad students."

"Well, I'm grateful to him, whoever he is, for tying up your loose ends."

Maya looked up at him with warmth and acceptance in her eyes. "I love you," she said.

"I'm sorry I ran away. I think I got used to running, to hiding, when things got hard. But when I got to Colorado, it didn't seem like home anymore. You're my home. And I'd like to stay here, with you."

Relief flooded Caleb's veins. Warm, sweet relief. He'd been trying so hard to go forward without her, reminding himself that he should be grateful that she'd come back into his life and turned it around. Telling himself that he was greedy to want more.

But he did want more. So much more. He wanted to love her again. To build a new life with her, here in their hometown. "You don't need to apologize to me. There is plenty about me that you'd be smart to run from. But I'm working really hard to get that stuff under control. To be a man good enough for a woman like you. I promise you, I'll do it, Maya. I'll make it my life's work to be the kind of guy you deserve. I just want a chance to love you. Forever this time."

Tears welled in her eyes, making the brown glitter. "I'd like to love you forever too. If you don't mind."

"I really don't mind." He kissed her, savoring her sweet mouth, wrapping his arms around her tiny, mighty frame, breathing her in. She was here. With him.

A small tug on his pant leg had him setting her aside so he could look down. The smaller of the two puppies looked up at him with big black eyes. "Looks like it might be feeding time," he told Maya.

"Let's get them their dinner then," Maya said. "And then we need to go see Grandma. I think she's planning something to welcome us home."

Caleb opened his mouth to protest that he didn't need a homecoming celebration. That he'd been in Shelter Creek a few months now. But then he realized that Grandma Lillian was, as usual, absolutely right. He *was* finally home, now that Maya was here with him.

MAYA HELD CALEB'S hand as they crested the ridge and walked out into the open field. A full moon was rising, bathing every leaf, every blade of grass, in silver. They started along the path to where they'd met that first night, when they'd each thought the other was a mountain lion.

"It's gorgeous," she said, looking up at the sky.

"A harvest moon." Caleb came to stand behind her and wrapped his arms around her to hold her close. He kissed her hair. Her cheek. "I am so glad you are finally here for good."

Maya had spent most of the past month traveling back and forth between Boulder and Shelter Creek, packing up her cottage, cleaning out her office and supporting the professor who'd taken over her research project. As of yesterday she was officially here, living with Grandma for now, while Caleb finished remodeling his house on the ranch. Because no way was he going to let her live there until, as he put it, it was beautiful, like her.

They walked to the spot where Caleb had emerged from the bushes and Maya had fallen onto her back like a turtle.

Together they spread their picnic blanket on the ground and sat down. Caleb started unloading the backpack he'd carried. "Champagne, bread, cheese, strawberries and—wait, hang on…"

Maya craned her neck, trying to see. He'd insisted on packing the food for their midnight picnic himself, so she had no idea what he'd brought.

"Would you look at this?" Caleb held up a small square box. "How did this get in here?"

It was a ring box. Maya's heart leaped and she covered her mouth with her hands, as if she could somehow contain her surprise that way. It was hard to speak, because she was smiling so hard. He'd bought this for her. But with what? He was already putting any extra money he could find into his remodeling project.

"You shouldn't have done this. Not right now. Not when we're so low on money."

He took her hand in his. "You'll have to complain to Eva. She had it in her gallery and she insisted I take it. She told me I'm not allowed to pay her for at least a year. Not until the tax bill is settled and the house is done and I'm on my feet."

Maya felt tears rise. "That is so kind." Love for Eva, for The Biddies and for him had tears rising. "Okay, now I'm going to cry again. And I feel like I cry so much these days. Happy tears."

"As long as they're happy." Caleb rose to his knees in front of her. "I know you love being out in wide-open places like this. So I thought I'd ask you here, in hopes that you'll be more likely to say yes. You're everything to me, Maya. My home. My heart. Will you marry me?"

His words, the beauty of them, stole her ability to answer. He opened the ring box, and the band of diamonds glittered in the moonlight. "Will you please say yes?"

"Of course I will." It wasn't possible to stop the tears as he slid the sparkling ring onto her finger. Tears of hope and gratitude and so much more. She wrapped her arms around him and held on tight. She'd almost lost him again. Until she'd found the courage to come home for good.

A rustling noise in the bushes behind them stilled her. Caleb must have heard it too, because he put a finger to his lips. Slowly they let go of each other, slid apart and looked toward the sound, somewhere out in the shadows and brush.

Maya reached for the flashlight in her pocket and waited. It took several deep breaths and a whole bunch of pounding heartbeats, but eventually a form, long and low, emerged from the bushes and stepped into the path. "Let's stand up," Maya whispered to Caleb. He rose, and so did she, until they stood side by side, sending the message that they were not prey.

Caleb brought his arm around her, instantly protective.

Maya switched on the flashlight and there it was. Rounded ears, low shoulders, high haunches, endless tail. Its eyes fixed on them, glassy green in the light.

"It's wearing a collar," Caleb murmured. "Do you think it's *our* mountain lion?"

Maya tried to see the ear tag, but the puma was too far away, and the night was too dark. "It easily could be. We can check the tracking app later on."

"I bet it's our guy. I just have a feeling."

"It has stayed fairly close to your ranch since we collared it," she reminded him.

Caleb kissed her hair. "But it hasn't come *on* the ranch. Thanks to you and all your predator tricks."

She laughed quietly and the mountain lion backed away a few paces.

"See?" Caleb teased. "You're a lion whisperer."

"We should scare it away. We don't want it to get used to people. Or try to steal our picnic."

"I don't want it to go."

Maya tipped her head up to get a better look at him, raising her brows in exaggerated shock. "Caleb Dunne," she murmured. "That is the last thing I ever thought I'd hear you say about a mountain lion."

He laughed softly. "I guess things changed for me. Starting with a moonlit night, a whole lot like this one."

Maya went on tiptoe to kiss his cheek. "I'm glad things changed. For both of us."

Caleb pulled her against him. His arms were the comfort that Maya had longed for, all of those years apart.

In a flicker of shadowy motion, the mountain lion leaped into the bushes and was gone. Maya wasn't surprised. It was following its instincts, seeking the safety of solitude, out in wild places. It was back where it belonged.

And so was she. It had been a long road. But she'd finally made it home.

* * * * *

# Get 4 FREE REWARDS!

## We'll send you 2 FREE Books plus 2 FREE Mystery Gifts.

**Love Inspired®** books feature contemporary inspirational romances with Christian characters facing the challenges of life and love.

FREE Value Over $20

---

**YES!** Please send me 2 FREE Love Inspired® Romance novels and my 2 FREE mystery gifts (gifts are worth about $10 retail). After receiving them, if I don't wish to receive any more books, I can return the shipping statement marked "cancel." If I don't cancel, I will receive 6 brand-new novels every month and be billed just $5.24 for the regular-print edition or $5.74 each for the larger-print edition in the U.S., or $5.74 each for the regular-print edition or $6.24 each for the larger-print edition in Canada. That's a savings of at least 13% off the cover price. It's quite a bargain! Shipping and handling is just 50¢ per book in the U.S. and 75¢ per book in Canada.* I understand that accepting the 2 free books and gifts places me under no obligation to buy anything. I can always return a shipment and cancel at any time. The free books and gifts are mine to keep no matter what I decide.

Choose one: ☐ **Love Inspired® Romance**
Regular-Print
(105/305 IDN GMY4)

☐ **Love Inspired® Romance**
Larger-Print
(122/322 IDN GMY4)

Name (please print)

Address                                                                                    Apt. #

City                                        State/Province                          Zip/Postal Code

Mail to the **Reader Service:**
**IN U.S.A.:** P.O. Box 1341, Buffalo, NY 14240-8531
**IN CANADA:** P.O. Box 603, Fort Erie, Ontario L2A 5X3

Want to try 2 free books from another series! Call 1-800-873-8635 or visit www.ReaderService.com.

*Terms and prices subject to change without notice. Prices do not include sales taxes, which will be charged (if applicable) based on your state or country of residence. Canadian residents will be charged applicable taxes. Offer not valid in Quebec. This offer is limited to one order per household. Books received may not be as shown. Not valid for current subscribers to Love Inspired Romance books. All orders subject to approval. Credit or debit balances in a customer's account(s) may be offset by any other outstanding balance owed by or to the customer. Please allow 4 to 6 weeks for delivery. Offer available while quantities last.

**Your Privacy**—The Reader Service is committed to protecting your privacy. Our Privacy Policy is available online at www.ReaderService.com or upon request from the Reader Service. We make a portion of our mailing list available to reputable third parties that offer products we believe may interest you. If you prefer that we not exchange your name with third parties, or if you wish to clarify or modify your communication preferences, please visit us at www.ReaderService.com/consumerschoice or write to us at Reader Service Preference Service, P.O. Box 9062, Buffalo, NY 14240-9062. Include your complete name and address.

LI19R2

# Get 4 FREE REWARDS!

## We'll send you 2 FREE Books plus 2 FREE Mystery Gifts.

**Love Inspired® Suspense** books feature Christian characters facing challenges to their faith... and lives.

**FREE** Value Over **$20**

# Get 4 FREE REWARDS!

## We'll send you 2 FREE Books plus 2 FREE Mystery Gifts.

**FREE**
Value Over
**$20**

Both the **Romance** and **Suspense** collections feature compelling novels
written by many of today's best-selling authors.

# READERSERVICE.COM

## Manage your account online!

- Review your order history
- Manage your payments
- Update your address

---

*We've designed the
Reader Service website
just for you.*

---

## Enjoy all the features!

- Discover new series available to you, and read excerpts from any series.
- Respond to mailings and special monthly offers.
- Browse the Bonus Bucks catalog and online-only exculsives.
- Share your feedback.

*Visit us at:*
## ReaderService.com